Praise for *The Cherry Cola Book Club*

"If Fannie Flagg and Jan Karon's Mitford were to come together, the end result might very well be Cherico, Mississippi. Ashton Lee has created a magical town with characters who will inspire readers and bring them back to a simpler time and place. With both humor and moving passages, Lee has captured the quirkiness and warm-hearted people of the small-town south to a 'T.' Fix yourself a cherry Coke and savor this fun and moving book."
 —Michael Morris, author of *Man in the Blue Moon* and
A Place Called Wiregrass

"Down-home and delicious, *The Cherry Cola Book Club* combines everything we love about Southern cuisine, small-town grit and the transformative power of books."
 —Beth Harbison, *New York Times* best-selling author

"Lee's buoyant David-versus-Goliath tale zestfully illuminates a real problem confronting libraries and cities of all sizes."
 —*Booklist*

Praise for *The Reading Circle*

"Charm, wit and a cast of characters so real they could be your next-door neighbors make *The Reading Circle* a surefire winner. Ashton Lee's authentic Southern voice shines in the latest addition to the Cherry Cola Book Club."
 —Peggy Webb, *USA Today* best-selling author

"Lee has crafted another pleasurable and diverting tale."
 —*RT Book Reviews*

And praise for *The Wedding Circle*

"*The Wedding Circle* is the perfect completion of librarian Maura Beth's adventures. I have loved immersing myself in the charm of Cherico's small town doings and feel as if all the characters are people I know well. What a happy read!"
 —Gloria Loring, singer, actress and author

Books by Ashton Lee

THE CHERRY COLA BOOK CLUB

THE READING CIRCLE

THE WEDDING CIRCLE

Published by Kensington Publishing Corporation

The Wedding Circle

ASHTON LEE

KENSINGTON BOOKS
www.kensingtonbooks.com

KENSINGTON BOOKS are published by

Kensington Publishing Corp.
119 West 40th Street
New York, NY 10018

All Kensington titles, imprints, and distributed lines are available at special quantity discounts for bulk purchases for sales promotion, premiums, fundraising, and educational or institutional use.

Special book excerpts or customized printings can also be created to fit specific needs. For details, write or phone the office of the Kensington Special Sales Manager: Attn. Special Sales Department. Kensington Publishing Corp., 119 West 40th Street, New York, NY 10018. Phone: 1-800-221-2647.

Kensington and the K logo Reg. U.S. Pat. & TM Off.

eISBN-13: 978-1-61773-342-0
eISBN-10: 1-61773-342-3
First Kensington Electronic Edition: April 2015

ISBN-13: 978-1-61773-341-3
ISBN-10: 1-61773-341-5
First Kensington Trade Paperback Printing: April 2015

10 9 8 7 6 5 4 3 2 1

Printed in the United States of America

In loving memory of my cousin
Ann Hampton Coleman
1947–2014

Acknowledgments

This series continues to be a pleasure to create. The cast of characters who assist me in New York is phenomenal. My agents, Christina Hogrebe and Meg Ruley, constantly help me fine-tune my drafts and give me superb literary advice. My editor at Kensington Books, John Scognamiglio, has been an inspiration to me from the time we signed the contract. The support he and his staff give me keeps me focused on producing the most polished manuscripts possible. I would also like to acknowledge the efforts of the foreign rights division of The Jane Rotrosen Agency for placing the series in Poland and Turkey. I get the biggest kick out of knowing that Europeans are sitting down and reading about the adventures of my Deep South characters. Also: Thanks to my cousin Bruce Kuehnle, Jr. for clarifying several legal points that have arisen in the series. To my sister-in-law, Nancy Carhart, for her crafts input. And to Gail Healy, Lucianne Wood, and Sissy Eidt: May I express my sincere gratitude for your delicious Southern recipes at the back of this novel. These ladies define Southern hospitality. Finally, to all the librarians around the country who have connected with me so positively about my heroine, Maura Beth Mayhew, cheering for her throughout every installment: I can assure you that Maura Beth loves you right back.

1

Baby Bumps and Wedding Woes

Maura Beth Mayhew was not going to let it happen again. Not a single member of The Cherry Cola Book Club would deter her from her mission this time. After all, it was beyond inexcusable to keep a literary giant like Eudora Welty on the backburner any longer—waiting in the wings like an unproven ingénue with only a few lines to make an impression on her opening-night audience. The standing ovation notices had been in for ages.

"No, ladies and gentlemen," Maura Beth continued playfully, lifting her chin and shaking her auburn curls for extra emphasis as she stood behind the podium in The Cherico Library, "the time has come to tackle *The Robber Bridegroom*. We've honored Margaret Mitchell and Harper Lee, among our female legends. It's only fitting that we now pay homage to an icon like Miss Welty. So, let's open our doors wide for Eudora, shall we?"

There was plenty of gentle laughter and head nodding among all those in attendance, followed by unanimous approval of the previous proposal to make *The Robber Bridegroom* the club's next classic Southern read. Maura Beth was pleased that all the regulars had shown up for this midsummer meeting in her cramped little library still smelling of fresh paint from the recent spring storm damage repairs. Most importantly, the big hole that a direct lightning strike had ripped open in the roof had been patched, even if some of the thoroughly soaked children's books had yet to be replaced. But at least the musty odors and the unsightly stains had been vanquished, and some semblance of normalcy had been restored to the outdated facility tucked away at 12 Shadow Alley.

Maura Beth took a cleansing breath and happily surveyed the audience sitting before her in the makeshift semicircle of folding chairs. Then she began making her mental notes.

Miss Voncille Nettles and her widower beau, Locke Linwood, had recently announced their wedding plans and were still holding hands like smitten teenagers, even though they were both on the verge of entering their seventies. There was no mistaking their fondness for each other, nor the extent to which the prickly, but still handsome, Miss Voncille had thawed and mellowed in the face of Locke's gentlemanly ardor. Ah, the transformative power of love!

Maura Beth's folksy girlfriend and owner of The Twinkle Twinkle Café, Periwinkle Lattimore, seemed to have recovered nicely from her ill-fated, second-chance dalliance with her manipulative ex-husband, Harlan; furthermore, she and her accomplished pastry chef, Mr. Parker Place—who had not come with her, however—had been spotted shopping and running other errands together around town. No one had yet perceived them as an "item" exactly, but it was obvious that they had become very friendly coworkers at the town's most popular restaurant. Rumor had it that he had even begun sharing cooking duties with Periwinkle to lighten her load in the kitchen, and no one thought she would ever delegate an enormous responsibility like that. Not where her fantastically successful Twinkle was concerned!

Maura Beth had now reserved a special corner in her temple of gratitude for wealthy retirees Connie and Douglas McShay, who were sitting directly in front of her. It was they who had generously donated part of their extensive acreage on Lake Cherico for the construction of the brand-new, state-of-the-art library that Maura Beth and Nora Duddney had managed to wangle out of the always scheming Councilman Durden Sparks. Only the three of them would ever know the truth behind his decision to pony up for the much-needed upgrade. As far as the general public was concerned, Councilman Sparks was the genuine hero in the proposition, donating the funds out of the civic-minded goodness of his heart. What wonders a little holding of feet to the fire over misappropriated funds had wrought!

Then Maura Beth turned her attention to Becca and Justin Brachle, respectively, the town's local radio show chef and real-estate tycoon. By now everyone in Cherico knew that they were expecting their first child. Imagine that—Becca "Broccoli" Brachle and her "Stout Fella," as she had nicknamed him, were going to become parents after ten years of wedded but childless bliss! That is, minus his "too-young-to-have-one" heart attack episode as a frightening reminder that life was indeed short.

And suddenly it dawned on Maura Beth why everyone had been so eager to approve the club read for the August meeting and get all the other official club matters resolved so quickly. That fawning cluster surrounding the Brachles the moment they had entered the library—including the wealthy spinster Crumpton sisters, Mamie and Marydell—was all about soliciting updates on Becca's pregnancy. Among the favored topics in small towns like Cherico, Mississippi, which women were expecting and how they were doing with their morning sickness and weight gain surely fascinated the greatest number of people. So, best not to keep them all waiting any longer. Time to retire to the long buffet table groaning with gumbo, chicken spaghetti, tomato aspic, baked custard, and chocolate cherry cola sheet cake, followed by the effortless socializing that had become the trademark of The Cherry Cola Book Club. True to form, it did not take long for the genteel inquisition to begin.

"I see you're not showing yet, dear," Mamie Crumpton said, in between bites of jalapeño cornbread. As usual, Mamie was overdressed for the occasion—her significant cleavage stuffed into an iridescent gown far better suited to an evening at Theater Memphis. Always trying to be the center of attention was, of course, her signature character trait. "You must be one of those lucky women who just don't put on a lot of weight. I had a first cousin like that. Why, the day Marcella Louise was about to pop, you wouldn't have even guessed it. As I recall, she didn't even have to wear maternity clothes. Must have saved a fortune!"

"Oh, it's a bit too soon for me, Miz Crumpton," Becca said, her petite figure still truly intact. "I'm not even out of my first trimester yet. But I'm looking forward to my baby bump all the same. After all this time, it's well worth the wait."

"Otherwise we're doin' just fine," Justin added, towering over her with his big frame and smiling the way expectant fathers do. Then he gestured in her general direction with his thumb and firmly set his jaw. "At least she is."

Becca gave him an exasperated glance and shook her pretty blond head. "Please, Justin. Enough about your feet!"

The kibitzing Maura Beth was intrigued and moved closer with a smile. "What's this?"

Becca pointed her plastic fork at him accusingly before resting it on her paper plate. "Oh, he keeps claiming his feet feel like a thousand bees are stinging him all the time. I'm willing to bet it's those snakeskin cowboy boots he wears night and day. That's got to be what's doing it. The snakes are getting their revenge!"

Justin looked unconvinced as he glanced down quickly. "Then how come when I take them off, my feet feel even worse? You know I've even been having trouble sleeping because of it."

Becca shrugged, flicking her wrist dismissively. "Okay, then we'll ask Dr. Healy about it when I go for my next visit."

"Now, what does your obstetrician know about feet?" he continued. "Unless they're tiny baby feet that show up in a sonogram. Seems like I was born wearin' a clunky size fourteen."

The group that had gathered around the Brachles was chuckling, and Becca said, "He's paying the price for all that line dancing he did all those years out at the Marina Bar and Grill with the boys."

Justin immediately did a passable imitation of taking offense. "Hey, there's nothin' wrong with a little boot-scootin' boogie now and then!"

With one question from Periwinkle, however, the focus of the gathering changed from the Brachles to Maura Beth herself. "That cute Jeremy of yours couldn't make it down tonight, honey?"

"Afraid not," she explained, barely able to disguise her disappointment. "He's up in Nashville packing for the big move in a few days. He's also getting rid of a lot of his bachelor guy things right and left. I pretty much told him he had to. For instance, he's hung this actual airplane propeller on the wall over his bed. Don't ask me where he got it. Anyway, he explained—and these were his exact words—that it was symbolic of his ability to rev up his engine. I told him straight out, 'I can vouch for the fact you definitely don't need that anymore, big boy!' and we both had a good laugh. But the truth is, until we move into a bigger place after the wedding, all the space we've got is inside that little efficiency of mine on Clover Street, and believe me, that's about as cramped as it gets."

"Couldn't y'all have timed things a little better?" Periwinkle continued.

"His lease expired, and we haven't been able to find anything suitable down here yet. So my place will have to do for the time being."

Then Periwinkle gave her a sideways, skeptical glance and folded her arms. "And how are your parents down there in Louisiana taking this early move in part? Or have you even told 'em about it?"

"I did tell them, and maybe I shouldn't have," Maura Beth said. "They're still giving me lots of flak about everything."

It was hard to imagine her socialite parents, William and Cara Lynn Mayhew, being less thrilled about her announced forthcoming wedding to Jeremy McShay. Actually, it was her imperious mother who had kept up the disdain in phone call after phone call once she had learned about the engagement: "Maura Beth, here you are making next to nothing as a librarian in that redneck town in the middle of nowhere, and you're going to compound that mistake by marrying a high-school English teacher? They make even less than you do. I can see it now—your father and I will have to send you money all the time so you can make ends meet. Of course, we'll be glad to do it, but is that the kind of future you really want? All of this is so far beneath you."

"Thanks for that huge bouquet of support, Mama," Maura Beth had stated as evenly as possible. She knew it was useless to do anything more than serve up a huge helping of sarcasm, but she would have given anything for a sunnier exchange every once in a while.

Then there was the issue of Connie and Douglas McShay, Jeremy's generous aunt and uncle, hosting the wedding at their lodge on Lake Cherico. Cara Lynn had immediately recoiled in horror at the prospect of her only daughter not reciting her vows at St. Andrew's Episcopal Church down in New Orleans, followed by the proper, seated gourmet dinner and reception at the terribly exclusive, live oak–shaded Three-Hundred Club.

Here, Cara Lynn Mayhew had risen up like a cobra about to strike, practically hissing through the phone: "Really, Maura Beth! Your father and I thought this rebellious phase of yours would peter out eventually—this wanting to be a drab little librarian to amuse yourself by shelving books and shushing other people's children. But we fully expected you to come back to us for your birthright. You're a Mayhew—a New Orleans Mayhew, one of the finest Uptown names. Not to mention my family, the State Street Danforths. I'm just glad your grandparents aren't alive for this. You deserve better than standing among those strangers at some tacky fishing lodge for that special moment in your life!"

Somehow, Maura Beth had managed to hold her temper and had even offered an olive branch. "Mama, they're not strangers. They're all my friends. And the McShays' home on the water is just lovely. Just think of Lake Cherico as a little Lake Pontchartrain without the sailboats. But Jeremy and I have discussed it, and we're willing to postpone the wedding until you've had a chance to come up here to Cherico and meet him and his family. They're all very nice, cultured, educated people, I can assure you. Besides, you've never once bothered to actually come and see what my life is like up here. Will you at least do that much for me?"

Maura Beth came out of her reverie, revealing to Periwinkle and all the other members of The Cherry Cola Book Club the outcome of that particular conversation. "I don't know how I did it, but I convinced my parents to come to *The Robber Bridegroom* review and meet all of you. After that,

God willing, we'll be able to finalize our wedding plans, and I will have made peace with my family."

Connie McShay did not appear to be taking these latest revelations very well, the worry clearly showing in the lines around her eyes. "Oh, Maura Beth, Douglas and I don't want to be the cause of friction between yourself and your parents. You know we'll be happy to withdraw our offer to host your wedding in an instant. Just say the word."

"That's very understanding of you, but it won't solve the real problem here," Maura Beth returned, sounding fiercely determined. "I've got to face my parents once and for all about the choices I've made for my life. They've got to understand that I don't necessarily value the same things that they do. It seems we've been at odds with each other for the longest time, and whenever I want to see them, I have to go down there. Maybe we can't resolve anything after it's all said and done, but I've got to give it at least one last try."

Miss Voncille offered up an odd little chuckle as she leaned into Locke Linwood and gave him an affectionate glance. "If it's not the parents causing all the trouble, it's the children."

Locke slowly shook his head of thick gray hair, looking suddenly forlorn. "What Voncille is referring to are my two very opinionated, grown children. At first we thought we had their blessing for our wedding, but everything seems to have fallen apart these last couple of weeks. First, my daughter, Carla, has had second thoughts. My son, Locke, Jr., in particular, is getting all bent out of shape about my getting married so soon after his mother's death. I told him, 'Son, it's been over two years, and whether you believe it or not, this is something your mother would want for me. I told him I wasn't going to argue any further and that Voncille and I intended to get married with or without his approval. He's making noises like he and his wife won't even be attending the wedding. Can you imagine that—after all I've done for him—

sending him to law school and giving them the down payment for their big house over there in the Delta?"

"It's very upsetting to us," Miss Voncille added, her usual vinegary demeanor somewhat watered down now. "We had both of the children and their spouses over for a home-cooked dinner, and I thought everything went well. But apparently, it was a surface appearance thing. Once they saw I was a real, flesh-and-blood person and not just a name mentioned over the phone, something must have clicked in their brains. Suddenly, Locke started getting calls and e-mails about who was going to inherit the house and this and that piece of furniture or which bank account and—well, I'm sure you get the picture."

"I guess I've found out who my children really are now," Locke continued, his voice full of disappointment and only a bit more forceful than a whisper. "I don't know who they take after with that attitude. Maybe greed skips a generation and then rears its ugly head again when it's good and ready. Their mother wasn't like that. I mean, Pamela wasn't overly concerned with material things, and I'm grateful for what I have and for what she left me, but I've always realized that I couldn't take any of it with me there at the end. Heh. I remember once Pamela said that she was reasonably certain Heaven was not going to be one big, climate-controlled, storage warehouse filled with family heirlooms."

There was a wave of appreciative laughter, but Mamie Crumpton quickly changed the mood of the room, dramatically heaving her bosom as she lifted up her cup of cherry cola punch. "Be that as it may, there are still a few dark clouds hanging over these weddings."

Maura Beth looked especially pensive for a few moments. "Sometimes I think we're all in rehearsal for a Tennessee Williams play with these dramatic developments. But I truly hope not. Most of his works didn't end well for the main characters, and I'd much rather be thought of as a Scarlett O'Hara than a Blanche DuBois. I don't know what's so appealing about that faded Southern belle concept anyway."

"Now I know things'll work out for ya, honey," Periwinkle said, nudging her friend playfully. "Don't get down in the dumps about this. Deep-six the Tennessee Williams scenarios. Why, we'll put on a show for your parents that they'll never forget when they come for their visit. We'll stage a feast at The Twinkle!"

Maura Beth brightened, as she frequently did when she was around her best girlfriend. "Oh, that would be wonderful. I really want them to get to know and love all of you the way I do!"

"Don't you worry that pretty red head of yours," Connie put in. "Matter of fact, it might be a good idea for your parents to stay with us out at the lodge. We have two wonderful guest rooms on the second story overlooking the lake, and our sunsets out on the deck are to die for. We'll show them there's more to our Cherico than meets the eye!"

"That's what I've been trying to tell my parents all these years," Maura Beth explained. "Unfortunately, they think New Orleans is the center of the universe, and they treat me like I'm living on an alien planet."

"Does your father like to fish?" Douglas asked. "If he does, I could take him out on *The Verdict* to see what we can reel in."

Maura Beth smiled, even as she was shaking her head. "Not to my knowledge. He's out there on the stands during duck-hunting season, though. That's always been his greatest conflict in life at that time of the year: whether to shoot ducks or cheer for the LSU Tigers on Saturday nights. Sometimes he even manages to do both. But fishing? I don't think so." Then Maura Beth screwed up her mouth as if reconsidering. "But Daddy is an attorney. Perhaps the two of you could compare notes on your careers. Maybe there'll be some bonding in that."

Now it was Douglas's turn to flash a skeptical smile. "Louisiana is so different from all the others states with that Napoleonic Code, though. What kind of law does your father practice?"

Maura Beth's brief little laugh sounded more like a hiccup. "Oh, he helps couples part company and split up their inventory, to put it politely. It's a big business these days!"

"Yep," Douglas added, clucking his tongue. "Good ole divorce—I like to think of it as Alka-Seltzer for a marriage gone sour!"

"Very clever," Maura Beth said, but quickly adopted a more serious tone. "If you and Connie wouldn't mind, though, I'd like to explore this business of my parents staying with you out at the lodge a little further. Perhaps you could stay a bit after the meeting is adjourned."

When everyone had finished their desserts of baked custard and chocolate cherry cola sheet cake a few minutes later, Maura Beth reminded the group one last time of the upcoming watershed event on the shores of Lake Cherico. "Now, don't forget to circle August first on your calendars, folks. If you're out of town on vacation, going to a wedding, or something like that, I'll understand, of course. But you know how much I'd appreciate it if as many of you as possible can be there for the new library's groundbreaking ceremony. When Councilman Sparks turns over that first shovelful of Northeast Mississippi red clay, we'll finally be on our way to getting a facility here in Cherico that we can be proud of, even if it'll always be one big mouthful to say."

Never being at a loss for words, Mamie Crumpton was quick to echo her sentiments. "I must admit The Charles Durden Sparks, Crumpton, and Duddney Public Library does go on forever and ever like a voter registration list. But Marydell and I were very pleased to make a particularly generous donation to the cause, weren't we, sister dear?"

As usual, dainty Marydell managed her quiet little "yes," along with a self-effacing nod.

But the third library namesake, Nora Duddney, had quite a bit more to say. "Of course, I was equally pleased to honor the Duddney family with my contribution, and I promise to round up as many of my friends as I can. And I may even bring an extra shovel in case our dear councilman claims he just happened to forget his. I didn't work as the man's secretary for way too many years without coming to the conclusion that his middle name should have been 'Devious,' not 'Durden.' "

After the polite laughter had died down, it was pudgy, affable James Hannigan, manager of The Cherico Market, who spoke up next. "Hey, I may even shut down the store for an hour so we can all come out and back you up." He gave Maura Beth his most mischievous grin. "And, yes, Miz Mayhew, you can not only put up the announcement on the bulletin board, but I'll talk you up with the shoppers over the PA system like I did for your library petitions."

"You worked absolute wonders at your grocery store, Mr. Hannigan. I think you got more signatures on your petition than anybody except our Periwinkle here. She even outdid the library."

"Hey, the truth is, everybody and his brother has to eat every day," Periwinkle added, lightly chucking her friend on the arm. "And I'm thankful that lots of 'em come to my little Twinkle all the time to do it."

"Amen to that!" Maura Beth said, the satisfaction clearly evident in her voice as she glanced around the room. "So everything is all set. Our August agenda will be that we're going to discuss and review *The Robber Bridegroom* right here and watch Cherico history being made out at the lake. I think The Cherry Cola Book Club is going to be accomplishing quite a bit next month."

"You know your parents better than we do," Connie said as she, Douglas, and Maura Beth sat in the semicircle of chairs, discussing the idea of hosting the Mayhews at their lodge. "But if tasteful accommodations are what they're expecting, our home should more than fit the bill."

Maura Beth winced ever so slightly. She knew her parents only too well, and she did not want to subject her good friends, the McShays, to anything less than their best social behavior. Surely they would not do anything to embarrass her. They were beyond such boorishness. After all, she'd seen her mother put on her best "Say cheese!" smile as she sashayed her way through many a dull cocktail or dinner party all over New Orleans.

"I'm afraid my parents have this false impression of Cherico—particularly my mother," Maura Beth explained. "It's that 'sophisticated provincial' thing that certain cities swear by. For instance, I've heard some New Yorkers dismiss the rest of America as flyover country, and I know for a fact that many a New Orleanian believe anything north of Lake Pontchartrain is culturally suspect. Or to be totally blunt—*Hee Haw* territory."

Connie laughed good-naturedly. "Oh, I understand that kind of thinking. But I'll let you in on a little secret." She bent near, her face lighting up, yet also looking determined. "All that 'putting on airs' stuff disappeared when people found themselves in my ICU up in Nashville. To a man and woman, they all just wanted to live to see another day, and it was my job to nurse them back to health and see that they got there if at all possible. I like to think that they took something away from being on the edge like that—maybe even became a little more tolerant of people who weren't born into the situation they were. It's cruel but true—the threat of flatlining is the greatest leveler there is."

In spite of Connie's last statement, Maura Beth was grinning. "So, are you suggesting we admit my parents to Cherico Memorial and hook them up right after they get here?"

"My goodness, but I do love your sense of humor, sweetie," Connie said, maintaining her gracious smile. "But I trust the good food and conversation out at the lodge will soften them up sufficiently. As you well know, Douglas and I are pretty good party-givers, but you have the final say on all of this."

Maura Beth reached over and took Connie's hand, making eye contact with Douglas at the same time. "I just wanted both of you to understand that I fully intend to get married up here no matter what. If my parents still don't get on board despite everything we do and say on their visit, so be it. This independent streak of mine is part of the reason I've stuck it out here in Cherico the way I have. The New Orleans social scene is what my parents wanted for themselves, and I had a generous helping of it growing up, believe me. But it's not what I want. I want something I can call my own, and now I know my legacy here will be The Charles Durden Sparks, Crumpton, and Duddney Public Library."

Douglas suddenly looked inspired. "They need to have your name on the building somewhere."

"Oh, they will. And yours, too. There'll be a big bronze plaque in the lobby with my name on it as director, along with Douglas and Connie McShay as benefactors. I'll see to that."

"Then are we actually full-speed ahead with our hosting your parents?" Connie asked.

Maura Beth contemplated silently for a few moments. "I think we've covered all the bases. My mother may be opinionated, but I've never known her to be rude in social situations. Frankly, I never thought she'd agree to come up here, but she did. Maybe there's a crack in that blue-blooded armor of hers. After all, I am her only child, even if I haven't exactly towed the line."

Connie patted her hand gently. "Something tells me it will all turn out just fine, and the spirit of Greater Cherico will prevail."

Connie's prediction stuck with Maura Beth even after the McShays had left her to turn out the lights and lock up. There were no more than 5,000 people in this little town that she had come to love so much. And once her beloved Jeremy had settled in with her, he'd only be a month or so away from his job teaching English at Cherico High. This was the life she had chosen for herself, and it was going to be her great adventure. In the end she was certain it was going to take her breath away. That was all there was to it.

2

From the Ground Up

The first of August was nothing if not the real beginning of Mississippi's dog days. Sporting triple digits and merciless humidity, it caused the population of Cherico to break out into rivers of sweat only minutes after stepping out of their air-conditioned homes and cars. Their morning showers and baths were therefore completely undone, disappearing as if never having taken place. In addition, there were no clouds of any kind overhead in the white-hot sky—and essentially no hope of rainfall, however brief. And yet, the new library groundbreaking would be taking place under such hellish conditions.

"You just wait," Maura Beth said to her sweet-natured, young front-desk clerk, Renette Posey. "I'll bet you one tasty lunch at The Twinkle we get a phone call from Councilman Sparks about the unbearable heat and putting things off until it cools down a bit. Hey, I only wish I didn't know him as well as I do."

The two of them were sitting across from each other in Maura Beth's cluttered library office, and they had already agreed that Renette would hold down the fort while Maura

Beth attended the groundbreaking later that morning out at the lake.

"You really think he'll try to postpone things?" Renette asked, blinking in disbelief. It was just part of her trusting nature—never thinking the worst of anyone until proved otherwise.

"I wouldn't put it past him," Maura Beth answered, leaning into her employee and narrowing her eyes. "Not that it would do him any good. We've got a contract to build that new beauty—signed, sealed, and delivered. Try as he might, he's not going to be able to wiggle out of that."

Renette's sigh was of the dreamy variety. "This is such an exciting time for you, Miz Mayhew. Imagine—just a year from now, we'll be in that wonderful new building with computers, a teen room, a full-time children's librarian, plenty of parking, and all the rest a real library ought to have!"

"Should have had years ago, of course. But every time I went to City Hall about all our deficiencies, I was ignored with a patronizing smile."

They both sank back in their chairs, happily engrossed in their visions of what was to come after so many years of struggle, so much so that they started noticeably when the phone rang.

"The Cherico Library," Maura Beth answered with crisp authority, once she had gathered herself. Then she briefly covered the receiver, and whispered loudly, "I would have won that lunch bet if you'd taken it!"

"Councilman Sparks?" Renette whispered back, her eyes widening playfully.

Maura Beth nodded quickly and then resumed her conversation. "Yes, it is a hot one today, Councilman. . . . Yes, you *could* fry an egg on the hood of your SUV." She and Renette exchanged conspiratorial smirks as Maura Beth listened patiently. "Oh, no, not at all, Councilman," she continued in response. "I can stand it if you can. You'd probably never guess it, but we Southern belles hide rotary fans beneath our hoop-skirts, you know. Besides, too many people all over Cherico have altered their daily routines in order to attend, and there's no hint of rain in the forecast. So I vote for bucking up and going out there to shovel it. As I'm sure I don't have to tell you, you're very good at that."

Renette suppressed a giggle, while Maura Beth wagged her brows. Then there was an extended period of silence while Councilman Sparks apparently went into some sort of monologue. Finally, Maura Beth said, "Yes, I'll see you in a few hours, Councilman. Looking forward to it as usual. Good-bye now." Then she hung up and adopted her most confidential tone. "Well, he says he wants to see me in his office after the ceremony is over. It seems he has some important questions about the new library he wants to discuss and resolve, whatever that means."

"Do you think you offended him with that shoveling remark?"

"I doubt it. He's pretty jaded."

"So what do you think he's up to now?"

"Anything and everything would be my guess. I like to think of him as one of those nesting dolls—you know, a different, smaller version of himself constantly being exposed. And I do mean smaller, and I do mean exposed."

Renette was temporarily amused, but then looked worried. "You don't think there's any way he can weasel out of building this new library, do you? I don't think even he could pull that off."

Maura Beth shook her head emphatically at the mere suggestion. "Oh, I can handle whatever this latest agenda of his turns out to be. I've had almost seven years' experience dealing with him, and I'm getting better and better at it all the time. If I hadn't learned from my considerable novice mistakes, we'd be in this god-awful building forever. I'm afraid I was a bit naïve about the way things worked around here for too long. With the way I was brought up, I thought it was bad form to challenge authority. Just part of my on-the-job training, I guess."

"I don't think anyone could blame you for that, Miz Mayhew. Councilman Sparks is a pretty intimidating man. I know I always get nervous when he pops into the library now and then. Why do I always think he's spying on us? Anyway, what are you going to look forward to the most when we finally move in out there?" Renette asked, rubbing her hands together and sounding a bit like a kid in a candy store.

Maura Beth took a moment and then pointed her finger at random spots on the wall. "Well, aside from watching this library rise from the ground up, I'd say that having an office with at least one big window would be first on my list. Maybe more than one. I've read that a little light and a view of the outside world can work wonders for the psyche. That and some color. I'm so sick of this off-white. Egg shells are for chickens."

Renette lit up, full of her girlish enthusiasm. "Ooh, what color would you paint your walls?"

Maura Beth was staring up at the ceiling, putting a finger to her lips. "I might just go crazy. Pink, or maybe even purple to match my walls at home."

"What fun!"

"Yes, wouldn't it be? I'll have light and color and some real space to put an end to all of this miserable clutter once and for all. This dark little closet I've been sentenced to all these years has almost made me feel like Maura Beth, the Vampire Librarian."

Renette laughed brightly. "Hey, with all the spooky, gory stuff the kids are hooked on these days, you probably could've made that work for you. Maybe you could've come to work in costume." Then she checked her watch. "Oops! I guess I'd better get back to the front desk. Good luck out there this afternoon, Miz Mayhew. Don't let Councilman Sparks trip you up."

"Not a chance," Maura Beth said.

But even as Renette left the room, Maura Beth couldn't help but wonder what the councilman had in store for her after the groundbreaking ceremony had become history. Might as well start psyching herself up for it now.

The unexpected expanse of white canvas took Maura Beth by surprise as she drove up to the somewhat overgrown groundbreaking site and parked her little Prius within shouting distance of the willow-lined lake. The noonday sun bearing down made the temporary structure all the more dazzling to behold. The McShays, looking dressed for summertime in their prudent white outfits, were already underneath it, waving and coaxing her to join them in its blessed shade. As there was no hint of a breeze, Maura Beth was right beside them in an instant.

"We knew you'd probably be the first one here," Connie said, as the two women embraced a few seconds later. "You even beat the councilman and his ever-present underlings."

"How do you like our little surprise?" Douglas added, hugging Maura Beth in turn as he pointed to the top of the canopy. "It's actually one of those deluxe football tailgating tents we rented just for the occasion. With football season just about a month away, they're pretty easy to come by."

Maura Beth was all smiles as she scanned the width and breadth of it quickly. "A brilliant move, I have to say. I wasn't looking forward to standing out in the sweltering heat while Councilman Sparks got in all of his photo ops. No telling how much shoveling he'll end up doing until he gets it just right for posterity. I predict he'll have "Chunky" Badham and "Gopher" Joe Martin snapping him from all different angles while the rest of us moan and groan."

"Well, we thought we'd do it up right in true Cherry Cola Book Club fashion," Connie continued, obviously quite pleased with herself. "We've got a bowl of cherry cola punch and some finger foods over there on the table to make sure everyone keeps up their energy levels."

Maura Beth gave the two of them her most affectionate gaze. "First you donate the land for the library, and now you jazz this up for us like this. I, for one, am so thankful you decided to retire here in Cherico."

"Thanks, sweetie, we are, too. But where's your Jeremy?" Connie asked, sounding somewhat distracted.

"Oh, he's on his way. He had a staff orientation meeting over at the high school this morning. Big doings since school begins next week. I can't believe how early the kids start these days. When I was coming along, we always went back closer to the end of the month, and Mama and Daddy said it was always after Labor Day for them. Summer vacation seems to be getting shorter and shorter."

Their conversation was interrupted by two staccato honks of a car horn, and they all turned quickly to see Jeremy generating a thick trail of reddish dust as he barreled down upon the site. He brought his yellow Triumph Spitfire—which he had nicknamed "The Warbler" after having lovingly reworked its 1971 engine—to an impressive, if herky-jerky halt; then he emerged from the front seat with a perfunctory wave of his hand and immediately began giving everyone the latest Cherico High update before anyone could even get out a word.

"Folks, I deliberately stepped in it just a tad bit today," he told them, serving himself a cup of punch as he sounded off. "That's a record for me. It took me a good couple of semes-

ters to get on the headmaster's nerves up at New Gallatin
Academy. But what else is new?"

Maura Beth's look of concern was genuine. If she had
learned anything about her fiancé in the time they had been
an item, it was that his fuse was exceedingly short. More than
once, he had gotten into trouble by not thinking things
through before he spoke. "What did you do now, Jeremy?"

He downed the entire cup in one great swig and then
quickly ladled himself another. "Basically, the same thing I did
up at New Gallatin with my nemesis, Mr. Yelverton. On one
of our breaks this morning, I brought up the possibility of his
approving literary field trips for my students. I said, 'Mr.
Hutchinson, Oxford's just about an hour and a half from
Cherico.' Then I suggested a bus trip to see Rowan Oak and
The Square and all the rest of William Faulkner's haunts. I told
him I thought it would really bring writing to life for my boys
and girls."

From the beginning, Maura Beth had admired Jeremy's
tenacity so much because she knew she could not live without a generous dose of her own. So she really had no choice
but to support him in all his endeavors, even if he wasn't always tactful in his approach. "And what did he say to all that?
Same as Yelverton?"

"All in all, I'd say his reaction was nothing short of hor-
rified. You would have thought I was asking permission to
blow up that school bus," Jeremy continued, trying to keep a
hint of levity in his tone. "Hutchinson gets this panicked look
on his face, clears his throat several times, and finally says with
his lips all puckered up, 'As you'll soon find out, we've got us
a real tight budget around here, Mr. McShay.' "

Maura Beth could almost guess what had happened next.
"Please don't tell me you challenged him about spending
money on the football team and its road trips like you did in
Nashville."

"No, not yet. But I fully intend to at some point. So, anyway, he says something to the effect that we should just try to get through the orientation first. He sounded for all the world like a politician running for office."

"You mean like Councilman Sparks always does," Douglas added with a conspiratorial tilt of his head.

"Exactly."

Maura Beth moved in closer and slowly massaged Jeremy's arm. She had discovered that he was more susceptible to her suggestions when she applied a gentle touch. "Maybe you should have waited until you got to know this man a little bit better before pushing all his buttons."

Jeremy finished off his second cup of punch and plucked a tuna fish sandwich from the artistic arrangement Connie had created on her big glass platter; but he did so rather clumsily, and the carefully balanced stack immediately tumbled into ruin. "Waiting to push his buttons is certainly one way to go. But I always like to know where I stand early in the game. I figure I plant the seed and then keep at it. In the long run, it'll help me make my case and maybe get just what I want."

Maura Beth was secretly pleased by yet another confirmation of Jeremy's considerable determination. A good, responsible husband should certainly possess that quality, among so many others. "Well, in that case, Mr. Hutchinson will never know what hit him when the time comes."

"Yep," Jeremy said, swallowing a mouthful of his sandwich. "Let's just continue the double-team. You keep tabs on Councilman Sparks, and I'll ride herd on Mr. Hutchinson."

By noon the crowd had swollen to nearly fifty people—too many, in fact, to fit beneath the shade of the tailgating tent, even if they had all made short work of the McShays' punch and sandwiches. Many of the citizens who had signed Maura Beth's petitions to keep the existing library open had shown up—including James Hannigan and his flock of Cherico Market employees. Of course, the Crumpton sisters—for once underdressed because of the heat—and Nora Duddney had been afforded the luxury of standing on either side of Councilman Sparks. As expected, he was milking the occasion for all it was worth. Also granted a respite from the midday sun was the project's architect, Rogers Jernigan, who stood as tall and spindly as one of the metal poles supporting the canopy. Even in the shade, however, he seemed to be sweating profusely, and his skin was sticking to his white shirt. Meanwhile, most of those who were not office holders, benefactors, or in some way connected to the library like Maura Beth were slowly roasting in the outside oven.

"My fellow Chericoans," Councilman Sparks began, surveying the gathering with his trademark display of dazzling white teeth. "Today, we begin a new era for our wonderful little town. When I turn over this first shovelful of earth, construction on The Charles Durden Sparks, Crumpton, and Duddney Public Library will officially have begun." He paused as pot-bellied fellow councilman Chunky Badham, huffing and puffing all the while, quickly maneuvered himself into prime camera-snapping position. Only after several frenetic "test" poses did Councilman Sparks actually plunge the shovel into the weedy ground, apply swift but significant pressure with his right foot, and deposit a little red clay mound beside the small hole he had created. He pointed to it dramatically, as if he had just struck gold. "Voilà!"

He resumed his speech in earnest after the polite applause of the crowd had died down. "From this small beginning our new library will grow from the ground up. And I do want to thank each and every one of you, ladies and gentlemen, for coming out here today. I realize this is not the most comfortable place to be right now. But let's look ahead, shall we? If we don't have too much bad weather this fall and winter, we expect everyone to be enjoying this new facility about this time next year, don't we, Miz Mayhew? Just under eleven months was the time frame quoted to us by the construction company, right?"

Caught slightly off guard, Maura Beth still conjured up her best smile and raised her right hand with her fingers crossed. "I believe that's the game plan. So everyone hold off on all those rain dances, if you would."

Councilman Sparks almost seemed to be conducting the burst of laughter that followed, as he raised both hands heavenward. Then he slowly brought them down to his side, apparently having invoked a generous helping of his godly powers. No tent revivalist could have done it better. "Yes, indeed. My vision of this project is very clear. Let me now share it with all of you. Imagine, if you will, being able to read your favorite novels with this glorious view of the lake at your disposal. Picture being able to walk out on the wraparound deck at sunset after you've done your research or read one of the many periodicals we'll have on display for your convenience. Our architect standing right here beside me, Mr. Rogers Jernigan, has assured us that this facility will be state of the art down to the last detail, and he has worked closely with our Miz Mayhew, getting the valuable input of Cherico's wonderful, degreed librarian. In addition, no expense will be spared in bringing these amazing blueprints of his to life. Our generous benefactors standing here beside us today have made all of this possible, doing more than their civic duty. Their contributions will be remembered for generations to come, as so many lives will be affected positively. . . ."

It was at that point that Maura Beth found herself tuning out the endless litany of clichés. It had been her frequent observation that whenever Councilman Sparks belabored something to a fault, he was very likely preparing to pull a fast one. It still amazed her that way too many people in Cherico had not wised up to his political method acting. Or, maybe they had but were just plain addicted to it—even wholly mesmerized by it. Put succinctly, the man was truly golden—getting continually reelected without a serious challenge.

Then, as everyone began dispersing when Councilman Sparks had finally wrapped up his performance, he took Maura Beth and Rogers Jernigan aside and spoke confidentially, putting his arms around their shoulders. "This little ceremony was all fine and dandy, but the three of us will need to put our heads together in my office this afternoon. I'm sure if we bear down hard enough, we can come up with some solutions to our problems. After all, we need to have the best interests of our fellow Chericoans at heart."

Maura Beth noted with a growing sense of trepidation that the politician and the architect were smiling, while she was not. But a walk to her car with Jeremy beside her was somewhat reassuring.

"You hang in there, Maurie," he told her, putting his arm around her waist and pulling her toward him. "Whatever this is about, just don't let them rattle you." His sweet little kiss sealed the deal. "And I'll see you back at the apartment for the blow by blow."

As she slid into the front seat and turned the key with a lingering smile, she fully appreciated what it meant to be a couple. In short, she no longer had to face anything alone.

3

On the Cheap and Off the Rack

At the moment, Maura Beth's meeting with Councilman Sparks and Rogers Jernigan was immersed in annoying déjà vu. How many times over the years had she endured similar inquisitions in the plush offices of City Hall? True, Chunky Badham and Gopher Joe Martin were nowhere to be found, but that made the current ordeal even more uncomfortable to endure. If nothing else, those two good ole boys usually provided much-needed comic relief with their frequent malapropisms and non sequiturs. No such luck today, however.

"There's something you need to understand, Miz Mayhew," Councilman Sparks was saying from behind his highly polished, massive desk. It had the effect of making him look and sound even more authoritative. "These blueprints of ours aren't written in stone. Perhaps we'd better let our distinguished architect here explain our concerns to you. Will you do the honors, sir?"

Councilman Sparks gestured toward Rogers Jernigan, who was seated across from him in one of the room's great leather chairs. "I'll be delighted, of course," he said, turning toward the nearby Maura Beth with a forced smile on his face.

But there was a nervousness about it that seemed to be ooz-ing from his every pore.

She winced the moment he spoke up. She had found working with him on a consulting basis to be pleasant enough, but it was the way he had continually deferred to Councilman Sparks that had never failed to get on her nerves. "Yes, Dur-den," he would say while the three of them were discussing the needs of a twenty-first century library. "I understand your point here. I realize there is only so much money in the till. You can count on me to keep that in mind." And on and on. She could not recall a single instance in which he had even come close to bucking City Hall's directives.

Summoning her best professional training, of course, she had endeavored to make Rogers understand things from a li-brarian's point of view. Although she had the gut feeling he was not really on her side no matter what she said, he had generally acquiesced in these sessions—perhaps just to keep the peace. But now here they were going over all of it again, and she feared the worst.

"You see, Miz Mayhew," Rogers continued in a decidedly patronizing tone, "as any architect will tell you, there are junctures in the construction of any building. By that I mean, once you reach a certain point, you can't undo things. Well, you can tear out walls and windows and such, but it will cost a ton of money and cause unacceptable delays. We certainly want to avoid that if we can. So, Durden and I would like to revisit a couple of items in the plans that we might want to change before we reach these junctures down the road in a few more months. For instance, there's this teen room con-cept. We feel that—"

Maura Beth straightened up and quickly interrupted, as her worst fears were confirmed. "What about the teen room? Are you proposing that we do away with it? I thought we'd resolved that issue once and for all. I can't believe you're bring-ing it up again."

Rogers cast a furtive glance toward Councilman Sparks, as if looking for validation. "You'll remember that we had quite a discussion about it the first time around."

"That's a polite way of describing it," Maura Beth said, re-calling how hard she had fought for it. Really, they had tried to work her to the bone, but somehow she had managed to stand up for herself and for her new library.

"The thing is," Rogers continued, "if we close up that space when the time comes, we could save a lot of money. It wouldn't be a problem to use that area for more shelving in-stead. That would even be a practical benefit to you. Besides which, don't you think teenagers are old enough to come into the library and make their own decisions without being di-rected to a special room?"

Maura Beth gathered herself, trying to slow down her quickening heartbeat. "Gentlemen, as I explained in some de-tail earlier, I'm trying to be proactive about the library's future readers. If we can get the children and teens to view the li-brary as a fun outing—maybe even the 'in' place to go, say, af-ter school—we've won the battle against the smartphones and tablets and all these other devices that can keep them from dis-covering the joy of holding a book in your hand and reading."

Councilman Sparks stepped in with a triumphant look on his face. "You're saying these kids can't read on these devices? I think you're on the wrong side of history if you believe you can stop them from buying and using all these gadgets. Besides, why should we be babysitters for these teenagers? Doesn't this amount to glorified daycare? And do you know how much money we could save by not putting that enormous flat-screen TV in there? How is letting them watch TV encour-aging them to read? If I know kids, they'll be watching all those DVDs and not giving books a second thought. I think you'll just be compounding the problem."

"But we'll be buying educational DVDs about learning languages, travel, history, documentaries—that sort of thing."

"Do we really need this extra item in the budget? Won't we just be sending them home to watch more TV?!"

Maura Beth had never seen Councilman Sparks quite this prepared and adamant before. He was like a guard dog pulling at a postman's trousers. But she knew only too well that it was all about the money that she and Nora Duddney had forced him behind the scenes to contribute toward the construction of the new library. Money that had never belonged to him or his family in the first place; that his father had stolen from the public funds intended to create Cherico's first library over seventy-five years ago. Now, it was obvious to her that he was trying to cut corners to put some of that ill-gotten loot back into his account.

"Councilman Sparks," Maura Beth answered, "was that grand speech you just gave out at the lake a bunch of hollow words? It certainly seems that way to me right now. You went on and on about how Cherico would be getting a state-of-the-art building. Do I need to remind you that this library will bear your name?"

"So what?"

"So it will reflect poorly upon you if this facility ends up actually not being state of the art. Your legacy will be tarnished, I can assure you, and I know you don't want that to happen."

That seemed to give the councilman pause, if only for a moment. "I can appreciate that. But these are legitimate questions I have here, Miz Mayhew. Please indulge me for a moment. For instance, what about this large space dedicated to . . . what was the term you used again, 'technicalities'? What the hell does that mean? Are you talking about unforeseen emergencies or something? This isn't a hospital, you know. We've got Cherico Memorial for that."

Maura Beth couldn't help but crack a smile. "As I explained previously, that would be technical services, Councilman. I don't just wiggle my nose like Elizabeth Montgomery to get the books on the shelves where they belong. Many's the long day I've wished it could be like that, but unfortunately it's not. The books have to be processed so we can scan them at the front desk and keep track of them. We have to add things like bar codes and MARC records—that's how we get them into the collection so the public can use them. We'll be hiring a full-time tech services librarian, and we'll need more book carts and tables and computers, for starters. But it's long overdue. I've had to do this all by myself the past six years, so I'm truly looking forward to delegating that responsibility."

Councilman Sparks whistled and then gestured over his head with a *Whoosh!* that let Maura Beth know everything she had explained had fallen on deaf ears. "I don't know about all this. I feel like you're the mechanic insisting that my car needs some part I've never heard of. Somehow I think you're taking advantage of us with all these fancy terms and stipulations."

Maura Beth felt something inside snap. If there was something akin to a composure bone in her body, it had just been shattered. But she wisely took a deep breath to let the crisis pass. She had no intention of taking this latest pronouncement lying down or letting it push her over the edge. "Since I came to Cherico six years ago, I've never been in a position to take advantage of anyone. My parents already think I'm crazy to stay here at my salary and do all the things I have to do to keep the library halfway up and running. But this new facility we're building out at the lake has been a silver lining for me. It's what's keeping me going. That and my upcoming marriage."

"Yes, that is a bit of good news for you," Councilman Sparks said with an exaggerated smile that quickly disappeared. "To that Mr. McShay you introduced me to today under the tent, I understand. And a fine-looking, responsible young lad he is, I'm sure. What was it he was going to be teaching out at the high school? Shop? Soldering? Or maybe woodwork? I know it must be rewarding teaching students how to make mailboxes."

Maura Beth recognized the dig but refused to let it bother her. "No, he's teaching English, as a matter of fact. He has some wonderful ideas about bringing literature to life for his students. He calls it 'Living the Classics in the Real World.' He first got the idea when he was teaching up in Nashville."

"Fancy," Councilman Sparks said with a smirk. "But I do feel I should warn you that our principal, Obie Hutchinson, is somewhat of a traditionalist when it comes to the curriculum. Readin', writin', and 'rithmetic, as he might put it. I certainly wouldn't put our Obie on the cutting edge of educational ideas."

Maura Beth gave him a fleeting smile but was determined to stay on point. "I'm sure Jeremy will work things out. He's going to be very patient about it all. But back to the subject of our blueprints, gentlemen. I can assure you that a tech services room and a teen room are not frivolous suggestions I've invented just to spend more money. I fully realize we have a fixed amount to work with, but when we accepted the bid of Thomas Grayson and Sons Construction, we all agreed that it came in under our ceiling by quite a bit. Doing things on the cheap at this stage is just not the way to go." The look of disdain on Councilman Sparks's face convinced Maura Beth that she needed to show her ace in the hole once again.

"Besides," she continued, raising her voice slightly, "Nora Duddney and I have agreed that we need to keep an eye on all things regarding the library, past and present. I'm sure you understand what I mean, Councilman."

While Rogers Jernigan looked puzzled, Councilman

Sparks immediately conjured up his best reelection smile and did not miss a beat. "City Hall has always appreciated your point of view, of course."

"Then are we finally agreed that the teen room, along with the tech services room and librarian, will be an integral part of our wonderful new facility? No fudging the plans and second-guessing down the road?" Maura Beth concluded with a saucy tilt of her head.

Councilman Sparks rose from behind his desk, leaned over, and offered his hand. "I think you've answered our questions to our satisfaction, Miz Mayhew. Hasn't she, Rogers?"

Still looking mystified, Rogers managed a perfunctory, "Uh . . . yes." And that was the end of that.

"This has been quite a day for both of us," Maura Beth said, back at her efficiency on Clover Street. She and Jeremy were seated next to each other on her rust-colored sofa, holding hands and gazing affectionately at one another. There were many times they found themselves doing that and saying nothing. But this time they had much to discuss. "We were both tested but came through with flying colors."

"This is just round one for me with Obie Hutchinson," Jeremy added. "But at least I let him know who I am."

Maura Beth drew herself up proudly. "Well, I think it's finally beginning to dawn on Durden Sparks that his glory days of intimidating me have come to an end. He got away with it for far too long; but as far as I'm concerned, I think I've slain that dragon. Or at least put out his fire."

Jeremy leaned in and gave her a light kiss on the cheek. "You are my princess warrior, Maurie."

The phone rang and Maura Beth hurried over to the kitchenette counter to answer it. She covered the receiver and loudly whispered the words "My mother!" in Jeremy's general direction as the conversation began.

"Were you in the middle of something?" Cara Lynn Mayhew asked at the other end.

Maura Beth enthusiastically gave the details of the groundbreaking ceremony in response.

"Sounds like something exciting went on up there for once," Cara Lynn continued. "I'm happy for you."

Maura Beth drew back in surprise but quickly recovered. "I can assure you I'm very happy, Mama. So, what's up?"

When Cara Lynn finally spoke up after a significant pause, she appeared to be playing a game of twenty questions. "Well . . . I was wondering . . . how I should dress for this upcoming Cherico outing? I mean, will I need any formal clothes? I'm thinking I probably won't. Does anyone ever dress for dinner up there?"

Maura Beth shot Jeremy an exasperated glance as she exhaled. She could picture her mother exquisitely coiffed and accessorized at this very moment, sitting at her antique writing desk; her makeup skillfully applied, and her tall, trim figure shown off to perfection by whatever designer outfit she was wearing.

"Mama, I know for a fact you have clothes for every occasion in that walk-in closet of yours. I've never seen you inappropriately dressed. You even look ready for the runway in your bathrobe with your hair dripping wet after you shower. Plus, everyone who is anyone at all knows you're the unquestionable fashion maven of the entire metropolitan New Orleans area."

"Thank you for that," came the perfunctory reply, "but this little Cherico of yours cannot possibly be anything like the Crescent City. Why, there's no comparison whatsoever. I was thinking I could get by with a few simple frocks if all I'm going to be doing is staying at a fishing lodge and visiting a library."

Maura Beth was growing weary of the gamesmanship and decided to turn the tables. "So you're thinking of appearing in something off the rack?"

The gasp at the other end of the phone was quite audible and genuine. "Maura Beth, what on earth would make you say a thing like that to me?"

"Oh, I don't know. Maybe the redundant nature of this phone call. We keep having the same conversations about everything, and you know good and well neither one of us is going to change her mind."

Another gasp followed. "So you'd rather not hear from your mother? Is that what you're saying?"

In spite of everything, Maura Beth indulged a smile. If she could back down Councilman Sparks no matter what he threw at her these days, she could handle her mother's trademark manipulations. "Now, you know that's not what I'm saying. Mama, I just wish you would try to be a little more open-minded when you and Daddy come up here. Why don't you pack like you were going to Europe for the summer? You've done that enough over the years."

The laughter that followed had a derisive edge. "Oh, surely you're not comparing Cherico to Europe, Maura Beth!"

"Mama, I don't know what else to say to you. Your hosts, the McShays, are perfectly lovely, generous people. All my friends are. You're going to have a wonderful time up here, if you'll just leave your preconceived notions at home."

There was hopeful silence. Then, "Well, perhaps there's no harm in that. But I had another question for you. Do you think your father and I should actually read *The Robber Bridegroom,* or can we just kibitz? I did all the book reports I ever intended to do in high school and at Tulane."

"Whatever you prefer. We have members of The Cherry Cola Book Club who come to eat and socialize, while others take the literary aspects very seriously. And then we have some who do both. If you'd be more comfortable just observing, then that's fine by me."

Cara Lynn's sigh was clearly plaintive. "Then I guess we'll just sit on the sidelines. I'll just think of it as another dull party. But I have to be honest and tell you that we're not looking forward to the long drive up. Five and a half hours of plowing through Mississippi."

"Mama, you're too much," Maura Beth said, more amused than disappointed. "They don't let the kudzu completely cover the interstates up here, you know. A few feet of concrete are still exposed so you won't lose your way. And if you don't feel like driving, you can always fly to Memphis and rent a car."

"No, thanks. The planes these days are like buses with wings. And they even charge you for the peanuts now. I can't think of anything I'd rather do less."

"Then it's all settled," Maura Beth added, wanting more than anything else to end the conversation before things got too out of hand and she was tempted to say something she might regret. "You and Daddy will drive up in two weeks for all the festivities and become the smash hit of Cherico. There's not a doubt in my mind."

"All right, then," Cara Lynn said, though not sounding wholly convinced. "If this is what you really want."

"Trust me, Mama. It really is."

There was no response at the other end, but Maura Beth could tell from the sound of her mother's breathing that she had something else on her mind. Finally, it came out.

"About your wedding dress . . ."

"Oh, I've narrowed it down to two since we talked about it last," Maura Beth said. "I'll have pictures of both of the ones I like best from Bluff City Bridal in Memphis. When you come up, you can help me make the final decision. One's an A-line design, and the other is an Empire."

"Empire?!" The disapproval in Cara Lynn's voice almost took on a life of its own. "Please tell me you aren't pregnant and that's the reason you didn't want to have the wedding down here!"

Maura Beth's initial surprise soon turned to exasperation, but she took a deep breath and steadied herself. "Of course not, Mama. You know me better than that. I just like the high waist, that's all."

There was more silence—at least thirty seconds of it—and Maura Beth even began to wonder if they'd lost the connection. "Mama? Are you still there?"

"Yes, I'm here."

"Listen, if you think the Empire dress will make people talk, we'll go with the A-line." Maura Beth was careful to keep a smile in her voice, but Cara Lynn seemed determined to channel the drama queen inside.

"There was . . . something else I'd like you to consider. I didn't bring it up last time because, well, I was so distracted by all of your other wedding decisions. I'm just the mother of the bride, you know."

Maura Beth continued to extend the olive branch. "Mama, you're so much more than that, and you know it. So please go right on ahead and tell me what's on your mind?"

"It's just that you and I are the same size. And I was thinking that maybe you might consider wearing *my* wedding dress. It's in wonderful shape since it's been in cold storage all these years with my winter furs. You've seen it in my wedding pictures, of course. It's sort of A-line-ish. And if you wore it, that would bring at least a little of our New Orleans tradition into the ceremony."

Well, there it was—full-blown. Maternal pressure as only

Cara Lynn Mayhew could conjure up. What to say and what to do? Delaying tactics definitely seemed the order of the day.

"Could I mull it over a bit and get back to you?"

"Yes, of course you can. I just thought I'd go ahead and put the bug in your ear."

"Oh, it's there, Mama. I can feel it crawling around."

Finally, a note of laughter from the both of them lightened an overwhelmingly leaden conversation. "Yes, well, you think about it and let me know. I could even bring my dress up on my visit and let you see it up close."

"Okay, Mama. I promise I'll get back to you soon."

After they'd hung up, Maura Beth stood beside the kitchenette counter frowning for the longest time. She wasn't even going to tell Jeremy about this latest development. It was just between herself and her mother, and she needed to dig down and make the right decision. An old, A-line-ish dress versus something brand-new and sparkling. Her mother's approval versus pleasing herself. Which was it going to be?

It was after Maura Beth's candlelight dinner of spaghetti, French bread, and tomato and avocado salad an hour or so later that Jeremy got the idea. "I don't know why we didn't think of it before," he began, while helping Maura Beth clear the cozy dining table that still managed to take up half of their living room. "I mean, all this time we've been focusing on your parents coming up for *The Robber Bridegroom* review. But sooner or later, the Brentwood McShays and the New Orleans Mayhews have got to get together. It's probably a good idea to get that over with before we leave for the honeymoon, don't you think?"

Maura Beth tried her best not to smile at his attempt at humor but couldn't help herself. "There you go again, Jeremy McShay. Such a grasp of the obvious."

"So, why not invite my parents down from Brentwood for the book club meeting, too? Let's be optimistic for a change. Maybe our mothers will really hit it off. For instance, they could talk about Mom's craft boutique down at the Cool Springs Galleria. It's exactly the kind of upscale store you said your mother likes."

Maura Beth began her task of rinsing off dishes. They had agreed to take turns, and this happened to be her night. "I don't know. Mama's not too much of an artsy-craftsy type, although she does love jewelry. She's more of a 'shop 'til you drop' girl—particularly when it comes to the right clothes."

Jeremy handed her another plate and snickered. "Well, then, they could talk fashion. That would give them something in common. Plus, Mom went to Sweet Briar, and you said your mother went to Tulane, right?"

"Only until she got engaged. She'd never admit it, of course, but that's why she enrolled in the first place. And sure enough, she met Daddy there while he was in law school."

Jeremy lifted his right eyebrow smugly. "So what's the big deal if she was on safari? You were the result, Maurie, and as far as I'm concerned, it doesn't get any better than you."

She turned to him briefly and flashed a flirtatious smile. "It's just that I was very serious about becoming a librarian at LSU. I had a completely different approach to my education. I knew exactly where I was going, and my parents haven't really gotten that into their heads to this day."

"Well, look at it this way. Dad taught psychology at Vandy for decades. That's three very good private schools among the in-law résumés right there. Chances are, they'll all hit it off."

"I certainly hope so. But do Connie and Douglas have enough space to accommodate the four of them out there?"

"They've got three huge bedrooms," he told her, "and you've seen how high the ceilings are downstairs. Uncle Doug always claims there's an echo in the place whenever anybody walks in and says, 'Hello!' No, I think our parents couldn't bump into each other if they tried."

Maura Beth turned from the dishes and caught Jeremy's gaze firmly. Neither of them was afraid to look the other straight in the eye when something important needed to be said. "I want you to understand one thing, though. You and I will bend over backward to welcome my parents and try to assure them that we know what we're doing. But if they still balk when all is said and done, it won't change my mind about our marriage. Sure, it would be nice to have their blessing. But if that doesn't happen, it's their loss. Not to mention, it's our life."

Jeremy gave her an impulsive hug and another of his lingering kisses. "That's my Maurie," he said, pulling back with a smile that was definitely on the sexy side of wicked. "Hey, why don't we leave the dishes for later and head on in to that purple bedroom of yours? I'll fire up this little votive candle I just blew out and take it in with us."

She didn't hesitate, quickly wiping her hands on the lavender dish towel hanging over the sink. "You just lead the way. I didn't make any dessert."

4

Sneaky Boys, Sneaky Men

An unexpected little drama at The Twinkle Twinkle Café was unfolding, and Maura Beth was there to witness it from start to finish. She, Periwinkle Lattimore, and Mr. Parker Place had huddled at one of the larger tables during the lull between the lunch and dinner crowds, and were planning the menu for the upcoming visit of the Mayhews and the Brentwood McShays. *The Robber Bridegroom* review and potluck was less than a week away, so there was a sense of urgency in their give-and-take; but everyone was in a cooperative mood, realizing the importance of the event. They had gotten as far as the first course when Periwinkle's trusty waitress, Lalie Bevins, emerged from the kitchen with her son, Barry, in tow. He was doing his best to pull away from her, but she was having none of it.

The family resemblance was very striking. Mother and son had the same round, rosy-cheeked faces and short stature. They parted company dramatically when it came to their dark hair, however; she wore hers slicked back in a ponytail tied with an ordinary rubber band, while he had engineered his into trendy-looking, short spikes. To further announce his presence to the world around him, Barry sported a blue-green tattoo on his right forearm that read in big block letters: **I'M STILL GROWIN'**

"Miz Peri, Mr. Place, Miz Mayhew," Lalie began, acknowledging each of them with an exaggerated nod. "I want y'all to hear this from the horse's mouth. Go ahead, son, tell 'em!"

Barry said nothing at first, flashing on his mother all the while.

"You're not goin' anywhere until you tell 'em!" she insisted, holding firmly on to his arm.

"What's this all about, Lalie?" Periwinkle asked, putting her pen and paper aside for the moment and rising from the table.

"His sassy little girlfriend is what," she answered quickly. "You tell 'em right now, Barry!"

"I didn't think it'd be such a big deal, Miz Peri. Honest," he finally managed. "It was just one baked custard is all. I sneaked one to my girlfriend, Mollie, when she came in yesterday. I'll pay for it myself if you want."

While Periwinkle seemed to take the confession without blinking, Maura Beth could not have been more surprised to hear it. She'd received nothing but glowing reports from Periwinkle about The Twinkle's first home delivery boy. Indeed, the brand-new Twinkle in a Twinkle takeout service was catching on, and Barry Bevins was getting rave reviews from all over Greater Cherico in the form of unsolicited phone calls from satisfied customers. And so far, he had yet to run a stop sign or red light, been caught speeding, or made so much as the tiniest dent in The Twinkle's white-panel van.

Maura Beth sat back and marveled at the way Periwinkle skillfully handled the situation. "Well, Barry, you must be goin' out with an invisible girlfriend because I didn't see her in here yesterday, and my eye doctor says there's not a thing wrong with my vision. So what's the real story here?"

"Umm . . . well, Miz Peri, Mollie came in the delivery door in back when you and Mr. Place were on a break."

Periwinkle raised an eyebrow. "Was this the only time you've helped yourself to food without telling us?"

He appeared to be considering his options—his eyes darting around like pinballs before he finally spoke. "Well, there was one more time. But that's all, I swear it. And please don't blame Mollie. She didn't ask me to do it. I was just tryin' to impress her, I guess. But, well, she did tell me once that she'd like to try something that had sherry in it. She, uh, dares me to do things a lot."

"You realize you can't be sneakin' food from the restaurant, young man. But if you'd asked, I would have worked out something for you—like maybe half price because you're an employee."

"Are you . . . gonna fire me?" he asked, blushing bright pink and staring down at his sneakers.

Periwinkle exchanged glances with both Maura Beth and Mr. Place but somehow managed a stern smile. "I believe in second chances because our customers have told me you're gettin' their food to them on time. Miz Connie McShay out at the lake swears by you."

Barry looked up, brightening considerably. "Yeah, she's my biggest tipper. Same order every time—lotsa tomato aspics."

Periwinkle maintained her somber tone. "You understand that the second chance I'll give you is based on no more freebies from the fridge when nobody's around, don'tcha?"

"I think you should dock him, no matter what, Miz Peri," Lalie put in, her nose in the air. "He needs to learn him a lesson. I didn't bring him up to steal from people, especially from someone who's been as good to me as you have. It's prob'ly 'cause his father and me got divorced when he was little. I've tried to do my best with him on my own."

"Tell ya what," Periwinkle said, taking it all in with a serene demeanor. "You pay half price for the two you stole, Barry, and I'll consider we're even. Have we got a deal?"

"Yeah, we got a deal. Thank you, Miz Peri," he answered, looking very relieved as the two shook hands.

"And you don't have to sneak your girlfriend in the back door, either," Periwinkle added. "You bring her in through the front so we can visit and get to know her a little better. That is, if you're serious about the relationship. I have to assume you are, the way you're movin' my custard on the sly."

"Yes, ma'am, I am," Barry told her with conviction in his voice. "I mean, I'm sixteen now, and I have this real good job here. Hey, there's nothin' I like better than drivin' all around town. I sure never thought I'd get paid for it and get such awesome tips. These two high-school buddies a' mine, Scott and 'Crispy'—well, his real name's Lawrence, but he likes bacon so much we all call him Crispy—anyhow, my buddies are so jealous of the money I'm makin.' And then they both wish they could be goin' out with a hottie like Mollie Musselwhite. It's so sweet—I got it all over 'em."

"You keep at it, son. I can assure you that being a hard worker will impress any sixteen-year-old girl. And when it comes to tips, here's the best one I can give you about women in general: We're all of us on the lookout for solid, responsible men," Periwinkle told him.

"Well, I think it's a good thing we nipped this in the bud," Lalie said, getting in a final word. "It was Mollie's mother who called me up and put me on to it, and I brought it straight to ya as soon as I heard, Miz Peri."

"For which I thank you." She paused to reflect, briefly bit her lip, and then nodded. "So, I think we're done here."

At which point Lalie and Barry headed back into the kitchen and Periwinkle resumed her seat, gathering her notes in front of her once again. "Now, where were we, folks? I believe we'd whittled it down to either a cucumber and red onion salad or my tomato aspic for the first course."

"I vote for the cucumber and red onion," Mr. Place said. "Not quite as heavy on the tummy in this August heat, you know. By the way, that was well done back there with Barry."

Periwinkle's smile was clearly not of the surface variety, and she even winked at him at the end. "There's nothin' I can't handle, Parker."

Maura Beth quietly observed the two of them throughout the rest of the meeting. It was the subtle things she couldn't help but notice: a stolen glance now and then; the tone of voice they used with one another; even reaching out to touch in what could only be described as a flirtatious manner. It was becoming apparent that they were probably moving beyond the friendship stage. Periwinkle had even suggested as much to Maura Beth recently. "Parker's just such a change from Harlan and those sneaky ways he tries to take advantage of me," she had revealed at one point. "But Parker's pastries aren't the only thing sweet about him, and I think I'm ready for that kind of man in my life right now."

But Maura Beth also wondered frankly just how open they were prepared to be about their relationship and what steps they might take next. Yes, it was the millennium, but it was still the small-town South and all that came with that. A burgeoning romance between a black man and a white woman might not attract the attention it once did, but it still wasn't the sort of thing it was wise to flaunt. Not to mention that he was still living with his elderly mother, Ardenia, on Big Hill Lane, and Periwinkle still drove home every night to her house halfway between Cherico and Corinth, thankfully with audiobooks from the library to keep her company. Was some sort of epic change looming on the horizon?

★ ★ ★

Periwinkle was pleased with all the decisions she, Maura Beth, and her Parker had made earlier regarding the upcoming dinner for the parents of the bride and groom. The menu had been set: cucumber and red onion salad; followed by spice-rubbed, grilled chicken breasts with homemade chunky salsa; and finally, Parker's key lime icebox pie for dessert. Despite what she had heard about Maura Beth's parents, she couldn't imagine that anyone could possibly be picky about delicious fare like that. After all, her livelihood was based on the truism that everyone spoke the common language of good food.

Now it was time to close up and drive home at the end of yet another successful day of business at The Twinkle. Her Parker had made it known from the beginning of his employment that he didn't much like her being the last one standing at ten o'clock every night, and he had intervened as the gentleman he was.

"I don't mind staying a half hour longer to lock up with you," he had insisted that first time on the job. "I'd feel better about things."

"Hey, I've done it for years, and I'm a big girl," she had told him. "I have mace on the premises, and I took a self-defense class a few years back. You just go on home and look after that sweet little mother of yours. You give Ardenia my best, now." And with a carefree wink, she had sent him on his way ahead of her—even if their send-offs these days had now escalated into long, heartfelt hugs, followed by delicious little pecks on the cheek.

In fact, the warm, fuzzy feelings generated by their latest good-bye were coursing through her veins as she turned the back-door key and headed toward her Impala. She always parked it in the slot beside the big, rusty-looking Dumpster, which for some reason she had come to think of as a stout sentinel looking after her precious Twinkle. She was also daydreaming about the humorous text she had received during the dinner service from up-and-coming country singer, Waddell Mack, telling her that he planned to stop by The Twinkle next time he was passing through Cherico on his way to Nashville. i hear ur place is word of mouthwatering, the text had concluded, causing her to break out into laughter to the surprise of everyone working in the kitchen. Why, if he actually showed up and ate her food, she might just have to start a wall of autographed celebrity pictures! That might really put The Twinkle on the map!

Thus, her guard was down when the long shadow cast from a nearby streetlight fell ominously across the asphalt stretching out in front of her. In an instant, her arms were encircled and pinned behind her as a gruff male voice declared: "Guess who, Peri?"

She felt like she had been stabbed with a hypodermic full of adrenaline as she got out a couple of piercing screams for help. But the voice immediately intervened. "Stop all that yelling, Peri! It's just me, Harlan!"

He loosened his grip, allowing her to break away from him. Then she spun around, her eyes filled with contempt. "What the hell do you think you're doing?! You scared me to death sneaking up on me like that!"

"It was just a joke. I didn't mean anything by it. But seriously, I need to talk to you," he said, softening his tone a bit.

She brandished her car keys in front of his face. "Some joke! You see these? I was fixin' to put your eyes out with 'em. Or give you a swift kick to that almighty junk of yours you prize so highly. What on earth's wrong with you? You wanna talk to me—you call me up like a normal human being and say what you gotta say. Or you show up in broad daylight when there are witnesses around. Whadda you mean stalkin' me like this in the parking lot?"

"Stop making such a fuss. I wanted to get it straight from you," he continued, exhaling as she lowered her keys.

"Get what straight from me?"

The lines in his face definitely hardened. "Don't you play so innocent with me, Peri. You know damn well what I'm talking about. Is it true that you're seeing that . . . that—"

She cut him off quickly, thrusting the keys at him once again. "Don't you dare say that word to me! Don't you even think about it!"

His laughter was dismissive. "I was gonna say . . . *that pastry chef.* See? You got all huffy for nothing."

"Oh, you don't fool me. I'm sure you were thinkin' it, and it's not the least bit funny," she said, backing away from him slightly. He was still intruding too much on her personal space. "It's no business of yours if I am good friends with Parker or what's goin' on between us. But let me remind you that you and I are divorced, Harlan John Lattimore, and that means it's over and done with. I thought I made that crystal clear to you when I turned down that so-called second proposal of yours a few months ago. Fact is, you're still the same irresponsible, pretend cowboy you always were. You'll never grow up—not in our lifetime. You oughtta try to see yourself as everybody else does for a change."

He inched closer to her face again, and she could smell that he had been drinking. "Spare me the lecture, Peri. Hell, I just can't believe you'd prefer this black man to me," he continued, contorting his lips into a sneer. "You keep this up, and it'll ruin your business for sure. It's one thing to hire this man to make some extra money on his desserts. I get that part. But it's another thing entirely if you're seen all over town acting like some damn fool, giggly teenager on her first date. Makes me sick just to think about it. You don't think people are talking about you behind your back? I'm only telling you all this for your own good, I hope you realize. Talk about looking at yourself in a mirror!"

Now it was her turn to laugh him off. "Yeah, I know you've always had my best interests at heart. Ha! That's why our marriage lasted so long. But you keep this stalkin' stuff up, and I'll get a restraining order against you. I mean it, Harlan. I don't have to take this foolishness, so you better get over your jukebox-playing, line-dancing, womanizing self. I don't wanna see you around The Twinkle even if you haven't eaten for a month and you're flat out starvin' to death. You're not welcome here on my property, and that's my fair warning."

He lifted his chin dramatically, twitching his nose as his eyes narrowed to slits. "If that's the way you want it, then, Miss High and Mighty!"

"Call me whatever you want. But you just remember those two big words, Harlan: *restraining order.* You'll get off my case here and now if you know what's good for you."

He mumbled something under his breath and started to walk away. Then he turned on his cowboy boot heels at the last second and wagged a finger at her. "You can't get rid of me so easily after all we've been through. And don't come crying to me when all this doesn't turn out the way you thought it would!"

"Believe me, I won't," she said, snickering. "And your veiled threats don't scare me the least little bit."

She watched him storming off into the darkness and suddenly realized she needed to catch a breath. Her blood was racing, and she felt more vulnerable than she had in a very long time. When she had finally calmed herself, she slid into the front seat of her car and sat behind the wheel thinking about what had just happened. Should she tell Parker about the distressing incident? The last thing she wanted was any kind of confrontation between the two men. That might bring the black versus white issue to an ugly conclusion.

She started the car and then turned on the air-conditioning, finding unexpected comfort in the rush of white noise it produced. Maybe if she just told her best girlfriend, Maura Beth, and sought her advice, leaning on her shoulder for once. What about her mother over in Corinth? Or perhaps she should just say nothing and hope for the best. Surely Harlan was just talking a tough game and trying to soothe his wounded male ego. It was easy to picture him as nothing more than an aging buck with a huge set of antlers, posturing and snorting at the air; then flicking his tail and running away into the woods to hide at the first sign of being stood down.

5

Bye Bye Broccoli

Jeremy and Maura Beth were sitting across from each other at the breakfast table a few days before the big visit of their parents. "You still have no clue what Becca's surprise girlie luncheon—as you keep calling it—is all about?" he wanted to know. It wasn't the first time he had pressed her on the subject.

She was momentarily lost in thought and then looked up from her cereal with a wry grin. "Hey, cut the woman some slack. She's pregnant and probably crazed with hormones. That's the best I can come up with right now. All she would tell any of us was that it was going to be me, Connie, Periwinkle, and Miss Voncille—the original core of the book club."

Jeremy took a sip of his coffee before throwing out his latest theory. "Okay, try this one on for size. I have to be good at reading the minds of all my students, you know. That's how you maintain control in the classroom—you anticipate the next moves of those fermenting teenaged brains. So, I was thinking that Becca might have an important announcement to make, and she wants her very bestest girlfriends at her side for a big dose of courage."

Maura Beth put down her spoon as her face fell. "Oh, no!"

He had a superior smirk on his face. "Hey, I'm well aware *bestest* isn't proper English!"

"No, it's not that, silly. It's the baby," Maura Beth continued. "I hope nothing bad has happened. She and Stout Fella have been waiting for ten long years to get pregnant. Oh, now you've got me thinking all sorts of terrible things!"

Jeremy adopted her sudden tone of despair. "Geez, I hadn't even thought of that angle. Sorry. I didn't mean to upset you." He took another moment. "But you said she was the usual bubbly Becca over the phone."

"Yes, she definitely was. I didn't even give her invitation a second thought at the time."

He dug into more of his cereal. "Well, it's probably nothing. And you'll know in a few more hours," he added, finally. "Maybe it's just some straightforward good news, and she just wants to share it with all of you first."

Then Jeremy changed the subject as they cleared the table. "Gotten any new e-mails or phone calls from your parents about the book club visit?"

"Nothing," Maura Beth said. "I'm just continuing to hope for the best when they get here. After Mama's last long-distance, diva performance about what clothes she should bring, I decided I'd rather not hear from her until she actually darkens our door. Silence really can be golden sometimes."

"Well, at least my mom and dad are excited about it all. I know for a fact they've always loved everything about Uncle Doug and Aunt Connie's lodge. And so should we, considering that's where we first met last year."

That brought a reflective smile to Maura Beth's face. "Yep, we were clicking on all cylinders that evening by the fireplace. Can't remember a single disagreement we had, and we trotted out all the deal breakers—politics, religion, pop culture, you name it. Plus, your parents have just been fantastic to me.

They helped me out so much with my book-club ideas up in
Brentwood, and your mother's been a sweetheart over the
phone ever since. Can I please just go ahead and adopt them?"

He gave her a chuckle as he rinsed out his coffee cup at
the sink. "No worries, Maurie. They'll be your in-laws soon
enough."

"And I'm really looking forward to that," she said, leaning
into him affectionately. "We're getting married no matter
what my parents throw up against the wall."

As Maura Beth drove her Prius along the gravel road lined
with pink crepe myrtles that led to the Brachles' sprawling,
multicolumned country estate, she was suddenly reminded of
the lack of affordable housing throughout Greater Cherico.
She and Jeremy had been looking for something larger—just
anything at all—for weeks now. But the only new construction within a ten-mile radius was going on out at Justin
Brachle's high-end lake development, and those were exclu-
sively the mega-budget projects of the wealthiest citizens.
Meanwhile, there didn't seem to be much of a market for a
new apartment complex of any size anywhere, especially since
Cherico was not growing. For the time being, Maura Beth's
efficiency on Clover Street would have to do; she and Jeremy
would just have to go the extra mile to avoid getting on each
other's nerves in such a small space. For the most part, they
were managing things nicely. Except that she was still somewhat upset by Jeremy's suggestion over breakfast that had led
her to think a tragedy of the highest order might have befallen
the Brachle household.

So when Maura Beth followed Becca into her chandelier-
hung dining room a few minutes later and saw that her petite
girlfriend was still not in maternity clothes, a nearly palpable
feeling of panic exploded somewhere deep inside her. It spread
from the core of her being all the way out to her fingertips,

and she could only hope that the concern was not reading on her face. There was also the problem of thinking of just the right thing to say if the pregnancy had indeed gone awry. She had never been in this position before and wasn't looking forward to the pressure.

"Always good to get together with the famous Becca Broccoli in her beautiful home," Maura Beth said, as she admired the pastel blue quatrefoil drapes, Wilson china place settings, and centerpiece of lush green hydrangea cuttings. "And what are you serving us today that smells so heavenly?"

"Oh, it's just my easy-peasy chicken spaghetti. It should be getting close to golden bubbly in a few more minutes," Becca told her. "Hope you're good and hungry. I doubled the recipe, and I'm expecting you girls to take home any leftovers. I mean it—I've got all my Tupperware lined up back in the kitchen."

"I'm sure I'll do my share of damage," Maura Beth said, matching the smile on Becca's face. So far, nothing seemed to be out of kilter, but appearances could be deceiving.

In order, Connie, Periwinkle, and Miss Voncille swept in—all fashionably dressed and coiffed—and they were soon enjoying Bloody Marys and chatting amiably. But it was when Maura Beth saw Becca sipping her cocktail that her heart truly sank. She knew there was no way a responsible pregnant woman would be consuming alcohol. In that case, it was obvious that Becca was putting up a remarkably strong front while steeling herself for the unpleasant revelation that she had indeed lost the baby.

When the time came for everyone to sit down and start enjoying their food, Maura Beth was so preoccupied that she merely pushed hers around her plate. Being the consummate hostess she was, of course, Becca noticed. "I hope there's nothing wrong with your spaghetti, Maura Beth. Did I go overboard with the cayenne pepper this morning? I've been in a spicy mood lately," she said, her voice the epitome of Southern hospitality.

Maura Beth looked embarrassed and thought on her feet. "Oh, no, Becca . . . it's delicious as usual. I guess I wasn't as hungry as I thought I was. But don't worry. I'll pick up the pace."

Becca smiled brightly and then chimed her spoon on her water glass a moment later. "Well, ladies, if I recall my *Alice in Wonderland* correctly, the time has come to talk of other things. I always enjoy getting together with you, of course, but I had another purpose in mind today. I have an important announcement to make, and I trust you'll all bear with me. This isn't going to be a particularly easy thing for me to explain, but I want you to hear it from me and not on the street."

Maura Beth briefly shut her eyes and tried to calm herself. So Jeremy had been right all along! Becca was truly putting on a brave show for the benefit of her dearest friends, bless her heart.

"You four Cherry Cola Book Club members are the first to hear the news," she began, having everyone's undivided attention. "Well, other than my Stout Fella, my big, lovable Justin. I haven't even told the WHYY station manager yet, and I don't think he's going to like me much when I've done the deed. But here it is, ladies. I'm quitting radio and shutting down *The Becca Broccoli Show*. I'm putting the old girl and her helpful hints to bed."

Expecting to hear something entirely different as a result of the dramatic buildup inside her head, Maura Beth was having significant trouble processing the information. Thus, her response was a genuine non sequitur. "But I saw you drinking a Bloody Mary, Becca!"

The others exchanged bewildered glances, but it was Connie who managed to speak up. "What does that have to do with the show?"

"Well . . . I . . . the alcohol . . . the pregnancy," Maura Beth said, struggling to explain herself. Everything suddenly sounded foolish to her even as it was all coming out of her mouth. How in heaven's name had she led herself down the garden path and been this far off in her thinking? She couldn't blame it all on Jeremy. Was the unthinkable happening? Was she becoming the same sort of drama queen her mother had always been and continued to be? Heaven forbid!

Becca's riff of laughter immediately dissolved the confusion in the room. "Oh, I see what you were thinking. But mine was a Virgin Mary, sweetie. Some extra Tabasco was all the kick it had. I thought you all knew that. I wouldn't dare touch even a drop of booze."

Maura Beth decided to save herself further embarrassment and change the subject quickly. "Oh, of course you wouldn't. Don't pay any attention to me. I seem to be rambling today. Anyhow, you were telling us about wrapping up *The Becca Broccoli Show.* But you haven't told us why yet."

"Yes, tell us," Periwinkle said, still frowning at Maura Beth with a skeptical, sideways glance. "I've gotten some of my best food tips from listening to you, Becca. People all over Cherico swear by you. Hey, even The Twinkle's menu swears by you, girl!"

"I know I do," Miss Voncille added. "Whenever I want to impress Locke with a new dish, I tune you in and get my pen and paper ready. He thinks I'm an absolute genius in the kitchen."

Becca surveyed her friends quickly and gave a delicate sigh of satisfaction. "Well, there are two reasons really. The first is the little one growing inside me. In just over five months I'll be a mother with a precious baby to look after. As you all know,

I've been wanting that for a long time, and now it's finally going to happen. Frankly, I just don't think I'll have the time anymore to keep coming up with all these recipe ideas, much less show up at the radio station early every morning, what with the diapers I'll have to change and the formula I'll have to fix."

"That sounds so familiar. I remember those hectic days when Douglas and I were on Lindy's two o'clock bottle schedule. My goodness, we thought we would never get a wink of sleep again. The truth is, a baby turns everything upside down," Connie observed, reaching over to rub Becca's arm gently.

"That's what I've been told, but I don't think I'll mind in the least."

"No, you won't. But I think I heard you say there were two reasons. What was the other one?" Connie continued.

This time Becca's sigh was drawn-out and weighted with worry as her face clouded over. "It's because of my Stout Fella. As some of you probably know, he's been having these horrible stabbing pains in his feet that just won't go away." She paused to gesture at the floor with her index finger several times. "I've been teasing him that it was all due to wearing those ridiculous cowboy boots of his. Ha! He thinks they help him with his real-estate deals somehow. Talk about your superstitious beliefs! Unfortunately, it turns out he has neuropathy. In fact, he has a condition called *insulin resistance,* and he's got to completely change his eating habits. I mean from top to bottom. I'll have to do a complete makeover of the pantry."

"But he's lost all that weight already," Maura Beth pointed out.

Becca frowned and waved her off. "No thanks to me in the first place. I've been fixing him tons of carbs and sweets ever since we got married. Hey, we've both even laughed about the way he 'islands' his ice cream all the time. But the neurologist up in Memphis said that he could actually reverse this insulin condition if he lost even more weight and paid strict attention to his sugar and carbs intake. I've got to try to help him do that now."

"This sounds almost like diabetes," Maura Beth said.

"It isn't yet, but that could be the eventual result if we don't do something quick. I just hope it's not too little, too late," Becca answered, sounding both maternal and determined.

Connie looked puzzled as she patted her big hair. "But haven't you been including more healthy recipes in your shows lately? Why, Voncille had us all over for breakfast to listen to that very first one where you told your audience you were putting the broccoli back in *The Becca Broccoli Show.* We just thought that was the cutest thing we'd ever heard."

Becca waited for the nods of recognition and polite titters to die down. "I appreciate that, but the basis of the show is still plenty of comfort food with carbs and sugar, and that's not what Justin needs right now. The way I see it, my first obligation is to my husband and child. The show's been a wonderful creative outlet for me—really, it's been a great ride. But I think it's run its course."

The table went silent for a while as everyone took it all in.

"All I can say is, I'll miss you on the radio," Miss Voncille said, finally. "In fact, I know good and well I've become addicted to it. I set my alarm every morning so I can get up and hear it. Oh, yes, Locke mumbles and complains, but then he turns over and goes right back to sleep while I head out to the kitchen to have my coffee and listen to you."

The others were nodding in agreement as Becca quickly replied. "I'm flattered. But I do believe I have something that'll take care of your withdrawal symptoms."

Miss Voncille beat the others to the punch. "Oooh, quick! Tell us!"

"Well, I've almost finished my *Best of Becca Broccoli* cookbook that I told y'all about last year at our very first Cherry Cola Book Club meeting. I promise it'll be out before the baby comes."

Maura Beth's sudden inspiration caused an audible gasp as she lightly clapped her hands several times. "And you simply have to have a signing at the library. You'd be our first!"

Becca acknowledged the suggestion with a gracious nod. "I'd be delighted, of course. We'll nail down a date soon."

Maura Beth finally felt herself relaxing now that her misguided perceptions had been thoroughly shown up and tossed aside. She also realized that she was actually hungry and began eating in earnest. True, the spaghetti was on the lukewarm side, but she wasn't going to make a fuss. It was more than enough that Becca's baby was still tucked away safely. All was right with the known world, both inside and out.

Over after-luncheon coffee and dainty amaretto cookies, the talk shifted to the latest on the upcoming weddings, and Maura Beth offered up a somewhat condensed version of her concerns and expectations when she was prodded. "I suppose I could avoid all controversy and give in to my mother's demands for a hometown service," she was saying. "Of course, it would mean going down to New Orleans and dealing with all of her high-maintenance friends, not to mention a hundred-something distant cousins who probably showed up last at my christening. The genealogical aspects of all that just boggles my mind. If I have to deal with our Cudd'n M'Dear and her ilk, I think I might explode!"

Connie managed a pleasant smile while speaking emphatically. "Well, you know Douglas and I are looking forward to meeting your parents, but we don't have to have the ceremony at the lodge. You can change your mind at any time. I promise we won't be upset."

"Maybe they'll surprise me and actually respect my wishes," Maura Beth added. "At any rate, Jeremy and I are hoping for a meeting of the minds when the two families get together."

Miss Voncille dramatically threw her hands in the air. "I certainly hope it works out, but, ladies, I have to confess that Locke and I have just about decided to leave things the way they are. Of course a wedding at this time of my life would be a dream come true for me, but Carla and Locke, Jr. continue to be unbelievably mean and nasty to us. If anything, they've gotten worse, and it's really hurt Locke deeply. As for me, I have a brand-new respect for those who decide not to have children!"

"So you're saying you might not even get married? I thought everything was all set for late August at the Episcopal Church," Maura Beth said.

"It was at one time. But we just might not get married at all. Just the other evening I looked Locke straight in the eye and I told him that if his money and property were going to cause all this friction, it would be fine with me if he left me out of the will whether we're married or not. After all, I have my pension and a little put by. I've gotten along just fine all these years on my own."

"That's awfully high-minded of you," Periwinkle said. But there was clearly reservation in her voice. "I'd just like to add that you can't let people intimidate you like that, Voncille, particularly if they're close to you and think they can get away with it. Believe me, I know what I'm talking about. If you and Locke really want to get married, you should go for it. Stand up for yourselves no matter what happens. You gotta draw the line somewhere." For a moment it looked as if Periwinkle was going to add something further but apparently thought better of it and merely shrugged her shoulders.

That seemed to have a sobering effect on the group, and

Maura Beth decided to change the subject and lighten the mood. "Well, folks, have we all read our Eudora for the book club review this weekend?"

Everyone said they had—except for Periwinkle, who indicated she was on the last chapter and turning the pages as fast as she could. "Since you didn't have an audio for me to check out this time, I had to sit down and actually read a book for once. I was a little outta practice since it wasn't one of my menus, you understand," she added, winking smartly.

"Speaking of menus, I assume everyone has their potluck assignments straight," Becca said. "Of course I'm bringing the shrimp gumbo in honor of your parents, Maura Beth."

"Frozen fruit salad!" Connie called out, raising her hand quickly.

"My biscuits and green pepper jelly as usual," Miss Voncille added, sounding a bit more restrained. "I know it seems like I'm in a rut, but it's what I do best. So why mess up a good thing?"

Maura Beth was up next. "And I believe I'm doing another chocolate, cherry cola sheet cake."

"I'm fixin' grilled chicken breasts!" Periwinkle blurted out, but then cocked her head with a frown. "Oh, wait . . . that's for the dinner at The Twinkle the night before." She was obviously concentrating now. "For the review, I believe I'm supposed to bring parmesan-stuffed mushrooms."

"Very good, gang," Becca said. "It sure looks like all of us are on the same page then."

The words stayed with Maura Beth long after the luncheon had ended and she was driving home reviewing everything in her head. She could only wish the weekend would be a matter of menus and that a clash of personalities would not enter into it.

6

Divas at Dusk

The drill was starting to get to Jeremy, but he was reluctant to annoy Maura Beth by saying anything. He knew she was well-intentioned; it was just that she was relentless, and he could only memorize so many pointers at one time.

"Now, on to politics," she continued, glancing at her notes as the two of them sat up in bed the evening before both sets of parents would be arriving. "Daddy goes back and forth all the time. Sometimes he attacks the Democrats—others times, the Republicans. It all depends upon the issue. He says it's because he likes to keep all his options open as a registered Independent. On the other hand, I'm not sure Mama has ever even voted, so I don't know what you can do with that."

Jeremy glanced her way with a weak smile and shrugged. "I don't either. But here's one for you. Does she complain about the shape the country's in?"

"No, not that I can recall."

"Well, at least she's consistent. The old adage is that if you don't vote, you don't have the right to complain."

"Yes, but maybe you could just avoid political discussions until they've both gotten to know you better." Then she flipped a page of her notepad. "Now, I think religion will be a little bit easier to navigate. As you know, they're both devout Episcopalians. That's why they're so upset with me about wanting to get married up here at the lodge instead of at St. Andrew's. But you're relatively cool with the Episcopal Church, aren't you? Not carrying grudges of any kind, I assume."

"None whatsoever, especially since I'm a lapsed Methodist these days," Jeremy said, unable to avoid snickering. "Although if Henry the Eighth and John Wesley squared off in a prize fight, I'd probably put my money on Wesley in a two-round knockout. I think Henry the Eighth would be a little out of shape. I seem to recall portraits of him with a giant turkey leg hanging out of his mouth."

Maura Beth's laugh seemed a bit forced, but then she suddenly became quite animated. "Oh, and I just thought of another important little tidbit for you. Please don't bring up Hurricane Katrina and the insurance companies. Daddy was on the wrong side of some of those lawsuits, and it wasn't pretty, let me tell you. I was still at LSU at the time and thought I'd never hear the end of it. Every time he e-mailed me, there was another diatribe to wade through."

Jeremy decided it was time to pull the plug. "Listen, Maurie, this is beyond fascinating, but all these categories are starting to make me feel like I'm cramming for *Jeopardy!* or something. I think you're worrying about this first impression business way too much. Being scripted is fine when you're teaching kids English, but it may not be all that great an idea when you're meeting your in-laws for the first time. If you've noticed, I haven't exactly given you a homework assignment to complete about my parents."

Maura Beth put her notepad down on the purple sheets and caught his gaze. "That's because there wasn't any need to. I've already met them, and the three of us already know we get along. It's like I've known Susan and Paul McShay all my life. I want to look as elegant as your mother does when I get to be her age, and who wouldn't like a retired Vanderbilt professor of psychology in the family when it comes to advice? They're both so together, I can't stand it. But the bottom line is, I just want my parents to like you as much as yours like me. Is that too much to ask?"

"In . . . a . . . perfect . . . world . . . no," he told her, deliberately taking his time. "But we don't live in one, unfortunately. Besides, you're the one who's been saying we're going to get married no matter what. Let's just trust that we'll do and say the right things here." He leaned over and gave her a soft, reassuring kiss.

"I'm sure we will," she said, pulling away slightly to catch her breath. "It's just that my mother can be so difficult at times. I think Councilman Sparks may be easier to deal with when you come down to it. And then, even though I've always gotten along better with Daddy, there's this semichangeling thing that keeps bugging me. I know it's ridiculous, but since I really don't look like either one of my parents, I've always wondered if somebody might have just dropped me off at their doorstep, or there was some kind of mix-up at the hospital."

Jeremy inched a bit closer, putting a protective arm around her. "Hey, I remember thinking that myself way back when. I'm sort of a combination of my parents—uniquely me."

"Yes, you are unique. But do you think I'm crazy?'

"No, I think lots of children play around with that scenario at some time or other in their lives."

Maura Beth looked amused. "Well, they say the gene for red hair is way recessive anyway."

"That's the spirit. You're a delightful throwback. So don't give that mix-up thing another thought. But you bringing up Councilman Sparks reminds me—anything new from City Hall about the library?"

"Nothing since the attempt to get me to erase the teen room and the tech services area from the blueprints. Not a peep out of His Royal Highness, I'm delighted to report. They'll be pouring the slab soon. I figure my dream library is a done deal once the concrete is cured."

"Well, there you go," Jeremy said, his voice oozing confidence. "You put Councilman Sparks in his place. Now I realize he didn't give birth to you, so that mother-daughter thing isn't in play. But I think you'll rise to the occasion tomorrow when your mother finally shows up. And I promise you—I won't put my foot in my mouth if I can possibly help it. I'm a keeper, remember?"

That led to another kiss, and this time she was the one who initiated it.

"How about I light another candle?" he said, moving down her neck with his lips. It had become a romantic convention of theirs—this flickering candle business on the nightstand whenever they decided to make love. "Enough of this coaching. Let's just play and have some fun. The evening's still young."

When Maura Beth saw her mother and father step out of their silver Escalade around three o'clock the following afternoon in front of the lodge, she inhaled the steamy August air and firmly grabbed Jeremy's arm. She needed that physical connection with him now more than ever, particularly after she saw how her mother was dressed. Yes, the outfit was simple and form-fitting, complementing Cara Lynn Mayhew's still-stunning figure and long legs. But it was also as black as pitch—as if she were going to or had just come from a funeral. It was a long-established fashion fact that this carefree socialite wore only bright, colorful designs in public. Was there a message in there somewhere? Surely not. Especially since Maura Beth had weighed her options carefully and decided to wear

her mother's wedding dress, hoping—perhaps against hope—
that it might dissolve the ongoing tension between them once
and for all.

"Keep your wedding dress in storage with the furs,
Mama—at least for now," she had said over the phone two
days before. "I don't need you to bring it up here. I'm going
to wear it proudly because you want me to."

For the first time in—oh, forever—Cara Lynn had sounded
genuinely pleased about something where the two of them
were concerned. "Well, what a nice surprise!"

"It's what you wanted, wasn't it?"

"Yes, of course." Then came the disclaimer. "Of course, I
could have wished you would be wearing it down in New
Orleans. We could still make it the social event of the season."

But Maura Beth had risen to the occasion, letting the
zinger bounce off her thick skin. "I only hope I'll look as
lovely in it as you did."

And Cara Lynn had been unable to top that, genuinely
thanking her daughter for the compliment. They hadn't spo-
ken since then, but Maura Beth liked her chances of making
this first visit a successful one, even if her mother *was* wearing
black.

Meanwhile, her father had stepped out wearing a gray
business suit and one of those trendy purple ties that Maura
Beth found so jarring on men these days. Purple ties and pink
shirts, even on some of the talking-head news and sports
anchors—what was that all about? She was at least thankful
that her Jeremy was a no-frills, white shirt kind of fellow.
Well, he did have a couple of yellow polo shirts in the closet
they now shared. But she was happy to say they looked very
sporty on him.

Fortunately, she came out of her spontaneous fashion review just in time to embrace her father, who was the first to
approach her and hold out his arms. "Hi, sweetheart! My lit-

tle girl is looking just wonderful!" William Mayhew exclaimed.

Maura Beth could sense that the strength of his hug was genuine, while his tone of voice was warm and relaxed. As for his appearance, the years continued to be kind to him. He had remained trim and athletic-looking with a full head of dark hair, although it had begun to gray significantly. Never what anyone would consider classically handsome, his masculine resolve had always been attractive to women; and he had enjoyed his share of them before settling down with his trophy wife.

"You're looking great yourself, Daddy," she told him. "I hope the drive up wasn't too tiring. I know it's a long way to come."

But Cara Lynn preempted her husband instead of greeting her daughter. "The interstate wasn't so bad, but this last part on the back roads seemed like we were lost in a foreign country. I don't know how many times I kept checking the map to make sure we hadn't taken a wrong turn."

"Good to see you, too, Mama," Maura Beth said, initiating their embrace and ignoring the last remark.

"Your father's right," Cara Lynn added, standing back for an assessment with the suggestion of a smile. The problem was, there was a certain skepticism in that suggestion, as if she didn't quite approve of whomever or whatever was in front of her. In fact, it had become a trait of hers that more than a few people found off-putting. "You do look quite pretty with your hair pulled back off your face like that. I've always thought you should show off your forehead instead of wearing bangs. It's just not age appropriate."

"I'll take that as a compliment, Mama. But you can thank my stylist out at Cherico Tresses. Terra works wonders with me all the time. She's a gem." Then she nudged Jeremy forward a bit. "Well, here he is, folks," she continued. "The pride of the McShays. The Brentwood, Tennessee, McShays, that is. You'll be meeting all the McShays in a few seconds."

William offered his hand and that masculine smile of his at the same time. "Hello, son. I'm sure you've been thinking this day would never get here."

"I guess Maurie and I have been counting it down, sir," Jeremy answered. "But it's a pleasure to meet you both at last."

Cara Lynn maintained a polite distance, settling instead for a perfunctory nod and a grin. "The same here, Jeremy. But who's Maurie?"

"Oh," Maura Beth said, caught off guard. "That's his nickname for me, Mama. I thought I'd mentioned it to you before."

Cara Lynn maintained the rigid posture of a mannequin. "I don't believe I recall it, no."

"Well, let's don't dawdle out here in this heat," Maura Beth continued, eager to switch subjects. "Jeremy's parents and your hosts are all waiting inside to meet you with a little something to drink. They thought it might be slightly overwhelming to descend upon you all at once."

"The way people do on a train platform or at an airline terminal," Jeremy added, clearly expecting some reinforcing laughter from the matter-of-fact inflection he was using. His face fell quickly, however, when he was greeted only with silence. Even Maura's Beth's hopeful smile and arched eyebrows failed to rescue the moment.

"What about our luggage?" Cara Lynn asked with an abruptness that seemed unnecessary. "We have quite a lot on the back seat and in the trunk. I really didn't know how much I should bring."

"Oh, don't worry about that, Mama. These strong men will bring all of it in for you after you've had a chance to catch your breath with a nice refreshing cocktail. Wouldn't that hit the spot?"

Cara Lynn exhaled with a hint of resignation. "As a matter of fact it would. Lead the way."

But they had taken only a few steps when the front door flew open, and Connie greeted them with outstretched arms and a smile typical of all Southern women who make playing hostess their specialty in life. "Welcome to Cherico and to our home! We're so happy to see you. I'm Connie McShay, Jeremy's aunt."

The rush of relatives continued as Douglas joined the group for another round of introductions. Once they were all inside, Paul and Susan McShay stepped up for more handshakes and hugs; and after the guests had been shown to their room to freshen up, everyone settled on sofas and chairs in front of the empty fireplace, sipping wine or something stronger. Then came the inevitable, awkward small talk.

"Your home is so spacious. I like it very much," William said with a sweep of his hand. "I don't think I've ever seen such high ceilings. How high are they, if you don't mind my asking?"

Douglas puffed himself up. "Twenty-four feet. I wanted twenty-six, but my architect said we'd need reinforcing beams across the span if we went any higher. I guess I was aiming for the sky."

"Yes, this was strictly Douglas's project," Connie added, hoisting her glass of Chardonnay toward the roof. "He's the fisherman in the family, and this is his idea of heaven. As for me, I just like to look out the windows at the water—especially at the sunsets. You wouldn't believe the colors!"

"Sounds lovely," Cara Lynn said, but with no real enthusiasm.

Maura Beth could have wished for a little more warmth

from her mother—what else was new?—but for the time being, things were going as well as could be expected. Nonetheless, she decided to try and liven things up. "Did I tell you that Susan runs a little crafts boutique at the Cool Springs Galleria up in Brentwood, Mama? She even designs some of the jewelry she sells, I believe."

Susan put down her Dubonnet and ran with the opening. "I do now. At first, I thought I would just cater to the artsy-craftsy crowd and be a supply store for them. That's why I called my little endeavor Beads and Crafty Needs. But as I got to know some of my customers better, I decided to try some of it myself. With my Jeremy and Elise all grown-up now, what's an empty nester to do? But anyhow, I like to think I've gotten quite good at it—I braid my own silk cords for the necklaces I make using a technique called kumihimo. Quite a mouthful, isn't it?" She paused for a girlish giggle. "And then I use jasper, amethyst, and jade to make some lovely pendants, if I do say so myself. They're among my best movers."

Maura Beth was pleased to see a genuine spark of interest spread across her mother's face, banishing the glazed, weary expression she had carried into the lodge with her.

"Oh, I just adore pendants. So few people know how to accessorize these days," Cara Lynn offered with genuine animation.

"Isn't that the truth?" Susan answered, leaning forward in her chair with a wink. "I have to cringe when some of these women walk into my shop with all this . . . bling, I believe they call it nowadays. And let's don't even talk about these piercings. Oh, the places they'll put them without a second thought. I keep wanting to ask, 'Does that hurt?' "

Both women chuckled richly; then Susan continued. "But don't think for a second I'm letting the men off the hook, either. Some of them come in looking just like pirates. It's all I can do when they buy beads to refrain from asking if they're going to make another pair of dangling earrings or stick them in their navels and then go terrorize a cruise ship."

Everyone was laughing now, and Maura Beth felt her residual nervous tension melting away as she locked eyes with Jeremy. This effortless banter right off the bat was exactly what she had been hoping for. At the very least, the meeting of the in-laws was off to a promising start.

Susan continued the feeling of camaraderie that had enveloped the room. "Cara Lynn, I always travel with a few of my jewelry catalogues. They're upstairs in my suitcase, as a matter of fact. I'd be delighted to show you some of my work later on when we get a moment."

Cara Lynn clasped her hands together excitedly. "Yes, I'd love that. Let's be sure and find the time."

"Well, we're having dinner early at The Twinkle. That's Cherico's restaurant of choice, you know," Connie put in. "I'm sure there'll be plenty of time when we get back. Believe me, Cara Lynn, you're going to love Susan's work. I have one of her jade pendants in my jewelry box. Matter of fact, I think I'll wear it to The Twinkle this evening."

Maura Beth sat back, admiring the ongoing ebb and flow. Mostly flow. Had she died and gone to heaven? Here were these two larger-than-life, diva personalities getting along famously. Perhaps her decision to wear her mother's dress had turned the tide in her favor. Or even in Cherico's favor. Was it barely possible that she had worried about the wedding for nothing?

A couple of hours later, the dinner at The Twinkle was humming along. Periwinkle had taken Maura Beth aside and reassured her from the get-go. "We've shut the place down for two hours just for you, girlfriend. I've got my full staff work-in' for ya tonight—myself, Parker, Lalie, Barry, and my part-time cook and waitress to boot. No excuse for slow service this go-round. We've got it all covered."

And that had definitely been the case—at least through the salad and entrée courses. The compliments had flown throughout the meal, and Maura Beth had detected no sign of her mother turning up her nose at the cuisine. In fact, she had even congratulated the chef the moment she tasted the homemade salsa generously heaped atop her grilled chicken. This was the Cara Lynn Mayhew—indeed, the mama—who she had been waiting for since adulthood.

So now there was only Mr. Place's key lime icebox pie left to serve to the eclectic mix of diners. There were several polite refusals in the form of, "I'm just too full," or something similar when the dessert plates were whisked out, however; but it pleased Maura Beth no end that her mother was not among those who wanted to push back from the table.

"I don't know about the rest of you, but I've made up my mind to splurge a little this weekend," Cara Lynn declared, admiring her slice of pie almost as if it were expensive jewelry.

"Dig in, Mama. You won't be sorry," Maura Beth added. "Mr. Place is the best darn pastry chef from here to Memphis, and he's been a wonderful addition to The Twinkle."

It was then that Barry Bevins rushed out from the kitchen, heading straight for Periwinkle, who had just placed the last dessert plate in front of William Mayhew. "Miz Peri," he began, slightly out of breath, "we just got us a real big takeout order way out in the boonies. Do ya want me to go ahead and deliver it as soon as possible, or do ya need me to hang around a little longer for this party?"

"We're almost through here, Barry," she told him. "We don't ever wanna keep our customers waiting. You head on out as soon as the kitchen gets it fixed. We've got our reputation to uphold."

"I must say I'm impressed. You do seem to be the only game in town, Miz Lattimore," Cara Lynn observed as Barry scurried away.

Periwinkle was beaming. "Oh, please call me Periwinkle. But I will say we do try awful hard, especially with our new delivery service. Cherico's never had anything quite like it—except for the pizza place, of course."

Then Cara Lynn took her first bite of pie and everyone thought she would swoon. "Ohhh! This is insane!"

"Isn't it scrumptious?" Connie added, her face lighting up as she leaned in. "I have no business eating it with my figure, of course. But I just can't resist."

Maura Beth continued to watch it all unfold with a satisfaction that had now morphed into outright smugness. Why, there wasn't a thing to worry about the rest of the weekend! There was now no reason to believe that her parents, particularly her mother, would not see her side of things regarding the wedding. The potluck and review of *The Robber Bridegroom* at the library tomorrow would clinch the deal. There would be an informed, intelligent discussion of a literary classic and the iconic Mississippi woman who had written it. Her parents would clearly see that both The Cherry Cola Book Club and the new library she had inspired were proof positive of the good works she was doing in Cherico, and furthermore, of how neatly their daughter blended into the fabric of this quirky little community. They would finally understand that their universe and hers might be worlds apart, but that there was nothing wrong with that. The two could coexist because father, mother, and daughter were truly a family. At long last.

★　★　★

The sun was getting ready to slip beneath the Lake Cherico horizon just as everyone returned to the lodge from the catered dinner at The Twinkle.

"Oh, quick!" Cara Lynn shouted in front of one of the great room windows, pointing toward the water in the distance. "Let's hurry out to the deck so I can see this for myself!" Then she grabbed Susan by the arm. "You come along with me, Miss Crafty Beads!"

The others followed, and soon everyone was outside, mesmerized by the gaudy, swollen display that could not decide which among the shades of orange, pink, and gold it preferred. At any rate, the brilliance of all the colors was short-lived as the sun finally blinked out, signaling the end of another late-summer's day in Cherico.

"You certainly didn't exaggerate," Cara Lynn said, turning to Connie. "That was like a scene from a movie."

Connie briefly gestured at the horizon. "Wasn't it? And I never get tired of it. I feel I'm getting my money's worth out of my retirement every time I see it."

"Well, now that the show's over, does anyone have room for a nightcap?" Douglas asked, turning around and pointing to the great room. "I'm your bartender, if you're interested."

Several people immediately took him up on his offer and headed back in, but Cara Lynn stayed behind, taking Susan aside at the last second. When everyone was well out of earshot, she said, "Please stay a moment with me. There's something I'd like to talk to you about."

Susan gave her a quizzical glance but remained at the railing. "Is it about my catalogue? I could go bring one down right now if you'd like. I'm sure you'll find something that suits you."

"Yes, we must look it over together—if not tonight, then tomorrow. I adored Connie's pendant. You are obviously quite talented." Cara Lynn was looking out over the water now, as if searching for the right words. Finally, she turned to Susan and lowered her voice. "I don't know how you feel about this lodge wedding that my daughter has cooked up, but William and I are not very happy about it. Maura Beth is our only child, and we want to give her a big wedding with all the trimmings down in South Louisiana. It will be part of the New Orleans social scene. I just don't think having a ceremony on the deck of a fishing lodge is very proper, even if we staged it at sunset. Tell me, do you think we're being unreasonable?"

Susan looked decidedly uncomfortable, forcing a smile. "I can understand your position, Cara Lynn, but shouldn't this be between you and your daughter? For what it's worth, I can tell you that Jeremy is fine with whatever Maura Beth wants to do. I think most grooms are a bit intimidated by weddings. I know my Paul was. My mother and I just told him what to do, and he did it."

"That may be, but I was hoping to talk her out of this idea of hers," Cara Lynn continued. "Wouldn't you and Paul like coming down to New Orleans for a traditional wedding? St. Andrew's is such a beautiful old high church, and there's nothing like a reception at The Three-Hundred Club. It's just the grandest stage you could ever imagine—just dripping with tradition. I've been looking forward to this all my life, and I just don't understand what Maura Beth can be thinking of with this fishing lodge idea of hers. She's always been so stubborn, of course, but maybe you could talk to Jeremy about it?"

"What do you mean?" Susan said, a subtle edge to her voice.

"If you could impress upon him how much a hometown wedding would mean to me—have him put in a good word for our position with Maura Beth. Maybe she'd listen to him. Maybe he could turn this thing around for us."

Susan's nervousness took the form of an extended sigh. "Cara Lynn, I think this is all very awkward for me. Paul and I have never been able to tell Jeremy what to do, either. We warned him that he wouldn't be making much money teaching English, and that some of the principals, headmasters, and superintendents he'd be dealing with might be nightmares. That's turned out to be the case, as a matter of fact. But he has this great passion for literature—he says he wants to improve the culture. He firmly believes it's taken a swan dive. And frankly, I think he's nailed it. Every time I see what's on television and what's playing at the movies I realize how low the bar has been set these days. And as for the wedding, I think we just have to let our children set their own agendas."

Cara Lynn's tone of voice took on a slight chill. "I see. Then you won't try to help me with this?"

"I don't think it's my place," Susan began. "And I have to tell you—I'm a bit surprised by all this. I thought the four of us were getting along just fine up to now. The men seem to be hitting it off in there with their after-dinner drinks, and I would imagine that Connie and your daughter are both starting to wonder what deep philosophical discussion we're having out here without them. So why don't we hurry on in and join the others, okay?"

Cara Lynn flashed a smile that was anything but sincere. "Yes, of course. And I trust this little chat we've had won't be repeated. I guess I went out on a limb expressing my opinions here so openly to you."

"You're the mother of the bride. You have every right to. But if you don't mind, Cara Lynn, I think I'll stay out of this."

Was it the B & B Maura Beth was sipping in a corner of the great room, or was it the sight of her mother and Susan McShay chatting so intensely out on the deck that was giving her such a warm, fuzzy feeling? It was obvious that these two

Southern divas had become fast friends. Could it get any better than that? They were no doubt outside thinking up ways to make her wedding even more spectacular now that it was clear her mother had shown up planning to cooperate and get with the program. Perhaps Susan would be adding something artsy-craftsy to the wedding bouquet, and they were discussing other unique and colorful favors for the ceremony. What a revelation it was all turning out to be!

"What are you grinning about?" Jeremy asked, sitting in an adjoining chair and brushing up against her leg.

She pointed to their mothers out on the deck, then to the men whooping it up across the room. "The truth is, I'd give anything to be a fly on the railing out there. Not to mention that Daddy is over there by the fireplace telling his god-awful bawdy jokes, and your father and uncle seem to be birds of a feather with it all. What's not to like about that?"

He swirled his snifter of Courvoisier and tilted his head. "Yep, I'd say it's going pretty smoothly. And you're right—I can hear those punch lines from here. They're pretty stale."

"Never mind that. I think *The Robber Bridegroom* review tomorrow will be the capper for your new in-laws. They'll see that The Cherry Cola Book Club is my greatest achievement to date."

"But it'll soon take a backseat to the new library," Jeremy added, hoisting his snifter.

"Well said. You don't know how long I've waited for my parents to appreciate why I've always wanted to be a librarian. It's ridiculous that they've made me feel defensive about it."

Maura Beth's smile grew even wider as her mother and Susan McShay finally came in from the deck and joined Connie for what looked like more girl talk. "I think we're going to be just fine," she told Jeremy, observing their body language from afar. "And that's not my cordial talking."

7

Trouble in Takeoutland

Barry Bevins was beginning to worry. He thought he knew all the back roads in and around Greater Cherico, but now he had to admit it. He was lost. He'd been driving around in the fading light for over fifteen minutes, trying to locate the takeout order address. He'd even called The Twinkle on his cell phone to reconfirm it.

"Yes, Barry," Periwinkle had told him. "You don't have it written down wrong. 305 Littlejohn Lane is what I'm showing here. You're on the right road. I'm sure you'll find it soon. But give me another shout if you need help."

Barry ended the call and then focused on the folly of it all. This was what came of Miz Peri buying a used panel van instead of something new that had a GPS system. And his mother had refused to let him get a fancy cell phone with that particular app. Too expensive, she had told him. But perhaps this latest incident would persuade her to let him upgrade.

Nonetheless, he was becoming so rattled that he turned off the Hunter Hayes CD he'd been listening to right in the middle of his favorite country music cut—"I Want Crazy." Well, he certainly seemed to have gotten his wish. The dilapidated houses out this way were getting fewer and farther between with each minute of travel. The last mailbox he'd been able to make out as he passed it in the fading light had read: 212 Littlejohn Lane. But this was no city street filled with next-door neighbors who were always ready to lend a hand. It was one of those winding country roads—the kind with no line of sight and the sort of dangerous curves that could cause careless or drunk drivers to have wrecks. But when it changed from smooth asphalt to bumpy, noisy gravel, Barry knew it was time to turn around and ask directions. He'd remembered his mother's comments on that particular subject once. "Men never stop and get help. I know that shiftless father of yours never did!" she'd declared.

So it was with no small degree of apprehension that he pulled over to the side of the road and slid out of the front seat of the van as he approached the little shack at 212 Littlejohn Lane. There were lights on inside, but the place had seen better days—if it had ever had any at all. The flimsy columns seemed to be struggling to hold up the roof, and there was clutter everywhere along the sagging front porch: an old tire leaning against the wall, a couple of rusty folding chairs, a watering can, stacks of magazines weighted down by bricks, and several terra cotta flower pots filled with dirt but with nothing growing in them. There was also a faded sign staked in the middle of the weedy yard that read: BEWARE OF DOG. Thankfully, there was no barking to be heard, and it even flashed into Barry's head that the dog had either died or wised up and wandered off for greener pastures.

He had not even reached the porch steps when a tall, slim man opened the front door and stepped out. Backlit the way he was with Barry looking up at him, he was just a dark figure with vague features, and therefore somewhat disturbing to behold. Echoes of slasher movies filled his head.

"Kin I hep ye?" the man said, his voice thin and high-pitched.

Barry froze in his tracks, swallowed hard, and took a deep breath to steady himself. "Yessir, I think I'm lost. Can you tell me where 305 Littlejohn Lane is? I have to deliver some food to a Mr. Donny Derbin, and it's gettin' cold. The food, I mean. Not the weather."

The man cackled. "Ain't no sich address, son. Ain't no Mr. Derbin out here, neither. Road turns to gravel about a half mile farther down. After that, it's just yer piney woods and whatnot roamin' around in 'em."

"You sure?"

"About the whatnot?"

"No, sir. About the address."

"Son, I've lived out here all my life. Even after my wife died, I stayed put outta respect to her memory. Believe me, I'd know if anyone new come out this-a-way." The man cackled again, turning up the volume this time. "I hate to be the one t'tell ya, but I think somebody's played a joke on ye, son. Somebody's done got the best of ye."

Instantly, Barry knew the man was right. He had that same queasy feeling in the pit of his stomach that he got every time his math teacher, Miss Yeomans, was about to hand out one of her famous pop quizzes—which he had yet to pass.

"Ye know how to git back to Cherico from here?" the man continued.

"Yeah," Barry answered, shaking his head in disgust at his predicament. "But thanks for your help." Then he started walking back to the van but turned just as he passed the yard sign. "By the way, mister, if you don't mind my askin'—what happened to your dog?"

"Heh?" the man called out.

"Your dog? The 'Beware the dog' sign you got here?"

There was more cackling. "Oh! Never had me one. Just figgered the sign'd be enough to keep people from stealin' my stuff!"

"Gotcha," Barry said, cracking a smile as he wondered who in hell would be remotely interested in anything he'd seen on the front porch or that might be hidden or hoarded inside. "You have a good night now."

The man's cackling rose to a crescendo. "Come out this-a-way and visit me anytime, y'hear?"

"Umm-hmm," Barry answered, still smiling.

So now there was nothing left to do but give The Twinkle another call, let them know what had happened, and then head on back.

"Well, I'll be damned!" Periwinkle exclaimed when he gave her the rundown. "We've never had that happen before!"

Barry was sitting on the front seat, shaking his head with the cell phone held to his ear. "No, ma'am, we haven't. Whaddaya make of it?"

Periwinkle hesitated briefly, but then came out swinging. "I'm thinkin' I have a real good idea what's going on, son. But you let me handle it in my own way. You just get back here safely now!"

Barry told her he would, put the phone down on the passenger seat, and then started the engine. He was totally preoccupied with what his employer had said as he drove along, slowly retracing his journey out from town. But not so much that he failed to notice the vehicle that came up fast behind him, seemingly out of nowhere. Had it been lying in wait for him somewhere on some side road, just waiting for him to pass by? That was definitely a creepy thought. Whoever was driving it had their high beams on, and it was nearly blinding him. He put his hand in front of the rearview mirror, trying to block the light and instinctively slowing down. Then he took a chance and braked quickly a couple of times, hoping to get his pursuer off his tail. That only brought an angry-sounding flurry of honks from behind. The driver flashed his headlights several times in a row before settling on the high beams once again. More images of slasher movies flashed into Barry's head.

He was beginning to panic as more adrenaline coursed through his veins. He realized with a growing sense of alarm that he was out in the middle of nowhere, driving in the dark with someone following him who might be drunk or maybe drugged out or something even worse than that. If he pulled over to the side, would the other car do the same? Who knew what could happen then? It would probably be useless as well as dangerous to try and outrun him. But at least he had his cell phone and could call for help. He picked it up and punched in The Twinkle's number on speed dial while carefully steering with one hand.

"Miz Periwinkle," he began, with the vehicle still tailgating him, "I think I'm in big trouble!" Then he gave her all the harrowing details, breathing hard in between sentences.

"Damn him!" Periwinkle cried out without even thinking about what she was saying. "I can't believe he's gone this far! Listen, Barry, whatever you do, don't stop. I'll call the sheriff's department for you when we hang up. Lon Dreyfus'll send someone out your way pronto. One of his deputies'll put a stop to all that. Are you still on Littlejohn Lane?"

"Yes'm. It goes on for miles out here. I'll be on it a while longer," he told her, squinting in an attempt to lessen the effect of the glare behind him. He might as well have had a comet on his tail.

"All right, then. You hang up and concentrate real hard on your driving. I promise you, I'm gonna get him off our backs if it's the last thing I do. This is probably all my fault. I should've just gone on ahead and gotten that restraining order when I had half a mind to."

"Get *who* off our backs, Miz Periwinkle? Who you gonna restrain?"

"Never you mind. Just you hang up and pay attention, son!"

Barry tossed the cell phone on the seat again and took another deep breath to try and calm himself. This was a nightmare, and he was even starting to fear for his life. The car behind could have passed him many miles back. They were the only two vehicles on this little-used road. So at the very least, harassing him was clearly the objective here. If this sort of thing came with the job, no amount of money was worth it. If he made it back to The Twinkle in one piece, he was seriously considering quitting right then and there. He even started practicing his resignation speech out loud as he tensely gripped the steering wheel. If nothing else, it kept him from contemplating a world of worst-case scenarios.

Suddenly, salvation appeared in the distance in the form of flashing blue lights, rapidly heading his way. And even if he got arrested for speeding, so would the insane tailgater behind him. He could feel the relief flowing from his hands gripping the steering wheel all the way down to his foot, which had practically melted into the gas pedal. All he had to do was not take his eyes off the pavement in front of him. Just a minute or two more, and he would be saved. If he could just hold on . . .

Periwinkle's intention had been to finish off the last ten pages of *The Robber Bridegroom* for the review tomorrow during the lull between the lunch and dinner services. It was downtime she always looked forward to in the midst of her busy day. An hour or so for a long, tall glass of sweet tea, putting her feet up on her office desk and "just chillin'," as the kids were fond of saying. But a couple of unexpected food delivery emergencies had tied her up and scotched her plans. It had been that sort of day.

Earlier during the lunch service there had also been an uneasy moment when she had just happened to look up as she cleared away the salad plates for the young couple dining at the small table near the front window. She could have sworn the man standing across the street in boots and jeans and staring directly at The Twinkle was her Harlan; but she could not be completely sure because whoever it was had his wide-brimmed cowboy hat pulled down so low over his face that his features were in shadow. Nonetheless, the tall physique looked familiar, and the idea that her ex might still be stalking her made her shudder. By the time she returned with the entrées, however, the man was gone.

And now, after hanging up with the sheriff's dispatcher in the midst of the current crisis, reading *The Robber Bridegroom* was the last thing on her mind. It was all she could do to keep Lalie Bevins from becoming hysterical about the developing crisis on Littlejohn Lane.

"Don't worry," she kept saying to her distraught waitress. "There's a patrol car going out there right now. I'm sure everything'll turn out just fine. It's been my experience that those flashing blue lights always put the fear of God in people. Hey, it's always made my stomach fall to the soles of my shoes whenever I see 'em in my rearview mirror."

But Lalie was inconsolable, working her hands into a nervous tangle and hyperventilating as the entire staff gathered around in the kitchen to support and comfort her. "How do you know, Miz Peri? There are some crazy drivers around Cherico. And there's one of 'em out there right now botherin' my little boy!"

"The officer'll call us as soon as everything's resolved," Periwinkle continued, nervously chewing her gum and gently patting Lalie on the shoulder. "And I just know Barry'll be okay. He's a smart kid."

"Well, I *don't* know. Maybe we shouldn't send him out so late at night like this," she said, absentmindedly wiping her hands on her apron as if they were wet. Anything to try to smooth away the awful stress that had enveloped her.

"It's not a bad thought, Peri," Mr. Place added. "We could cut off the delivery service after seven if you want to. These addresses are always easier to find in broad daylight."

Periwinkle took the suggestion under consideration, but she had no intention of sharing her nagging suspicions with the rest of the crew. Namely, that it was Harlan John Lattimore up to no good out there on the back roads of Cherico. That it was he and his petty scheming that had sent Barry on this wild goose chase of a delivery. After all, she had chosen not to tell anyone, not even Maura Beth, about the altercation with him a while back. Oh, there was that one time she had picked up the phone and started to let Maura Beth in on everything, but she had relented at the last second. She knew Maura Beth was all caught up in her wedding plans and the little psycho-dramas that accompanied dealing with her parents. Plus, there was the upcoming *Robber Bridegroom* review and all the preparations it entailed. So, for the moment, it was much more important to be supportive of Lalie and to trust that they would all soon be greeting her son alive and well and none the worse for wear. The worst-case scenario was just unthinkable.

"Yes, the daylight helps," Periwinkle said, but her tone was noncommittal. "Meanwhile, I think we have a couple of desserts to serve to our customers out there, so let's follow through, gang. Parker, would you please take care of that for us and give Lalie a little rest?"

"Thanks," Lalie managed, trying her best to smile. But her eyes gave her away, darting around the room looking for a safe haven somewhere. Her efforts were futile, however. It was clear that she would not be able to rest until her baby boy was once again safely in the fold.

The next ten minutes passed more like sixty. Periwinkle

and Lalie stayed near the kitchen phone, both hoping it would ring and yet dreading what news might come. They were unable even to make small talk during the wait, and only the occasional clatter of dishes being stacked nearby broke the silence.

When the call finally came through, Periwinkle exhaled deeply and picked up the receiver. The moment had arrived. Then she nodded and briefly held it away from her ear. "He's fine, Lalie. You can breathe now!" she called out. "He's on his way here right now. Should be just a few more minutes, and he'll walk through that door and you can hug him all you want."

"Oh, thank the Lord!" Lalie exclaimed, the relief almost seeming to rise from her visibly at the exact moment her shoulders slumped and the air rushed out of her chest.

Periwinkle continued to listen to the officer at the other end, her face a study in surprise. "What?! I can't believe it!" she cried out at one point. "Why, that's just a low-down, miserable, dirty trick!"

Lalie grew alarmed again at Periwinkle's incredulous tone. "What is it? Is my Barry still okay?"

Periwinkle nodded vigorously, held up one hand, and whispered. "Still just fine. Tell you all about it in a minute. Just hang on."

When the call was over and Periwinkle began to explain to everyone what had happened in some detail, reactions among the kitchen staff were mixed. Mr. Place cocked his head and suppressed a smile, while Lalie and the others just shook their heads. Not long after, Barry sauntered in through the delivery door, looking as if he truly did not have a care in the world and the crisis had never happened.

His mother soon wiped the lopsided grin off his face, grabbing him by the shoulders, staring him down, and stopping just short of giving him a good shaking. "You gotta get you some nicer friends, young man," she told him. "Guess you know you had us all scared half to death. I'm too old to be put through the wringer like this. I'll have enough gray hairs soon enough!"

"But I didn't mean to," he said. "At one point, I was really scared, too." Then he broke away from his mother and turned to Periwinkle. "Right in the middle of it all, I said to myself I was gonna walk in here and tell you I was quittin', Miz Periwinkle. But I guess I got me the last laugh, huh?"

"Reckless driving is no laughing matter, son," she told him. "But we're all glad you're safe. I just have to agree with your mother, though. I don't think you should hang around with Scott and Lawrence anymore. I'd say they're bad news after what happened tonight."

"Crispy," Barry chimed in. "We call him Crispy 'cause of the bacon, remember? He hates it when we call him Lawrence. Once he even punched me on the arm when I up and forgot. It really hurt, too. He's a big guy, and he packs a wallop!"

"Some friend," Periwinkle observed.

"Well, I think you should call him Lawrence as punishment for what he and Scott did to you tonight," Lalie added, putting her hands on her hips. "I don't think it's the least bit funny them callin' in that fake order and tailgatin' you like that. If y'all had wrecked out there, no tellin' what coudda happened. We'd prob'ly all be over at Cherico Memorial right now in the waitin' room on the edge of our seats. Really, son, I shudder just to think."

Barry could only shrug his shoulders at his mother's lecture. "Yeah, but they got a ticket for reckless drivin', so I don't think they'll ever try somethin' like that again. That officer was pretty rough on 'em after we all got pulled over. So I got out of the van and walked back, and he was tellin' 'em they were lucky they weren't spendin' the night in jail. Then he asks Scott why they'd even do a dangerous thing like that, and Scott goes, 'We were just messin' around is all.' Then Scott says he and Crispy were tired of me lordin' it over 'em with my job and money and goin' out with Mollie Musselwhite and all. He even pointed his finger at me, like that was gonna do him some good with the cop. Ha!"

"Like I said, son," Lalie added, pointing her own finger at him, "you need to get you some nicer friends. I never did like those two. Wild as berries in a briar patch. That crazy Scott with that one danglin' earring he wears and then talkin' you into your tattoo and all. They aren't welcome in my house anymore, I can tell ya that. No more a' them comin' over and eatin' me outta house and home like they've been doin'. 'Specially that big fat tub, Lawrence!"

Barry corrected her again. "Crispy!"

"Now, you listen good. I don't wanna hear that silly name one more time, do you hear me, young man, or you're grounded?!"

Barry looked and sounded thoroughly disgruntled, waving at his mother as if he were swatting a fly. "C'mon. Those guys aren't that bad. We've mostly've had a' lotta good times together."

"I don't care what all y'all did or didd'n do together. They aren't welcome, and that's my final word," Lalie told him, shutting her eyes and shaking her head emphatically.

Periwinkle collected her thoughts after everything had been talked out and everyone was pitching in with the final kitchen cleanup. For once—and possibly just this once—she had been wrong about Harlan, jumping to her hasty conclusions the way she had. Perhaps it was her assumption that he was the man across the street that had influenced her. But she was now doubly thankful she hadn't told the others about her recent encounter with him. That would only have muddied the waters and caused more gossiping behind her back, and she did not want that kind of distraction going on in her kitchen. She had The Twinkle's sterling reputation to uphold.

In the end, it had all turned out to be nothing more than a lot of hyperventilating about a foolish teenaged prank. More importantly, she realized that nothing had really changed. There was no actual threat to her takeout and delivery service as she had feared for a couple of stressful hours, and it was time to turn her thoughts to the food she would be preparing tomorrow for *The Robber Bridegroom* review at the library.

Then, too, with luck and reading in bed a little later than usual, she would finally finish those last ten pages of the novel. True, she hadn't followed some of it particularly well up to now, but she fully intended to hold up her end when the serious discussion got under way. Ultimately, this brief distraction would not deter her one iota from helping Maura Beth and Jeremy clear the deck for what was certain to be the most unusual wedding Cherico had ever staged.

8

Adoring Eudora

There was no getting around it. Maura Beth felt like a bucketful of cold water had just been splashed in her face, and she immediately began rethinking her unbridled optimism of the evening before. The first inkling that she might have been living in a fool's paradise was her mother's flabbergasted expression when she walked into The Cherico Library for *The Robber Bridegroom* festivities, somewhat overdressed for the occasion. The woman had never been really good at hiding her emotions; she was often tactless in dealing with her peers, believing that her wealth and social position insulated her from any wrath her behavior produced. So when the Mayhews and all of the McShays arrived from the lodge a good fifteen minutes before The Cherry Cola Book Club review and potluck was to begin, Cara Lynn did not hesitate to reveal her first impression to her daughter.

"I don't know what to say, Maura Beth. *This* is where you've worked all these years? *This* is what you've been raving about in all your phone calls and e-mails?"

Trying her best to remain calm during what amounted to a kamikaze attack, Maura Beth scanned the group with a diplomatic smile. "Yes, this is my labor of love, Mama. To each her own, I always like to say."

Connie quickly came to her rescue. "Maura Beth has done wonders with the place, Cara Lynn. What I mean is, she's made it so much fun to come here for these outings. We're so proud of our Cherry Cola Book Club. It's brought us all together, and we've learned a lot along the way. And best of all, Cherico is going to get a brand-new library, thanks to your daughter."

"And not a moment too soon from the looks of things," Cara Lynn said after another disdainful sweep of the cramped lobby filled with metal folding chairs. Then she pointed to the two black-and-white posters of Eudora Welty that Maura Beth had positioned on either side of the podium. On the left side was the youthful Eudora, while the distinguished, elderly version graced the right. "Is that by any chance the librarian who worked here for years before you came? Looks like the job just wore her out. No makeup, no hairdo, nothing."

Maura Beth decided to rise above her mother's sudden cattiness. Having Councilman Sparks stirring things up in previous book club meetings had prepared her for such unwarranted behavior. "That's very clever of you, Mama. Of course, we all know that Miss Welty's great talent was a matter of the prose she wrote. I don't think she was ever very concerned with how she photographed. At any rate, there's the buffet table just waiting for us across the room. We have our usual favorites—chicken spaghetti, gumbo, and the like; and a few new treats such as hot fruit, cashew cheese log, and clam canapés that Periwinkle and Mr. Place brought us from The Twinkle. So shall we all head on over and serve ourselves? I don't know about the rest of you, but I'm starving."

"Nice work there, Maurie. You handled it like a pro," Jeremy whispered to her out of the side of his mouth as they led the way to the food and drink.

That was all Maura Beth needed to hear to remain calm and focused on the task at hand. Jeremy had become her rock on so many different levels, and when he gave her arm an affectionate squeeze, she knew there was nothing her mother could say or do to knock her off-course. Nonetheless, she was honest enough to admit to herself that she was disappointed by her mother's snippy remarks. Where was the gracious, bubbly woman who had been so chummy with Susan McShay last night at the lodge? Had she merely been an illusion?

It did not take long, in fact, for Maura Beth to notice that her mother and future mother-in-law were keeping their distance from one another. Her years of librarianship, which included figuring out the behavior and preferences of her patrons as they came and went, were serving her well here. The two women sat on opposite ends of the front row of chairs with their husbands in tow once they had helped their plates. Finally, Maura Beth put her speculation on the back burner and informally opened the discussion about *The Robber Bridegroom* while everyone continued to balance their plates on their knees. Ordinarily, she would have waited for all the eating to be over and done with and then taken to the podium, but she felt the need to get the bad taste of her mother's testiness out of her mouth.

"So, let's get right down to it. What did y'all think of Miss Welty's work?" she began, as she precisely speared one of Periwinkle's stuffed mushrooms with her fork. "In other words, who adored Eudora?"

"I did!" Becca called out, raising her hand and wiggling her fingers. "Even though it was a little over the top in parts. I thought all the characters were larger than life, and I was especially intrigued by the concept of a gentleman robber like Jamie Lockhart. I didn't know there could even be such a thing. If you steal for a living, you're not a gentleman in my book."

"Things were different way back then in pioneer times," Maura Beth pointed out. "The concept of law enforcement was a bit iffy, which made life rough along the Natchez Trace for travelers. So, would you agree with those who insist that *The Robber Bridegroom* reads more like a fairy tale than anything else?"

Becca nodded emphatically. "With characters named Big Harp, Little Harp, Mike Fink, and Goat, I'd say so."

Then Jeremy took the floor. "It's certainly been compared to the Brothers Grimm, and the good versus evil part is easy to identify. But I would definitely agree that life along the Natchez Trace was rough. Back then, travelers from Nashville to Natchez had actual bandits like Big Harp and Little Harp to deal with. Some lost their money, others even lost their lives. That's established historical fact. Eudora Welty just expanded and embellished the truth a bit from her knowledge of Mississippi folklore. And quite colorfully, I might add." He paused for a barely audible chuckle. "Of course, there were no park rangers to protect people the way they do today. I can vouch for the fact that the biggest threat to safety out there now is the occasional flying deer." He pointed to his rib cage. "I still have a slight hitch from that bad wreck I had. But my doctor says it'll disappear over time."

"I believe in angels on our shoulders at critical times," Maura Beth added, her eyes tearing up slightly. "I think you're living proof, Jeremy."

The remark seemed to pour a layer of good feeling over the gathering; but not long after, Miss Voncille drastically changed the tone of the discussion. "I did enjoy the novel, but it made me think long and hard about the fairy-tale aspects you just mentioned, Maura Beth. I've found myself applying that to my own life. Mainly, that I think Locke and I ought to consider giving up this fairy-tale notion of getting married at our age, even though I'm the one who's been lobbying him so hard for it. I never thought I'd be saying something like this, but there it is."

Locke rested his fork on his plate and turned her way. "Maybe this isn't the time and place to discuss this, Voncille."

"Perhaps not. But there are all sorts of complications when too many characters are involved in anything, whether it's in a novel or real life," she answered. "Locke Jr. and Carla are determined to keep us apart, and I don't like the feeling of being the villain in all of this."

"But you aren't. They are!" Locke protested.

"That doesn't stop me from feeling the way I feel!"

"Maybe we're wandering off the subject a bit here," Maura Beth said, mindful of her role as the even-tempered moderator. "Perhaps we should get back to the plot of our read here."

But Miss Voncille had evidently touched a nerve, and Periwinkle stepped in to pick up on her theme. "I think Voncille makes a good point, though. When Harlan and I got married, I know I thought I was living a fairy tale. I was a princess, he was my prince, and the entire universe revolved around us. Okay, so maybe there wasn't the sort of plotting and horse trading that went on in *The Robber Bridegroom,* but looking back on it all, I can clearly see that I wasn't near in control of my life as I thought I was. I mean, you get all these gifts and good wishes, and there's wedding cake and then rice thrown at you when you leave for your honeymoon. You're on this incredible adrenaline high. But where's the course you should take for the reality of marriage? Who prepares you for that? I know my mother hugged me, and told me, 'Everything'll be just fine, darlin' girl.' That's what she always calls me. But things didn't turn out to be just fine. I think weddings are like fairy tales, plain and simple. But some of 'em don't have happy endings."

"I don't want you to take this the wrong way, Periwinkle,

but that seems a little too cynical to me," Connie said, sounding a bit irritated. "Douglas and I have always worked out our problems, haven't we?"

"Work being the operative word," Douglas agreed.

"Same for us," Becca added, gesturing toward her Stout Fella. "I mean, isn't that the real point of a wedding? The fantasy part fades quickly, but you take that first step and then start the business of working hard at your marriage. At least, that was our approach."

Stout Fella nodded with his biggest, most boyish, grin. "Amen! I think I've learned that the hard way!"

Then Maura Beth steeled herself as she saw her mother leaning forward in her chair and frantically waving her hand a few times. She'd witnessed that sense of urgency in her mother's demeanor many times before, and it was never a good sign. "My opinion is that weddings can be very disappointing if they're not done right. They have to be thought through and not just thrown together any old place. I'm speaking about propriety and tradition here. And not only that—"

William Mayhew interrupted, grabbing his wife's arm and shaking his head. "Cara Lynn . . . don't. Not here."

"No, I'll have my say," she continued, clenching her teeth as she loosened his grip. "I haven't come all this way to be a mousy little wallflower in the background. I'm the mother of the bride, for God's sake. Unless you're planning to get married over and over again like Elizabeth Taylor did—and I'm sure she didn't intend for things to turn out that way—a wedding should be a once-in-a-lifetime affair. It should be unforgettable and beautiful and full of pictures you can paste into an album you can show off to your grandchildren when you get old. It should have the perfect setting. And so what if it costs a lot of money? If you have it, you should spend it— even lavish it on your only daughter. Parents wait all those years to see their children get married and settled in life, and their opinions and ideas should count for something. I don't see why this is so difficult to understand."

Maura Beth closed her eyes while quickly trying to figure a way out of her contentious dilemma. She even briefly imagined Eudora Welty herself overseeing the whole book club meeting from her perch in literary heaven and clucking her tongue in despair. Why, this was nowhere even close to what she had intended to convey with her fanciful novel! So, how had they managed to veer so far off track? It was almost as if Councilman Sparks were in the room again, stirring things up the way only he could manage—but this time wearing a Cara Lynn Mayhew mask. Oh, the irony of it all!

"Mama, I think we should discuss this later in private," she finally managed. It was clear from everyone's downcast facial expressions that they were all very uncomfortable with the latest exchange between mother and daughter.

Then it was Jeremy's turn to try to rescue the situation, clearing his throat and speaking very emphatically as he reverted to teaching mode. "Getting back to the novel, I think the plot is a bit on the grisly side at times. First, you have Jamie saving Clement from being murdered and robbed by Mike Fink. Then we learn all about Clement's past where his first wife and sons were captured and tortured. It's the sort of fairy tale that stops just short of the blood and gore you'd expect when a giant shows up stomping around and shouting, 'Fee-fi-fo-fum!' "

Maura Beth's laugh was clearly forced, but she was grateful for the change of subject. "Good point, Jeremy. Who has something else to add? Come on, now, don't be shy."

Unexpectedly, and before anyone could say anything further, Cara Lynn put her plate down on the floor, sprang up from her chair, and headed toward the door in a huff, her nose way up in the air. "Come on, William. Take me back to that lodge!" she demanded. "I've had enough!"

Maura Beth immediately got to her feet as well. "Wait, Mama. Please don't leave like this!"

William turned to his daughter at the last second with a pained expression on his face. "I'm so sorry, sweetheart. There's just not much I can do when she gets this way." Then he headed after his wife at a fast clip, mumbling unintelligible things under his breath.

As was the case with nearly every previous meeting of The Cherry Cola Book Club, unforeseen circumstances had brought things to a screeching halt. It never seemed to fail, and no one—not even a stupefied Maura Beth—knew what to do or say for the longest time.

Finally, Mamie Crumpton, who had been uncharacteristically quiet so far and mainly concentrating on her plate of food, spoke up. "Your mother seems to have a very short fuse, dear."

Maura Beth couldn't help but blush, hanging her head. "Unfortunately, I can't remember when she didn't."

"I'm afraid this is all my fault, Maura Beth," Miss Voncille suddenly insisted. "I shouldn't have wandered onto the subject of marriage the way I did. I should have stuck to reviewing the novel."

"I guess I'm equally to blame," Periwinkle added. "I went on and on about my bad marriage experience, and we weren't here to talk about that. I think I just added fuel to the fire."

But Maura Beth was having none of it. "Nonsense! From the very beginning I've encouraged outside-the-box angles for our reviews. If that's where the discussion led us, then so be it. I just have to apologize to all of you for Mama's behavior. She's very upset with me because I won't see things her way about my wedding. I assure you, this has nothing to do with any of you. She was bound and determined to have her say, no matter what."

"If I could, I wanted to say that—well, your mother feels very strongly about this," Susan McShay offered with some reluctance. "I thought we were getting along so well, but she really got her back up with me last night. I was very surprised at how adamant she was about having a church wedding down in New Orleans. I won't go into some other things that were said."

Maura Beth's little sigh of resignation summed it all up. "Appearances really can be deceiving, can't they? I wanted so much to believe that the two of you were getting along famously last night."

Susan looked despondent, shifting her weight in her chair. "I wish that had been the case, sweetie. She didn't even want one of my jewelry catalogues when all was said and done. As a matter of fact, she barely spoke to me all day today. Just a quick nod at the breakfast table."

"I don't want to sound so pessimistic here, but perhaps it's just not worth it," Connie said. "I mean, having your wedding at our lodge out on the deck. I've said it before and I'll say it again, Douglas and I don't want to be the cause of this kind of friction between you and your parents. We don't want to have to live with that."

"But it's mostly my mother who's the problem," Maura Beth admitted. "She's tried to make me think that Daddy feels the same way she does, but I don't think that's true now. It's up to me to find a way to resolve all this with her—not you, Connie. You and Douglas are just innocent bystanders."

Connie offered her most reassuring smile, reaching over to take Maura Beth's hand. "We just want you to enjoy your special day, whatever you decide to do."

Mamie Crumpton suddenly started chuckling to herself, her generous bosom vibrating all the while. "I can't speak from experience since I've never been married, of course, but listening to all this controversy, it seems to me that the people who elope have the right idea. That way, you don't give people time to drive you crazy telling you how, when, and where you should get married."

"You may have a point there," Miss Voncille said. "I never thought I'd have to jump through so many hurdles."

"As a practical matter, a justice of the peace is just as good as a minister, priest, or rabbi," Mamie continued. "A little on the drab side, of course, but the ceremony will get the job done—just without the fuss and fanfare."

Miss Voncille looked as if she might seriously be considering the suggestion and appeared ready to say something further, but apparently thought better of it and merely shrugged her shoulders at Locke.

From that point on, Maura Beth tried her best to get the focus back on *The Robber Bridegroom,* but her heart wasn't really in it. There was also a lack of enthusiasm among the others, as everyone sensed that the air had been let out of the proceedings. Only Jeremy was able to rise to the occasion with his insights, being the advocate of great literature that he was.

"I'm a big believer in archetypes," he said. "And there are plenty of them in *The Robber Bridegroom.*" But it wasn't enough to keep interest from flagging even further, as yet another meeting of The Cherry Cola Book Club unexpectedly fell short of expectations.

Nonetheless, Maura Beth kept things together long enough to propose a couple of titles for their October read; and when the vote was taken, *The Member of the Wedding* by Carson McCullers won out. "It's a wonderfully poignant, coming-of-age story," she told everyone. "Very Southern. Truly heartbreaking—especially for any woman who remembers the low points of her puberty."

A bit later, Maura Beth felt both frustrated and guilty as she and Jeremy busied themselves switching off lights and locking up together. "The thing is, I don't think we adored Eudora in the first-class manner she really deserves. I let everything get out of control, and we practically forgot all about her. Oh, sure, we bandied about a few bits and pieces of the plot, and the food was delicious as usual; but this was definitely not our best Cherry Cola Book Club outing."

"Oh, I don't know. I think Miss Welty would be gracious enough to understand and forgive us," he pointed out. "How cool is it that people are still discussing her work long after she's been gone? I think writers have the best kind of immortality. Don't get me wrong now—I love my teaching. I wouldn't want to do anything else with my life. But what I wouldn't give for a little writing talent myself!"

Maura Beth turned and gave him an expectant glance. "Have you ever sat down and tried to write? The world is full of people who say they have a novel in them or something like that. But they're just a lot of talk. They never actually do anything about it."

Jeremy suddenly looked a bit sheepish. "Actually, I have. I wrote a couple of short stories once, but I tore them up right after I'd finished. I just didn't think they were very good."

"You didn't let anybody read them?"

"Nope."

Maura Beth briefly pursed her lips. "Hmmm. Well, my opinion is you should write something else and let me read it this time. As a librarian, I have a very good eye. Maybe you're better than you think."

He considered briefly and exhaled. "Okay, then. Maybe I will. I'll let you be my critic."

"I'd be honored. Now, I've got to buckle down and solve my problem. I'm sure you realize I'm going to have to force a showdown with Mama. This tension between us has been building up for years. I've got to settle things once and for all. No more putting it off."

Outside under the portico, Jeremy paused, and said, "You need me for backup, Maurie?"

Finally, after an incredibly stressful evening, Maura Beth was able to smile. "Thanks, sweetheart, but this is one of those mother-daughter things that will require lots and lots of space. When the two of us get together, there's no room for anybody else within a ten-mile radius."

"Sometimes, Southern women get too close and go boom!" Jeremy exclaimed, making a playful, explosive gesture with his hands.

Maura Beth gave him an impulsive hug and then pulled away, looking wide-eyed and wary. "I know you were just trying to be funny, but I sincerely hope it doesn't come to that."

9

The World's Oldest Teenagers

Locke couldn't imagine what had gotten into his Voncille. She had been giggling to herself off and on in the car all the way home to Perry Street from the library. When he'd asked her what was up several times over, she wouldn't tell him a thing. She just kept on giggling like a schoolgirl with a secret she was just itching to spill, but in her own good time. More than once, she even had to avert her gaze and cover her mouth, she was so full of herself.

Finally, he'd had enough, and after they had just entered the kitchen, he said, "Okay, Voncille, once and for all, what is so damned funny all of a sudden? What's this inside joke of yours?"

She headed straight to the counter to turn on the coffee-maker and heat up the carafe. "I guess I do need a nice black cup of something sobering like this."

Locke managed to look amused in spite of himself. "That's one of the more ridiculous things I've ever heard. You can't possibly be drunk on that cherry cola punch."

This time she laughed out loud. "No, but the way things went at our book club meeting tonight, I kept wishing that punch had been spiked. You have to admit, it got pretty rough at times. But at least one good thing came out of it all, and Mamie Crumpton, of all people, pointed the way."

"Will you stop being so mysterious and tell me what in the world you're talking about?"

She gestured emphatically at the telephone. "I mean, we're going to call up Henry Marsden right now and get married as soon as he can work it into his schedule. A justice of the peace ceremony will do just fine, thank you. Then we're going to pick a spot on the map and run off for our official honeymoon. And we aren't going to tell a soul about it—not your children, not even Maura Beth and our book club friends. They can all think we've been captured by aliens, but we're going to get this out of the way. I say enough of this going back and forth with Carla and Locke, Jr. We had it right the first time. We don't need their blessing. We're going to elope, and that's all there is to it. And if you want my further opinion, I think Maura Beth should stop trying to please that overbearing mother of hers—she and Jeremy should just do the same thing and start living their own lives."

"You intend to call her up and tell her that?"

"Well, no, I don't. But the way I see it, she ought to be able to figure it out for herself. Not that differences between parents and children are all that easy to handle. I've been in her position myself."

Locke was stunned as he tried to take it all in. "So now you *do* want to get married again after that fiery speech you gave at the library? I'd like to think this will be your final decision. After all, you spent a lot of time getting me to see the light, and I finally did. Then for a while there, you just gave up the ghost and wanted the status quo. Are you telling me you'll have no regrets about that sweet little church wedding we were planning?"

"None whatsoever. As a practical matter, we hadn't even gotten to the invitations yet, so I promise you, this is it," she told him, folding her arms for emphasis. "Getting married shouldn't be this difficult for anybody. We've had our license for a while now. We just need someone to perform the ceremony. Lord knows, there are enough youngsters full of hormones out there who don't give getting married a second thought and rush into it with mostly disastrous results. Or *have* to get married, which usually implies something even worse. That's what I was giggling about. I was thinking to myself, 'Here we are, both of us pushing seventy, and we've gotten way too caught up in what your children think—' "

He interrupted with a look of resignation, shaking his head. "They came at us pretty hard. Blindsided us, really."

"That's an understatement. And I understand how hurt you are. Anyway, about my giggling. If we do something like run off and elope, we'd be acting like the world's oldest teenagers, and that particular image just makes me very happy at this stage of my life. I know my parents wouldn't have liked it at all, and that makes me even happier. After all these years, I think I'll finally be my own woman and free of their constant disapproval of me and the way I wanted to live my life."

"And what a very special woman you are," he told her. "You've been exactly what I've needed. In fact, I know we've both changed for the better since we've been together."

His compliment found its mark, causing Miss Voncille to blow him a kiss. Then she glanced over at the warming carafe and decided it was time to pour herself some coffee. As she reached up into the nearby cupboard, she turned his way, and said, "Would you like some, too?"

"Yes, I believe I'll join you."

They stood there for a while, slowly sipping and concentrating. "Well, here's something to consider. Can you put up with Henry Marsden's constant whistling?" Locke said, finally. "He's not the only justice of the peace in the world, you know. We could find someone else and drive over to Corinth or even up to Memphis—whatever you'd like."

"Oh, there'll be just a few minutes of it at the most," she answered, cracking a smile. "I suppose the poor man could solve his problem if he'd just get himself a new set of dentures, but judging from all the years I've known him, it doesn't look like he's going to do that anytime soon. He seems to like himself the way he is. Ssso I can ssstand it if you can."

"Now that's very clever!"

"Oh, I suppose so, but I'd never make fun of him that way in public." Then with a surge of energy, Miss Voncille clapped her hands twice, sounding like an excited schoolgirl. "Let's just go ahead and call Henry up right this minute and see how soon we can get this show on the road!"

Locke's expression was full of polite skepticism. "Speaking of the road, where is this wonderful little spot on the map we're going to spend our so-called honeymoon? Any suggestions?"

"Oh, I don't know. Let's be adventurous about it. We can just drive somewhere. None of this 'booking in advance' nonsense. I loved that old *Route 66* TV series where they'd just get in their sports car and have a new adventure every week— acted like they didn't have a care in the world. We could do something like that. You could go get your atlas off the back seat, and we could thumb through it state by state. Or maybe I'll close my eyes and we'll go wherever my finger lands. Who knows?" Uncharacteristically, she started waltzing in place with arms outstretched, her salt-and-pepper head tilted back and her eyes affixed to an imaginary partner. "I want you to look and see if I'm first on your dance card, Locke. I'd better be!"

Her spontaneity was contagious, and he looked very much in love as took her in his arms and began leading her around the kitchen. "Why, I do believe you're my very first, and I think you and I make absolutely wonderful, seventy-year-old teenagers." Then he looked suddenly inspired, glancing briefly at the ceiling. "By the way, what are we dancing to tonight?"

She drew back for a moment and gave him a wry smile. " 'The Blue Danube'? 'The Merry Widow Waltz'? 'Tennessee Waltz'? I loved Patti Page's version back in the day. I don't know. You pick one. You can even hum it for us. I don't care as long as we keep on dancing."

Miss Voncille was not about to be bothered by Henry Marsden and his sibilance on this, her wedding day that had been so long in coming. The pleasant buzz she had created for herself by ten o'clock the next morning in his institutional-looking office was a potent mixture of expectation and the sort of fantasy she herself had decried during *The Robber Bridegroom* review at the library the evening before; in spite of the peeling green paint, a framed American flag whose colors were badly faded, and any number of illegible metal plaques and citations tacked to the walls. There was also one feeble attempt to add a ceremonial aura to the surroundings in the form of two white votive candles offering up their cloying, flowery scents at opposite ends of Henry Marsden's desk.

But it was as if none of those pedestrian things existed. For across from Miss Voncille stood her gentlemanly Locke, the epitome of distinguished and dashing in his three-piece gray suit and silver tie; while she felt like the queen of the ball wearing her champagne-colored cocktail dress and holding her makeshift bouquet of white crepe myrtle cuttings from Locke's front yard. What a last-minute inspiration that had been as she had rushed into the garage to retrieve his garden shears! After all, he had been tending to his trees for many years now. They were quite mature—their trunks having grown very gnarled and muscular as crepe myrtles will do— and snatching a small part of them to take with her as she became his wife was something she thought would be quite original for the ceremony.

Everything else continued to fade into the background, including Henry Marsden's impediment, the almost comical, big ears that protruded from the sides of his bald head and the cramped little room that would bear witness to their exchange of vows. Even his thin, mousy wife, Oralee, wearing a sack of a dress that hung on her bones while she played the role of witness on this steamy morning, seemed like little more than a theater prop.

And then Miss Voncille began reciting her own original words that would finally turn her into a married woman: "Locke Linwood, I come to you today of my own free will with joy in my heart so that the two of us can become one. When I least expected it, you appeared in my life, and I was wise enough to open my arms and let you in." The emotion in her voice was very evident, and she paused briefly to steady herself as she continued. "My long wait is over now. You've quietly touched my soul, and I look forward to the rest of my life with you."

Then it was Locke's turn to take the stage, and he did not miss a beat. Not even once did he look down at the small square of paper with scribbles tucked away in the palm of his hand—just in case his memory failed him. "Voncille Nettles, you will never know how much you've changed my life. I've always been a man of few words, but you make me want to tell the whole world how I feel about you. But I know the best way to do that is to take you as my wife and travel together from there. I can't wait for the journey to begin. Our sunrise is at hand."

Miss Voncille noticed that Oralee Marsden's jaw dropped as Locke finished up. Without the woman saying a word, that had to be high praised indeed. There was no question about it. These vows of theirs were verbal jewels, even if she and

Locke had pulled them out of their heads over coffee, biscuits, and green pepper jelly at the breakfast table only an hour before. The spontaneity of it all was taking Miss Voncille's breath away, but she was having no trouble handling it.

"The ringsss pleassse," Henry Marsden said next.

At that point absolutely nothing could stop Miss Voncille from smiling, although she noticed her Locke was wincing slightly. The sibilance of the last phrase had been particularly sharp and penetrating. Had there been a dog of any kind in the room, it was easy to picture its ears perking up, along with a pitiful whimper or two. But soon enough, the rings were exchanged, and the rote part of the ceremony with the "I do's" was over and done with.

Then came the final sibilance. "By the power vesssted in me by the Ssstate of Misssisssippi, I now pronounssse you husssband and wife. You may now kisss your bride."

Indeed, Locke's kiss was one for the ages. It was soft and gentle, lingering just long enough to convey genuine passion, yet stopping short of becoming a side show. As Miss Voncille pulled back staring affectionately into his eyes, the reality of it hit her. After decades of going it alone the best way she knew how, she was finally married. With the distant tragedy of Frank Gibbons and his MIA status still an immutable part of her, she was truly moving on at last. She was now Mrs. Locke Linwood, and it would no longer matter what his children said or did. If they came around as decent, loving people ought to, then fine. If not, at least she and Locke had stopped all the second-guessing and agonizing and done the deed.

"Well, off we go on our honeymoon," Miss Voncille told Oralee as everyone was shaking hands after all the paperwork had been signed at Henry's desk.

"If you don't mind my askin', where y'all goin'?" Oralee wanted to know. "Henry and I went to Six Flags Over Texas. A' course, that was way back when it was a real big deal. It sounded like it'd be lots a' fun, but I threw up on the roller coaster."

Miss Voncille winced at first, but then drew herself up proudly. "We don't even know where we're going. All I can tell you is, we're heading west from here. We'll just see where the road leads us."

Oralee looked flabbergasted, bringing her hands together. "Why, I never heard of such a thing. But I kinda like it. Y'all are so impulsive."

"Aren't we, though?" Miss Voncille leaned in and whispered playfully. "But please don't tell anyone we've done this. We're going to keep it under our hats for a while and let everyone know about it in our own good time."

"My goodness! Y'all make me wanna get married all over again," Oralee added. "Why don't we take our vows again, Henry?"

"Well now, Oralee," he told her, looking at her like she was out of her mind, "that'sss the lassst thing I want to do right now. You and I, we're jussst fine the way we are. We're too old for that kinda foolissshness. Not only that, but don't you get enough of all thisss? I mean, I'd think you'd want a break sssince you're ssstanding up for ssso many couplesss all the time?"

"You'd think, wudd'n you?" Then she turned to Miss Voncille once again, talking out of the side of her mouth. "But I've gotten pretty good at tellin' what's what. When some a' these people walk outta here, I know without a doubt they're not gonna make it. Don't ask me how I know it. After thousands a' ceremonies, I just do. Why, I wouldn't issue a fishin' license to some of these crazies!" She paused to enjoy a good laugh, wiping the corner of her eye with her finger.

"But you two, you've got that special twinkle. You had that snap in your step when you first come in. You definitely looked like you knew what you were doin'. Now you be sure and let us know where you ended up when you get back from your little trip. Why, just the idea of somebody takin' off on an impulse the way y'all are doin' is so romantic, I can hardly stand it!"

Miss Voncille gave her a quick hug. "I totally agree with you. It's so unlike me to do something like this. I've always been so organized and such a perfectionist about everything over the years—from my school teaching to my genealogy research at the library. If I hadn't cut my hair so short like this, I'd say I was definitely letting it down for the first time in my life."

The look of envy on Oralee's face was quite obvious, and the sigh that followed was overly dramatic. "Y'all drive safe now."

"Don't you worry about a thing," Miss Voncille said, as she headed for the door with Locke leading the way. "We're both very cautious behind the wheel, and when the sign says *yield,* believe me, we yield. And not only that, Locke's even been known to stop and ask for directions when he can't find an address or thinks he might be lost. Can you imagine? You know how stubborn men are about that. If they don't mind asking, they're definitely keepers. If nothing else, it means they'll actually listen to you once in a while!"

Locke turned back with a smirk. "I can't remember when I've dominated a conversation with you, Voncille. I'm wondering if anyone ever has."

"That's enough of that," she said, taking his comment in stride with a chuckle. "Let's go see what we can discover out there on the open road."

10

Concrete Proof of Life

"Now that I finally have you one-on-one again, I want you to follow me. I have something I need you to see," Maura Beth was saying to her mother out on the deck of the Mc-Shays' lodge the morning after *The Robber Bridegroom* potluck and review had blown up in her face. The two of them had just endured a tense breakfast of coffee and croissants during which everyone's conversation around the table consisted mainly of small talk with a generous helping of averted glances thrown in for good measure. It was obvious that no one cared to discuss Cara Lynn's hasty exit of the evening before, or the heated exchange that had sent her on her way in such a huff.

But Maura Beth could postpone the inevitable no longer. She had finally brought her napkin up from her lap, excused herself to Jeremy, her hosts, and in-laws, and issued a pointed invitation as she rose from her chair. "Mama, please join me outside for a minute, won't you?"

At first, Cara Lynn had continued to play the role of the outraged mother of the bride. "No, thank you, I've seen the view. I've already said how lovely I think it is. Your father and I need to get upstairs and start packing."

"This is very important to me. Please, Mama," Maura
Beth added with a gentle urgency in her voice.

William Mayhew had caught his wife's gaze and tilted his
head in the general direction of the deck, and she had relented.

"All right, then. But we have a schedule to keep to get
down to New Orleans at a reasonable hour."

Once out on the deck, Cara Lynn maintained her cantan-
kerous demeanor as she kept her gaze trained on the still,
brown water. "I've seen everything I need to see here, Maura
Beth. Yesterday, the grand tour of that matchbox apartment
you live in just broke my heart. I'd go out of my mind being
hemmed in the way you are. It certainly doesn't do justice to
the beautiful sofa we sent you. Besides, it's starting to heat up
out here already. Why on earth do I have to follow you somewhere in all this terrible humidity?"

"Because we haven't resolved anything. You and Daddy
are about to run off, and we're practically right back where
we started. We've been skirting around the issue of my wedding, and you know it."

Cara Lynn drew back in exasperation. "I don't see it that
way. You've made it clear that you're going to have your wedding right here where we're standing. And what your father
and I want is of no importance."

"That's just not true. I'm wearing your wedding dress because it's important to you."

"Yes, and I appreciate that. I really do. But why not agree
to come down to Louisiana and do things up right? Yes, your
friends here in Cherico are very nice and hospitable, but what
about the family and friends you grew up with? Don't they
mean anything to you at all?"

"You mean like Cudd'n M'Dear?" Maura Beth was staring down at the planks and shaking her head.

"All right. I'll give you that one. Cudd'n M'Dear is a bit

hard to stomach at times. I don't even think she means well when she goes off on one of her absurd tangents. But there are so many other people who have always taken a genuine interest in you from the time you were just a baby. Why won't you let your father and I give you a beautiful New Orleans wedding that you'll never forget?"

Maura Beth was determined not to get drawn into her mother's time-honored tactics and pressed on. "If you'll just come with me, Mama, I think everything will make sense to you. Connie and Douglas have already taken Daddy over to the construction site. Will you at least do that much?"

Cara Lynn made a big to-do of checking her watch and sighing. "If you insist. But we really do need to be heading back to Louisiana. I think we've overstayed our welcome as it is."

Maura Beth gestured in the direction of the steps leading to a winding path flanked by monkey grass. As they slowly proceeded, the trail became less and less defined, and the border of greenery eventually disappeared. Ahead lay only a thick stand of willows and hardwoods that screened the neighboring property from view. But just when a dead end seemed all but certain, Maura Beth pointed to an opening partially obscured by overhanging branches.

"It's right there in the clearing just beyond," she told her mother. "You go ahead of me, please. I don't want you to leave without seeing it. It's concrete proof of what my life is all about up here."

Cara Lynn obeyed, but not before giving her daughter a skeptical glance. Then she shaded her eyes as she began surveying the flat land in front of her. "What is it I'm supposed to see, Maura Beth? There's nothing there. It just looks like a graded lot to me."

"Look more closely right over there by the water," Maura Beth said, gesticulating emphatically.

"What? At that big, long slab? You mean that remark about the concrete was supposed to be taken literally?"

Maura Beth's pride clearly showed in the way she held herself and drew in a breath of the heavy morning air. "Yes, it might be just a concrete slab right now, but that's the foundation of Cherico's new library—and it wouldn't be going up if I hadn't come here in the first place and then fought long and hard for it. Won't it have a beautiful view of the lake when it's finished?"

"Yes, I can see that it will," Cara Lynn admitted. "The lake is very nice." Then she faced her daughter, finally dispensing with the last vestiges of the cold-shoulder treatment she'd adopted since the outburst at the library. "But I still don't get it, Maura Beth. Honestly. I mean, this fascination you have with being a librarian. I've tried to understand, but frankly, it all just eludes me. Of course, Daddy and I thought you'd stay with it for a while just to make a little money until you got married, settled down, and gave us grandchildren. We never dreamed you'd go to this extreme and turn your back on your upbringing the way you have."

Maura Beth could not suppress a light ripple of laughter. "Mama, you kill me sometimes."

"Why? What's so funny about what I said?"

"Here, let's get out of this bright sun first," Maura Beth said, moving into the shade of the trees once again and waiting for her mother to follow. "The part about money. I can pretty much promise you that nobody goes into the library business for the money. If they do, they're going to be sadly disappointed and disillusioned."

Cara Lynn was arching her brows dramatically and nodding her head furiously now, daring to disrupt her carefully arranged hairdo. "There, you've practically made my argument for me. What on earth is the big attraction? I know you're barely scraping by, and every single time your father and I have offered to help out, you get so upset with us. It seems we can't win with you, no matter what. Do you think there's some virtue in not having money? I know there are politicians out there who make a living running down the entire concept of wealth as if it's the greatest sin in the world, but I'm just not buying it."

Maura Beth had been waiting for this moment for a long time. Perhaps she could finally explain who she was to her mother in person, since all the phone calls, cards, and e-mails over the years had not put a dent in Cara Lynn's stubborn misconceptions. "Do you remember when you took me by the hand and enrolled me in the New Orleans' Library's summer reading program?"

"Yes, of course I do."

"Why did you do that? Do you remember?"

Cara Lynn looked more surprised than puzzled. "I don't know. I guess I thought it would help you read better and that would help you do better in school. I'm not sure I really give it that much thought at the time. The other mothers in my crowd were doing it, so I went along with it, too."

Maura Beth managed a gracious smile. "Well, I'm glad you did, regardless of the reason. As you know, I loved reading. I loved all my little picture books and read as many as I could get my hands on."

"Yes, I loved reading to you just before bedtime. It was sweet when you looked up at me and tried to repeat some of the words. Every time you tried to say, 'Once upon a time,' it came out, 'One tie tie.' "

Maura Beth detected a softening of her mother's attitude and decided to proceed. "And I loved it when you read to me, Mama. Things were so simple back then. I miss that simplicity. Can't we get back to that again?"

Cara Lynn put her hands on her hips, briefly looking up at the trees. "That all sounds nice, but I think you're the one who's made everything complicated. You won't budge on your wedding plans. Well, I guess that's not quite true. As you just said, you did agree to wear my dress down the aisle. There is going to be one, isn't there? An aisle, I mean."

"Yes, of course, Mama. Just not in a church. But please try to understand. The entire New Orleans experience, The Three-Hundred Club—it was all pleasant enough growing up. And I know it means a lot to you. I'm just not sure it means nearly as much to me. To be honest with you—well, it was almost suffocating at times."

Cara Lynn looked astonished as she brought her hands down to her side. "Having access to the finer things in life is suffocating? Having friends from nice families is somehow a burden?"

"No, that's not what I meant." Maura Beth took a few moments to work it all out in her head. She had never put her feelings into words quite this way, and she wanted to be careful not to make things worse. "It was just that you and Daddy seemed to have everything planned for me—from ballroom dancing class to where I should go to college to my debut— you never asked me, you just told me. What I might want never seemed to enter into the equation. And somewhere along the way, I decided that what I wanted was to be a librarian. To be around books and literature and all kinds of information. I liked the idea of having the answers, or at least helping people try to find them. Maybe that doesn't make a lot of sense to you, but it's the best I can do."

Cara Lynn threw her hands in the air, but it registered more like resignation than annoyance. "Well, I don't know who you take after with this business of doing things your own way and the rest of us be damned. I remember in the first grade when Miss Katie Hyde told you everyone was going to color with blue crayons that day, and she called me up later and said you refused to cooperate and were going to color in red. And you did, too. But she wouldn't even give you a bad deportment grade because she said you were so cute with all that red hair. She was sure that was why you wanted to use the red." Cara Lynn paused to reflect with a strange smile on her face. "It's that red hair of yours, you know. That recessive gene, wherever it came from. I've come to the conclusion that you redheads answer to no one but yourself. But you weren't content with that. You had to go and be a redheaded librarian to boot!"

Maura Beth was certain she sensed a significant crack in the armor and immediately seized the opportunity. "Aren't I just awful?"

Finally, they both laughed. Gentle laughter, to be sure, but a genuine release of much-needed tension.

It did not stop Cara Lynn from giving it one last try, however. "So there's absolutely nothing I can say or do to convince you to have your wedding in your own church in your own hometown? You're going to insist on having people traipse up here this long way for this little fishing lodge to-do?"

"Mama, it would mean so much to me if you and Daddy would go along with it. And I know for a fact that Connie will cooperate with you in any way you like. She only wants to please us. She's made that clear from the beginning."

"Oh, this isn't about her," Cara Lynn insisted. "She's been a wonderful hostess. It's not even about the testy words I had with Susan McShay. This is about you and me. Your father will do what I tell him to do. At least most of the time." Cara Lynn wiped her brow with the back of her hand. "Look, let's head on back into that air-conditioning before we both burn to a crisp without a drop of sunscreen on. Especially since you can now say I've seen where your new library is going up. And, yes, I think it's nice that you're responsible for it. I get it—concrete evidence of your life here in Cherico. Are they at least going to name it after you?"

They began to retrace their steps, this time with a little more urgency. "No, they're not. It's going to be called The Charles Durden Sparks, Crumpton, and Duddney Public Library."

"What? Who are all those people?!"

Maura Beth chuckled under her breath. "Rich benefactors."

As they reached the steps, Cara Lynn had her nose out of joint once again. "Well, you ought to insist that your name be in there somewhere. That is, if this library business means as much to you as you say it does."

"Of course it does. But never mind that. I'll be given sufficient credit when the time comes." Just before they reached the deck doors, Maura Beth gave her mother a brief, impulsive hug. "Can we at least say we've reached a truce on my wedding plans? I need to know that."

Cara Lynn pulled away slightly, and Maura Beth was relieved to see that there was a smile on her face. "Well, it's nice to know you need your one and only mother for something."

"Yes, yes, I do, Mama, and maybe this wedding is not exactly what you envisioned, but I want you and Daddy there. And I'd like very much for you to feel good about it all."

"But the truth is, I just don't know if I really can. You're asking me to turn my back on my upbringing. It's what I know. It's what I'm comfortable with. That's asking an awful lot of someone as set in my ways as I am," Cara Lynn said, a definite note of defiance in her tone. "I might as well be honest with you. I came up here fully expecting to wear you down or talk you out of all this. And even though I haven't succeeded yet, I usually get my way, sooner or later. You're very much mistaken if you think I'm going to let up on you the least little bit. And I mean what I say."

Maura Beth took her hand and gave it a gentle squeeze. "Oh, Mama, I was so hoping you'd at least try to be more flexible than this. I absolutely hate this feeling of being at war with you!"

So far, Maura Beth had had very little time alone with her father over the hectic weekend. He always seemed to be bonding with the other men over stiff drinks and stale jokes, but she was very pleased that Jeremy had been included in these macho huddles more often than not. It was a very good sign that father-in-law and son-in-law were getting along so well. In fact, Jeremy had gone out of his way to tell her so in the privacy of their apartment.

"He's a really good guy, Maurie," he had said. "Not at all the way I pictured he would be after everything you've been telling me. I think maybe you've been underestimating him."

But it was now less than an hour away from her parents' departure to Louisiana, and there were things Maura Beth needed to say to the first man in her life she had ever loved and admired.

Fortunately, the opportunity for a one-on-one conveniently arose when William Mayhew announced that he needed to run into Cherico at the last minute to gas up the Escalade. "Come on and go with me, Maura Beth," he told her just as he was about to exit the front door.

Once they were on their way to town, Maura Beth lost no time in catching up. "I hope you understand a little better what my life is like up here, Daddy," she began, testing the waters. "Maybe it doesn't make much sense to you, but it's what I've chosen for myself."

William turned briefly to flash a smile and then trained his eyes once again on the winding road. "The most important thing for you to remember is that your mother and I aren't always on the same page. I think it's exciting that you've struck out on your own the way you have. I should have told you that sooner."

"Yeah, I kinda wish you had. Mama's always made it seem like she speaks for both of you."

"She doesn't, though."

They hit a bump in the road that caused them both to lurch forward a bit. "Oops! One of our Greater Cherico potholes that Councilman Sparks is always fretting about," she said with a weary inflection.

"I've noticed you haven't taken the time to introduce us to him. Maybe that's for the best?"

"I think so. Although I'll probably invite him to the wedding. That is, if he doesn't mess with me and my library too much until then."

"That's my girl," William said, the pride clearly reflected in his tone. "You're a fighter."

"I think I probably get it from you, Daddy. You've argued and won a lot of cases in your time."

"That may be, but the truth is, I haven't been nearly as adventurous with my life as you have," he continued. "I fell in love with your mother, the ultimate Uptowner from State Street through and through—as you well know. Of course, I let her call the shots socially, and life has been pretty good for the most part. I never even thought about moving anywhere else—certainly not the way you have. I remember how your mother carried on so when you told us about getting your job here in Cherico. 'Now, where on the face of God's green earth is that?' she said. Then she never stopped shaking her head when she located it on a road map and gasped. You would have thought you'd been exiled to Siberia or some third world nation."

Maura Beth managed to find the humor in it all and then concentrated on the scenery in silence for a short while. There were pastures full of grazing crows passing by on either side, and it all brought a smile to her face. Those lucky, cud-chewing, milk-producing beasts! Never having to plan weddings and walk down the aisle and such. All they ever had to worry about was clearing a path to the nearest salt lick and wading into the nearest pond when the temperature soared!

"Daddy, do you think I'm doing the wrong thing by having my wedding up here? Am I annoying you and Mama no end? The truth now."

William actually looked surprised as he turned her way. "I don't think there's any right or wrong about it. It's your special day, and you should be entitled to have things the way you want, even if it's unconventional."

Maura Beth reached across and patted her father's knee. "The thing is, Mama acts so hurt and betrayed—even after I agreed to wear her dress. And, yes, I realize she's been doing her dead-level best to make me feel guilty. It's almost like a political campaign to her."

"Has she succeeded?"

"Well, no, not really. I have past experience on my side. I've been to lots of receptions at The Three-Hundred Club, and they're just so overwhelming. I mean, all of our distant cousins and family friends—like Cudd'n M'Dear, for instance—they'd be coming at me and gushing the way they always do. And not meaning a tenth of it, by the way. Mama just can't get enough of that 'darling, you just look divine tonight' stuff, but it turns me off—always has. I just don't want that. I want something quieter and less stressful."

He leaned her way and lightly chucked her on the shoulder. "That's just who you are, sweetheart. You're your own librarian without a pretentious bone in your body, and you should be very proud of that."

"Wow, Daddy! I suppose you know we should have had this conversation a long time ago."

"Yep, probably should have. I guess I just took it for granted that you knew I supported you."

"Sending me to school was one thing. Not giving me any

positive feedback on my major was another. Oh, well, better late than never, but the timing's just perfect," Maura Beth admitted, feeling a new surge of confidence. "I'm glad you needed to pump some gas so we could talk this out."

"Actually, I have a full tank, sweetie. I wanted this time together just as much as you did."

Maura Beth's first impulse was to leap across the seat and throw her arms around him, but instead settled for blowing him a big kiss. "Oh, I love you, Daddy!"

"I love you, too."

After another half mile or so of grazing cows and the occasional field of corn to break the monotony of it all, she said, "But what are we going to do about Mama? The way we left things this morning, I could tell she was still upset. There was . . . well, an uneasy truce. No, not even that. I know she's still plotting."

"That's to be expected, I guess. But you just let me handle your mother. I'll make her see the light. I'll come up with something, I promise." Up ahead, William spotted a gravel road, turned onto it, and began a series of reverse maneuvers to head back to the lodge.

Halfway there, Maura Beth broke the contented silence they were both enjoying. She simply had to know. "There's just one other thing I need to ask you, Daddy. It's very important to me. What do you think of Jeremy?"

He did not answer right away, but eventually said, "Hmmm."

"Oh, come on, now. Please don't do that to me. You're making me very nervous here."

William shot her a playful glance. "I was just kidding around. I think he's a very forthright young man. He speaks his mind. He talked to me about his interest in literature and writing, and I could tell he was sincere about all that. Not my cup of tea, this business of teaching the classics, but you can't fake that kind of enthusiasm. I guess I don't have to tell the both of you that there's not a lot of money in what you're doing, though. But I see what you're trying for. I played it safe as an Uptown New Orleans lawyer and never lacked for anything from the very beginning. Maybe I'm a little envious of the risks the two of you are taking. You don't have much now, but it doesn't seem to matter to you. Your mother and I always seem to be acquiring more things and going all over the map to find them. Well, she certainly does."

Maura Beth wondered if she looked as surprised as she felt at the moment. Why, the things two intelligent people could discover and reveal just by taking a short drive together through peaceful green pastures! "But I thought you and Mama were deliriously happy with your lives. You've never given me the slightest impression that you weren't."

"Oh, we are, for the most part," he told her. "Don't get the wrong idea. I just think this trip up here has truly made me understand what my daughter is all about for the first time in my life. That old library you love and fought for so hard that's just about had it, this new library going up because of you, all the ideas that you and Jeremy embrace. And what I mean by that is, you're more interested in discussing ideas with your friends in the book club instead of accumulating a lot of things. I think it's pretty refreshing, and I want you to know that your old man gets it, even if your mother doesn't. At least not yet."

"Oh, Daddy, I think that's the sweetest thing you've ever said to me. If you weren't driving, I'd give you the biggest hug."

"Plenty of time for that before we leave. We'll sneak one in," he told her as the lodge came into view ahead. Then he pointed emphatically toward it. "Well, there's your mother, already hauling out the suitcases. I guess she's made it pretty clear that she didn't want to stay a minute longer than she had to. But for the record, if she starts making noises long-distance about not wanting to pay for the wedding the way you want it, you just ignore her. Now, I don't really think she will, but just in case, you're golden with me."

Maura Beth and Jeremy were tallying up their triumphs as they lounged on top of her purple-quilted bed after the weekend had finally come to an end on Sunday evening. They were both pleased with themselves for the most part—especially Jeremy, who hadn't had to contend with a difficult parent the way Maura Beth had. The one thing they had been able to count on from the very beginning was the support they had received from Paul and Susan McShay, who were treating them to the Key West honeymoon.

"I just wish Mama had been more pleasant and not such a diva about everything," Maura Beth was saying at one point.

"It is what it is, but the most important thing we accomplished was to actually pin down a date there at the end," he reminded her. "I don't know who else has ever scheduled a wedding the third week in September, but it sure looks like we have. So Aunt Connie and Uncle Doug can start planning everything with you and your parents over the next three weeks."

Maura Beth, who was in the midst of painting her toenails their customary pink, tried to keep the skepticism out of her voice but failed miserably. "It may just be mostly me, though. Daddy's made it perfectly clear his pockets will be deep—which I appreciate no end—but he'll leave the planning to us women. And I have the feeling Mama will continue to be on the standoffish side."

"You're not suggesting your mother will have to be dragged screaming to the ceremony, are you?"

Maura Beth laughed in spite of herself. "No, she'll do the

socially acceptable thing in the end, but there's a part of me that really likes that image. I probably shouldn't be saying something like that, but the idea of my mother not getting her way for once does tickle my funny bone."

Jeremy started fanning his face and then slid to the foot of the bed. "Those fumes. I think I'm getting high!"

"Don't be such a baby. I'm almost through," she told him, briefly sticking her tongue out as she put the finishing touches on the little toe of her right foot. "Anyway, I wish we could come up with something else to win Mama over. Looks like wearing her wedding dress isn't going to be enough. We should put our heads together."

Jeremy apparently went right to work accepting the challenge and was soon snapping his fingers. "I just thought of something."

"Already?" She screwed the cap back on her nail polish, put it on the nightstand, and then began blowing in the general direction of her feet.

He hauled himself back up to the pillows and stretched his legs out again. "Yes, already."

"Well?" she said, in between puffs of air.

"Here goes," he told her, looking particularly proud of himself. "You tell your mother the wedding won't be complete until you have that rector of St. Andrew's down there in New Orleans officiating. What was his name again?"

"Father Will Hickock."

Jeremy snickered. "Oh, yeah. Imagine having to go through life with a name like that—especially if you're a priest. All the corny jokes and references—and maybe even some shoot-'em-up sound effects for good measure!"

"He's made it work for him, though. I was just a little girl when he came to St. Andrew's, but I'll never forget that first sermon he gave. He said, 'Howdy, folks, yes, I'm Will Hickock, and there's a new sheriff in town!' It seemed like the entire congregation laughed for at least five minutes, and from that point on, he had us all in the palm of his hand."

"Perfect! So if we're not going down there to get married, why not forget about the local rector and bring Father Hickock up here? Maybe that'll placate your mother a little bit more."

Maura Beth finally stopped fussing with her toes and thought it over. "That's not half-bad. I'll bring it up next time she calls about something incredibly trivial and tedious—and believe me, she will."

"Of course, we're back to square one if we can't get him up here."

A suggestion of panic flashed across Maura Beth's face. "That's true. He might be tied up and not be able to come. I'll feel much better about it all once we've finally exchanged our vows out on the deck of the lodge, no matter who's officiating. That day just can't get here soon enough for me."

He wisely took the cue and snuggled up against her, his arm around her shoulder. "It's going to be fine, Maurie. We've worked through a helluva lot already. Nothing will keep us apart. Not those deer out on the Natchez Trace, not your parents—I mean, nothing."

She looked up into his eyes and managed a tentative smile. "I believe you, of course."

"Is there a 'but' in there somewhere?"

She drew back, and the smile vanished. "But . . . I just wonder if you're ready for the rest of my family. Even in small doses, they're a lot to handle. Especially Cudd'n M'Dear."

Jeremy propped up his pillows and sat bolt upright so he could concentrate fully. "Yeah, what's the story on her—especially that name? It keeps popping up all the time in conversation."

Maura Beth briefly collected her thoughts and proceeded. "Well, she's the Queen Mother of Eccentricity, I always like to say. Makes people like Miss Voncille and Mamie Crumpton look dull and predictable by comparison, and that's saying a lot, of course. Mama told me that she couldn't stand any of the names she was saddled with at birth. Let me concentrate so I can get them all right." There was a pause during which Maura Beth was frowning and moving her lips. "Okay, here goes. Theodoria Agnes Montaigne Mayhew. There. She's actually on Daddy's side of the family. Anyway, at some point in her murky spinster past she decided to make everyone call her My Dear. Just up and did it one day. She sent out little notes written in calligraphy in all caps, and I remember her message word for word:

DEAR FAMILY: YOU ARE
CORDIALLY INVITED TO BEGIN
CALLING ME "MY DEAR" INSTEAD
OF BY ANY OF MY OTHER
HORRENDOUS GIVEN NAMES.

"Mama and Daddy kept theirs in the family scrapbook and showed it to me once. From time to time I'd sneak another peak, I thought it was so funny. It was quite well done—she must have spent days lettering those things. And then over the years, I think her name evolved into M'Dear, and someone added the Cudd'n. The upshot is, that's how things end up the way they do in the Deep South."

Jeremy gave her a peck on the cheek, and said, "I love me some Deep South. Cudd'n M'Dear it is, then."

"Yeah, you're all casual and cavalier about it now. But wait 'til you actually meet her when she comes up for the wedding and corners you somewhere when she's had a few. You'll be craning your neck, desperately looking across a crowded room for me to come save you. Believe me, it won't be at all like 'Some Enchanted Evening.' "

"Maybe she won't come."

"Ha!" Maura Beth declared in startling fashion. "Not a chance. If no one else shows up, she'll be here. She never misses weddings and funerals and anything that passes for a party. She lives for them all. You'll see!"

This time he leaned in and gave her one of his trademark passionate kisses. "It will be a wedding for the ages, witnessed by our unique circle of friends," he told her after they had both come up for air.

She sighed as if the weight of the world had been lifted from her shoulders. "Yes, our very own wedding circle."

They sat with that for a while and then Jeremy's eyes widened as he spoke up tentatively. "I-I haven't said very much to you about my sister, Elise . . . except that she's a college professor at the University of Evansville. Maybe she's our family's Cudd'n M'Dear—but in a very different way."

"Well, your mom and dad never seem to mention her very much, either. So what's her story?"

Jeremy briefly averted his eyes, taking a while to speak. "Leesie's pretty militant about most things—I mean, in a feminist way. She thinks I'm practically a Neanderthal because I don't vote the way she does, but I try to see the good in the candidate and don't worry too much about party labels."

Maura Beth shrugged. "So? Lots of people disagree on politics—and religion, of course."

"It's just that Leesie takes it to the extreme sometimes. She's hung up the phone on both Mom and Dad when they didn't agree with her about some hot-button issue. And . . . it's been years since I've seen Leesie. If she comes to the wedding, she'll be a handful to handle with all her opinions."

"*If* she comes? You mean there's a chance she wouldn't?"

"Knowing her, I'd say yes."

"I can't imagine a sister not coming to her own brother's wedding."

Jeremy managed a little chuckle that sounded completely forced. "Welcome to the McShay Family, Maurie. We're not all sweetness and light, either."

The remark brought Maura Beth up short, but she soon recovered. For now, it was enough that Paul and Susan Mc-Shay seemed to be the ideal in-laws. But maybe there was something she could do to help repair Jeremy's relationship with his sister.

11

Old-School Pros and Cons

It was perfectly acceptable to Maura Beth that the wedding plans had been scaled down significantly after the invitations had gone out and the "declines" were far outnumbering the "will attends" among the RSVPs. The last thing she really wanted was an extravaganza similar to what would have been staged by her mother down in New Orleans at St. Andrew's and in the hallowed halls of The Three-Hundred Club. They were now expecting less than forty-five people for the ceremony and reception at the lodge—most of whom would be attending from Cherico itself. Of course, Cara Lynn Mayhew had continued to carp long-distance, despite Maura Beth's concession on the wedding dress.

"Well, practically no one from the family is coming!" she had declared one afternoon in that exaggerated manner of hers. "And the ones who are have even called me up and asked if they needed to join Triple A to help them get to Cherico since they've never even heard of the place. I knew this was going to happen when you refused to have it down here in Louisiana. And nobody I've talked to is crazy about having to book a room over in Corinth and then drive back and forth on those back roads. There's just no decent place to stay in Cherico. I'm sure that's why more people have decided not to attend."

Maura Beth had stopped short of gritting her teeth and plowed ahead fearlessly. "That's not true about the family, Mama. Connie and I are keeping track of the acceptances quite nicely. There are at least twelve of our relatives in some form or another who are coming so far, including Cudd'n M'Dear."

"Yes, well, we could do without her. She'll upset the applecart and the punch bowl and everything else before it's all over and done with."

Maura Beth had held the receiver away from her ear momentarily and rolled her eyes at that one. Nothing the woman could ever do could possibly compare to all the flak Maura Beth was continually receiving from her own mother. Clearly, a change of subject was needed and quickly. "I'm sure we can handle Cudd'n M'Dear, Mama. Meanwhile, have you picked out your dress yet? I can't wait to see it."

"No, I haven't," Cara Lynn had answered, sounding thoroughly exasperated. "I just can't seem to decide what's appropriate. St. Andrew's would be one thing. The deck of a fishing lodge will be quite another."

"You're not going to wear that little black number you trotted out for your trip up to Cherico, are you?"

Cara Lynn had failed to see the humor in the remark, and the conversation had been cut short as a result. Mission accomplished—temporarily. But Maura Beth knew she had not heard the last of the complaints from South Louisiana.

Even on a scaled-down basis, however, progress was being made on the staging of the wedding at the lodge, thanks to some brilliant suggestions on Connie's part; and now the time had come to finalize the plans. Both Jeremy and Douglas were willing to leave it to their women to tie everything up with ribbons into a neat little package. So it was the afternoon before Labor Day that Connie and Maura Beth sat down on one of the great room sofas with a couple of Bloody Marys and their diagrams to put their stamp of approval on all the details.

"Let's review what we've decided so far," Connie said, after devouring one of the cocktail onions floating next to the lemon wedge atop her ice cubes. Then she briefly consulted the notes on the legal pad that was resting on her lap. "Your father will walk you down the aisle we'll fashion between all the folding chairs. Music yet to be picked out by you and Jeremy. But right now you're leaning toward anything except the traditional *Wedding March*. I agree. That gets so tiresome, doesn't it? And why not something different since we're not going old-school here?"

"I can't think of anything less old school than this wedding."

"Oh, I have news about Father Hickock," Connie said. "The latest is he may very well have to do a christening that weekend, but the parents haven't finalized the date with him yet. He could still end up coming."

"Well, let's keep our fingers crossed that he can make it. Now—one last time. You're sure you don't mind rearranging all your furniture?" Maura Beth added, gesturing at the various sofas and chairs with a sweep of her hand.

"Listen," Connie began, patting her hair and leaning in with great relish as if getting ready to divulge a secret. "This will probably be my one and only chance to turn this cathedral of a fishing lodge into something besides a house of worship for Douglas's many prized catches."

Maura Beth glanced over at the Tennessee sandstone wall crowded with framed pictures and nodded. "Point taken."

"Anyway, back to the wedding. Paul will be Jeremy's best man, of course. Renette, Nora Duddney, and Miss Voncille will be your bridesmaids. That is, unless my niece has changed her mind. Last time I talked to Susan, she said Elise still refuses to participate. I just think she's being very childish about the whole thing."

"She also told Jeremy she wasn't coming the last time he called her up and tried to persuade her. He's not very happy with her right now," Maura Beth said. "I think it's awful that a brother and sister have been that estranged for so long."

"It isn't just Jeremy, though. Elise has alienated herself from the entire family," Connie continued, shaking her head. "She takes teaching Sociology and Women's Issues at the University of Evansville way too seriously, in my opinion. She told us all a long time ago how militantly opposed she was to the institution of marriage as it exists today—at a family reunion, of all places. She insists it exploits women. You should have seen all the jaw-dropping with mouths full of hot dogs and potato salad. It's funny how someone who's never been married can be such an expert on the subject. Anyhow, Jeremy's as old-fashioned and romantic in his thinking as Elise is abrasive and counterculture, to use one of her favorite words. She slings it around constantly, even though it belongs to my generation, not hers."

"Nothing wrong with standing up for what you believe in," Maura Beth said, trying not to sound judgmental, although she knew his sister's inflexibility had hurt Jeremy very much.

"I think we should change the subject," Connie added, quickly scanning her notes again. "Now, let's see. You said Emma Frost has declined to participate because her husband is ill and is undergoing some tests? I hope it's nothing serious."

"They can't seem to figure it out yet," Maura Beth said. "It's really distracting Emma at the front desk, I can tell you that. But I completely understand her priorities. Family comes first."

"We'll just have to hope for the best. Oh, and I've been meaning to tell you just how sweet it was of you to ask Nora Duddney to be part of your wedding."

"She was so thrilled, of course. You should have seen her face light up. But I owe her so much. If it hadn't been for her help, we wouldn't have our new library going up out at the lake. I thought this was one way I could pay her back."

"Agreed. And weddings are a wonderful setting to meet people and then start up a romance. Maybe that'll happen to Nora."

Maura Beth had a distant, dreamy expression on her face. "She deserves it after all those years of being so isolated because of her dyslexia."

Connie nodded and then resumed her businesslike demeanor. "Now, on to your multiple matrons of honor who have accepted—myself, Becca, and Periwinkle." She paused to chuckle at what appeared to be an inside joke. "But no co-ordinated, pastel prom dresses for anyone to spend their good money on, thank God. Why, you can't even hand those god-awful things down to the next generation. We each dress as we please!"

Maura Beth joined the laughter. "Yes, pull-eez!"

"Then the moment finally arrives. You and Jeremy will recite your original vows out on the deck right at sunset with Father Whomever from either here or down in New Orleans. We'll time it like a military operation. The precision of it all should take everyone's breath away."

Maura Beth sat up straighter and crisply sounded off like a boot-camp recruit. "Check!"

"We leave the deck doors open wide so that everyone seated inside can enjoy that gorgeous Lake Cherico sunset as well. You'll be framed beautifully. Douglas will tape everything for posterity, that is, if he can finally figure out the new camcorder he bought."

"Check!" Then Maura Beth frowned. "Oh, what about the friendly neighborhood flies and mosquitoes?"

"We'll spray out there before everyone arrives, sweetie. One of those outdoor foggers works wonders, believe me. I've done it tons of times when Douglas and I have had the neighbors over. And the evenings should have that first hint of fall by then. It'll be perfect."

"Lovely."

Connie returned to her legal pad. "Now we've got Periwinkle and Mr. Place working up the hors d'oeuvres menu along with the champagne punch, and when I talked to her this morning, she said, 'Oh, he's designing your cake as we speak.' Those three tiers of crème de menthe you requested."

Maura Beth almost seemed to be shivering with delight. "Yes, yes, yes. His grasshopper pie in wedding cake form."

"I'm right there with you, sweetie. I can't resist anything he makes." She continued smiling down at her notes. "Then everyone has lots to eat and drink, and there'll be dancing to your favorite music if anyone cares to."

Maura Beth leaned in with a twinkle in her eye. "We finally decided on the music last night. It's going to be an all-Johnny Mathis outing. 'Chances Are' and 'The Twelfth of Never' and 'Misty' and whatever else is on his CDs. Slow and easy. I've never liked these herky-jerky workout bands that show up for receptions."

"How romantic! So Johnny Mathis was your idea?"

"Nope, Jeremy's. Aside from classical music, he just loves fifties ballad singers."

Connie's sigh suggested she was taking a trip down Memory Lane. "I'm kinda partial to that period myself, since that's when I first started paying attention to songs on the radio. 'Smoke Gets in Your Eyes' by The Platters was my absolute favorite. Anyhow, after all the slow dancing, you and Jeremy will change, wave good-bye, and head up to Memphis to catch your plane to Key West for your Hemingway honeymoon. Now surely that was Jeremy's idea."

"Yep, you know how he is about his literary haunts. If he could find a way to fly his English classes down there, he would. But he's also hoping he'll get some inspiration for the novel he wants to start writing."

Connie produced another sigh. "That Jeremy of yours is a keeper. Take it from me. Imagine starting out with a man with that kind of romance in his soul."

"I'm thinking he'll keep it, too. Maybe he's right about himself when he says he was born in the wrong century, but I get the benefit of it."

"Well, Douglas may be addicted to his fishing boat, God knows," Connie confided, "but he hasn't lost that special spark in the bedroom. Oh, I do love dishing about the men, don't you?"

Maura Beth looked supremely pleased with herself. "I have to admit, I'm not having a bit of trouble getting with the program, considering how new I am to it. I think it's finally beginning to dawn on me how close I am to getting married. It's been a long time coming."

Mr. Place—aka Joe Sam Bedloe—was driving home to his mother's house on Big Hill Lane with Periwinkle weighing heavily on his mind. Conflicting elements swirled around inside. On the one hand, there was the depth of emotion that had been growing daily for months now; but there was also the sense that he might be entering uncharted and even dangerous territory. She seemed to be having no reservations, though. After a long day of serving customers and planning Maura Beth's wedding menu at The Twinkle, there had been a stolen moment back in the kitchen around closing time when she had surprised him with her directness.

"All this wedding to-do has got me thinking about just how far we want to go with our relationship," she had said. "I'm trying to picture my mother's reaction if the two of us ever decided to do something like—oh, I don't know—get married. It'd be one of two things—one a' her hissy fits or she'd just shake her head and tell me I'm as headstrong as I always was, never listened to her when it came to the subject of men, and I might as well go to it and suffer the consequences."

Mr. Place couldn't help but visualize his own mother's reaction to such a conversation as he drove on through the mostly deserted streets of Cherico. He and Periwinkle had yet to sleep together, even though he was certain they would get there soon. But marriage? Well, that had truly startled him, even though he had fleetingly given it consideration once or twice. All that aside, had the time come to broach the nature of his relationship with Periwinkle to Ardenia Bedloe once and for all?

Oddly, the moment he walked into the living room to find his mother sitting in her favorite spot on her green afghan-draped sofa, he could clearly read the preoccupation in her face. Moving back in with her after losing his job up in Memphis had enabled him to zero in on her every mood without fail, so he quickly sat down beside her in solicitous fashion.

"Aren't you feeling well tonight, Mama?" he said, taking her hand. "Is it your arthritis acting up?"

She gazed into his eyes the way only mothers can do where their children are concerned. "No, baby," she told him, her voice radiating maternal affection. "No worse than usual for somebody nearly seventy-six." Then she began her nightly ritual. "Did you eat at The Twinkle? I know you say you do every night, but you look thin in the face. I can see too much cheekbone pokin' through."

He knew better than to resist the interrogation and complied quickly. "Yes, I ate. Some of my own gumbo. And I don't look thin in the face."

"You lost some weight. I know what I'm talkin' about."

"Okay, yes, a little. I've taken my belt in a loop. I've been working hard, that's all."

Ardenia looked dissatisfied but moved on with a wave of her hand. "I do have somethin' else I wanna tell you."

He gave her hand a gentle squeeze. "And what's that, Mama?"

"I think somebody followed me home from the gas station today. It's been worryin' me ever since."

He drew back, tilting his head as if he hadn't heard her right. "You sure about that? Maybe it was just somebody going the same way for a while."

"I mighta thought that, too. But I know near 'bout everybody here along Big Hill Lane, know what kinda car they drive and all. It was a big white truck behind me, and nobody out here own one."

They both sat with that for a while. "Maybe somebody was lost," Mr. Place said finally, perking up. "These back roads are pretty confusing."

"Could be. They turned around once I went on down the hill to the house. But I still thought it was mighty strange. I got this shiver up my spine like you do when you out in the yard and suddenly spy a snake nearby that you nearly step on."

"Could you tell anything about the driver in the rearview mirror?"

Ardenia shook her head emphatically. "No, they had that dark, smoky glass where you cain't see in. I tell you, that kinda glass is downright scary. Could be anybody in there up to no good."

He decided to try and lighten the mood. "Now, what am I gonna do with you, Mama? You had no business going into town to fill up your car like that in the first place. I told you, I want you to let me do things like that now."

She let go of his hand and puffed herself up to reaffirm her dignity. "You actin' like I cain't hold on to the steering wheel. Well, I got my arthritis under control, and I just got me a new prescription for my glasses from Dr. Casey, so I can see a whole lot better now. I can take care a' myself."

"I know you can," he told her, capturing her hand once again and stroking it gently. "But when I came down to live with you, I thought we agreed that if you kept an eye out for me, I'd do the same for you. I'm in good health and have myself a terrific job at The Twinkle. And I have you to come home to every night. Let me keep up my end of the bargain."

She turned away briefly and worked the muscles of her face into what amounted to a mask of a smile. "Well, long as you brought up The Twinkle again, I had somethin' else on my mind. I don't want it to seem like I'm interferin', though."

"What are you talking about, Mama?" But even as the words escaped his mouth, he knew only too well what she meant. They were just too bound up in each other these days for any sort of misinterpretation.

"It's the way you talk about her all the time," she began. "I was in love once myself. 'Course I coudda done way better than Sammy Bedloe, but that just the way it played out when I was a silly-head young thing and thought he would do right by me. He did give me a son, though, so I thank him for that. But it's no use you hidin' it from me any longer, baby. You love that Miz Lattimore. I know you do."

He said nothing at first but decided it was pointless to play games. "How long have you known, Mama?"

"Awhile now. You come home every night, and you might as well be bringin' her with you the way you carry on. 'Peri say this, and Peri did that. Peri wore this, and Peri told this funny joke.' It was just like that time you had that crush on little Bercelia Ann Jefferson way back in grade school. I thought you'd crumple up in a heap and die, you had it so bad for that little girl!"

So, she had beat him to the punch on the subject of his love life. But he smiled anyway. "I never could keep anything from you."

"You right, no way you could. But I'm still gonna worry. I know you think it the twenty-first century out there, but not in some folks' hearts. You and Miz Lattimore best be on the lookout."

He still couldn't stop smiling at the way his mother had his back for the zillionth time in his life. How could he be mad about that? Still, what she needed was a little perspective. "You remember how you worried about me when you sent me off to school that first day it was integrated? But nothing bad happened then or even up until I graduated. Miss Voncille was my homeroom teacher, and from the very beginning she saw to it that I fit in."

"Yes, baby, I may be old, but I'll never forget that time and how my heart hurt when I said good-bye to you at the door that first day. I didn't stop hurtin' 'til the bus brought you home, too. 'Til I saw you walk through the door with that pretty smile you got right now."

He patted her hand and drew back just enough to get a better look at her. "You are not old, Mama. At least not the way you mean."

"But I'm old enough to know that you and Miz Lattimore better think twice about everything," she added, her demeanor as serious as he had ever witnessed. "Somethin' else happen when I was at the gas station I need to tell you about. I really think you oughtta hear it."

"Now, you see, Mama, you going to the gas station is nothing but bad news. You let me take care of the gas tank from now on. I'm serious," he told her, trying for humor.

"You gonna let me tell my story?"

He nodded dutifully. "Go ahead."

"Well, while I was down there, I went inside to get me some milk 'cause we just run out. And there was this black teenager—don't know who he was, so maybe he wudd'n from around here—but anyway, there he was, wearin' his pants down so low you could see his underwear. Wearin' some plaid boxer shorts—which I had no business knowin'. I don't know why these kids think everybody want to see somethin' like that. But anyhow, this new clerk they got in there, he raise his voice, 'If you wanna buy somethin' in here, you better pull those pants up, boy!' "

Mr. Place could only shrug. "Maybe I would've said the same thing. I hate that look myself. I know we wouldn't serve anyone at The Twinkle who came in like that. Same if they came in barefoot or without a shirt. Seems to me there are certain rules of decency that should apply to everyone."

"But my point is, that clerk, he called him 'boy.' Seem like he was just waitin' to say it to him. That was the excuse, and it was some old school stuff right there. I know. I lived through it back in the day."

"I think you might be overreacting, Mama. I don't think that has anything to do with civil rights."

She looked incredulous while shaking her head. "No?"

"Listen. They got signs all over the place now that say, 'No shoes, no shirt, no service.' Even saw one once that mentioned pulling up your pants. Imagine having to tell people that. But it has nothing to do with race anymore. Besides, what's that got to do with me and Peri? Don't you want me to be happy? You've said that to me practically all my life."

"Now, I know you're not sayin' that to me," she said, her mood lightening a bit. "Here you are fifty-four years old and still not settled down. Course I want you to be happy. But when a black man and a white woman get too friendly in a small town like this, not everybody that crazy about what they see. You know I'm tellin' you the truth, baby."

"It's not like we're flaunting our friendship, Mama. And I wouldn't exactly say we're going out."

"You coudda fooled me. Sister Leola Perkins at the church told me she drove by and saw the two a' you carryin' on so in front of The Twinkle under the awning one afternoon."

His gaze grew both studied and skeptical. "Carrying on a conversation and taking a break was more like it. Maybe laughing and talking out on the sidewalk. It's a free country last time I looked. I don't apologize for that, and I'm not about to start running scared after all these years. This town has handled its race problems better than most around the South. You should know that better than I do."

She gripped his hand as tight as her arthritis would allow. "I just couldn't stand to see anything bad happen to you or Miz Lattimore, that's all. I don't care how old you get, you'll always be my baby boy."

He could see she needed the reassurance of a hug, so he gave her one that lasted a good fifteen seconds, followed by a couple of gentle pats on the back. "And you'll always be my mama. If it'll make you feel any better, though, I promise you that Peri and I will be as discreet as we possibly can from here on out. But, honestly, I don't think our customers are spending a lot of time trying to read between the lines when they see us working so well together at The Twinkle. Maybe they think it's just professional, maybe they don't. But that's where I disagree with you about the millennium. I think we've made enough progress that even if Peri and I do decide to spend the rest of our lives together, we'll be able to do it in peace."

"I hope you right, baby," she said with a sigh that left her slumping in place. "I guess I'm stuck back in the day when the Ku Klux marched in sheets all over the South and people bombed out the schools, burned crosses in folks' yards, and

and all like that. Maybe I should get my head outta that awful place for good. Just never did see you fallin' for a white woman."

"Surprised me, too, Mama." He cut his eyes to the side as he dredged up his recent memories. "At first, I was just grateful that Peri had hired me, since I needed a job so bad after they tore down the hotel up in Memphis. But then she went through all that trouble with her ex-husband trying to get her back, and it seemed like I was the one she always turned to for advice when she was so confused. After that, things just started to fall in place. I wasn't seeing her as a white woman. I was just seeing her as a woman who'd been hurt, and something inside me wanted to reach out and help."

"You a sweet, kindly man, and I know you got that from me. Sammy Bedloe was one mule-headed so-and-so who didn't care about nobody but himself. And when he up and left us one day like he did right after you turned three, I said, 'Good riddance, and please don't let the door hit you in that way too big behind a' yours on the way out!' "

They both enjoyed a gentle laugh; then he said, "I'm proud if I take after you, Mama. You taught me from the time I was a little boy how to look after myself in this crazy world, and that's how I know nothing bad will happen to me the rest of the way. I learned my lessons well."

She started tearing up and took off her thick glasses to wipe her eyes. "I know you did, baby, but no way on God's green earth could I stand it if somethin' did happen to you. I just couldn't go on—I want you to understand that here and now."

The unexpected burst of emotion behind her words gave him pause. Perhaps he and Periwinkle *had* been too cavalier about their friendship, making assumptions about acceptance that weren't warranted. Yet, what he had told his mother was also true: He had never lived in fear because of her strength and guidance. It all meant the conflict that had simmered on the surface of his brain during his drive home was far from resolved. And even though he had largely dismissed it as his mother's overactive imagination, there was something vaguely unsettling about her insistence that someone had been following her from the gas station to Big Hill Lane.

12

Arrivals and Departures

One week before her wedding was to take place, Maura Beth was summoned unexpectedly to Councilman Sparks's office for reasons unknown. "I want to share something very important with you. But you're to keep everything I reveal to you this afternoon in strictest confidence for the time being," he had told her over the phone as she was sitting at her office desk daydreaming about the big day that was fast approaching. In her current interrupted fantasy, none of the New Orleans area contingent were being a problem—least of all her high-maintenance mother. In fact, they were all applauding vigorously at the recitation of the breathtaking sunset vows, followed by cameras flashing with abandon and much consumption of champagne punch and other spirits.

Maura Beth had to admit she was intrigued by the phone call, since Councilman Sparks had volunteered nothing further; but from his relaxed tone, she could only hope that his news might be good for once. That it would not be threatening her libraries—both old and new—or her hard-won position in the community. Particularly not this close to her wedding with all the stress it entailed.

"Let me put you at ease," he began, once she had settled

in across from him a few hours later. "This has nothing to do with the library. Zilch, nada. Well, not directly anyway."

Maura Beth disliked the qualifier but pretended she had not heard it. "I think I've known you long enough to recognize good news when I see it in your face, Councilman. So tell me all about it."

He leaned forward, casting aside the usual photo-op affectations. "I guess you've heard that we went ahead and prepared the land north of town for industrial prospects? The Charles Durden Sparks Industrial Park is finally a reality. We, uh, found the money, so to speak."

"Yes, funny thing about that, huh? The library never had to be the sacrificial lamb you made it out to be, and I never should have had to go through all that petition nonsense. You politicians just love to pick on libraries when it comes to getting your way."

His laughter was directed at the ceiling, and it lingered a bit longer than was necessary. But when he caught her gaze again, he was all business. "That's why I wish you had come to work for me when I asked you to. You're such a perceptive person. Eventually, you get it all figured out every time. You'd have been a tremendous asset as my secretary. I just wish you weren't so damned straightlaced. We could have had some fun."

With a tremendous sense of satisfaction, Maura Beth noted that his latest inappropriate comments did not faze her in the least. She was getting so much better at handling his incessant, roguish self-importance. "Water under the bridge, Councilman. Or at least the road not taken, and that *will* make all the difference. At any rate, let's don't go there anymore. So, what's your big news?"

He settled back, holding a pen between his fingers as if he were smoking a cigarette. Oddly, it flashed into Maura Beth's head that it made him look slightly effeminate, instead of the power broker of Cherico that he actually was. Or maybe it was just that she was no longer intimidated by anything he said or did. She now saw him as the poseur he really was. "We have our first genuine prospect for the park, and we should know in about a month or so if they'll definitely be coming to town and locating the plant here. Their arrival would mean much-needed jobs for Cherico, and that will increase our tax base. In the long run that means more money for all the municipal departments—including that library of yours we're building out on the lake. So there's the indirect part, and that should make you very happy."

Maura Beth wanted to exhale physically, but she settled instead for mental relief and one of her most diplomatic smiles. "Well, that really is good news. My sincerest congratulations to you for all your hard work on behalf of Cherico. If you don't mind my asking, what's the name of this fantastic industrial prospect that just can't wait to come here?"

"Keep in mind that this musn't get out until they've signed on the dotted line," he reminded her. "But it's a new cowboy boot manufacturer that wants to expand—Spurs 'R' Us. Kinda kicky, huh?"

Maura Beth's laugh was genuine enough, even if she halfway wondered if he was joking. "I'd say so, yes. There's even a Broadway play called *Kinky Boots* that's all the rage now. Plus, cowboy boots do go over quite well in this part of the South. So, exactly how many jobs will they be bringing to Cherico?"

"Three-hundred and fifty, at first. But they have plans to expand to over six hundred within two years. It's all good. Why, Cherico could become the cowboy boot capital of the world, eventually!"

Maura Beth had never seen Councilman Sparks this happy and proud. It was almost as if he had just found out his wife was pregnant, and he just couldn't wait to spread the word. "I promise I won't say anything until I get the green light from you." She rose quickly and offered her hand, not wanting to stay any longer than she had to. Lingering with the man was almost always an unwise decision. "Congratulations again, Councilman. I applaud your vision."

"Nice to hear that coming from you, Miz Mayhew. I'm really not a bad guy, you know."

"We'll just keep that little secret between us," she said with a wink.

He escorted her to the door where they said their good-byes, and she was almost out of earshot when she turned back at the last second, crossing in front of Lottie Howard's desk. "Oh, by the way, Councilman, we haven't gotten your RSVP for the wedding yet. I assume you did get your invitation?"

He seemed to be genuinely astonished by her question, and she knew he was a man who was very seldom surprised. "Well, I know we got it because Evie mentioned it a while back at the dinner table. I thought she had gone ahead and taken care of it, though. I'll remind her. But, yes, we intend to be there to watch you tie the knot with your shop teacher."

"English teacher."

"Ah, yes. How could I forget?"

Maura Beth quickly conjured up a dig of her own as she gave him a saucy smile. "I'm sure you made a point of it. But, anyway, I wanted you to know that you'll get to meet lots and lots of my distant relatives at the wedding. That will be your punishment for all you've put me through lately."

When Maura Beth returned to the library, she was greeted by the intriguing sight of Nora Duddney and Renette laughing like girlfriends behind the front desk, their faces flushed bright pink.

"What are you two up to?"

"Miz Mayhew, meet my new assistant," Renette said,

pointing while still full of giggles. "No, I'm just kidding. Nora's just given me the best news, so I made her come around here so I could give her a big hug."

Maura Beth put her purse down on the counter and cocked her head. "So tell me already."

"Well, Maura Beth, I can hardly believe it myself," Nora said. "But I've met someone. It happened this past Wednesday at the church supper. Cherico officially has a new gentleman in town—Mr. Wally Denver, and he and I just seemed to hit it off while we ate our spaghetti and meatballs."

Maura Beth immediately joined the giggling. "Just like a scene from *Lady and the Tramp*, I guess. But I really am so happy for you. And when do we get to meet this Mr. Denver of yours?"

Nora emerged from behind the counter, and said, "That's what I wanted to talk to you about, if I could."

"Well, come, let's go into my office and have a seat."

No longer the dull, shy secretary of old, Nora cut to the chase once they had settled inside. "I was just wondering if I might bring Wally as my guest to the wedding. I mean, it doesn't say 'and guest' on the invitation, so I thought I needed to run it past you."

"Of course you can bring him. You didn't even have to ask. In fact, I can't think of a better way to meet him," Maura Beth said. "This really is such exciting news, Nora. No wonder you and Renette were cutting up so much."

"We're sister bridesmaids, after all!" Nora exclaimed. Then she leaned across the desk and gave Maura Beth a wink. "I can't believe how much my life has changed since I had the courage to join The Cherry Cola Book Club. It's all been smooth sailing since then. You know, just the other day I was thinking that your book club is way better than any therapy out there—plus, it's way less expensive."

Maura Beth leaned back in her chair, looking like she had

conquered the world. "That's some high praise, Nora. I've never thought of the book club quite that way, but you're probably right. It really does provide all of us with a great opportunity to get to know each other—and help each other out as we go along, too. But there's one more thing I'd like to say to you, Nora. You have truly arrived, and every time I see you, you're more confident than ever—why, you're practically glowing. I really am so proud of you."

Nora hung her head and blushed. "Thanks, Maura Beth. I don't think I could have done it without your encouragement."

Periwinkle hung up the kitchen phone at The Twinkle and stared straight ahead at the gleaming walk-in freezer across the way, her face a mask of bewilderment. She even took the gum out of her mouth and threw it in the nearby trash can. It was just after three o'clock—that blessed lull she always anticipated and truly needed to rejuvenate herself for the dinner service. Mr. Place stood at a nearby counter, mixing up the ingredients for chocolate ganache in a big silver bowl, but also noticing her pose out of the corner of his eye.

"What's wrong? Who was that? I thought you'd never get off the phone. You sure did a lot a' listening."

She moved closer to him but seemed to be having a great deal of trouble speaking. Then her bewilderment shifted into something resembling a pained expression.

"Peri?" he continued. "What is it?"

"That was . . . Harlan," she told him, her eyes downcast.

Mr. Place immediately stopped his stirring and drew himself up, his protective instincts apparently kicking in. "Now, what does he want? He better not be bothering you. I've got half a mind to give him a good talkin'-to. Maybe the two of us should've had it out long before now. After all, I know where he lives."

"No need for anything like that," she said. "He won't be bothering me anymore." She glumly pointed to her office. "Let's go in there and sit down."

Once settled inside at her cluttered desk, she continued to have trouble expressing herself, shuffling papers around absentmindedly as if trying to buy herself some time. Finally, she just blurted it out. "Harlan's leaving town."

"What!?"

With the worst of it behind her, the rest began to flow more easily. "He's . . . declaring bankruptcy. He'll close down the restaurant and go back to Texas where he came from. He—he wanted me to be the first to know. I mean, I knew The Twinkle had turned into some real competition for him, but I didn't think things had gotten that bad. I . . . I almost feel sorry for him and . . ." She trailed off, apparently lost in thought.

"Well, I guess that's that," he said, sounding almost flippant about it.

"I guess so, but it just seems like, well . . ." Again, she seemed to be wandering mentally.

"Now, don't tell me you feel guilty about this, Peri. It is what it is. You're a damned good businesswoman, and if he couldn't keep up with you and figure out a way to compete, then he had to suffer the consequences. As we like to say down here in the South, bid'ness is bid'ness."

Periwinkle was fine with his logic, but her heart was in a very different place. She knew Harlan had tried to manipulate her into a second marriage and had refused to sign the prenuptial agreement she had created to protect herself. Furthermore, he had made a nuisance of himself on and off ever since then, making her imagination work overtime that he still might be stalking her. She had threatened but never followed through on that restraining order. But somehow, she had thought he would always be around, out there by the lake with his stale jukebox tunes playing and drinking buddies trading their stories. Not exactly a viable option for her—but still there on the periphery of her choices. She suddenly realized that something about that notion had been strangely comforting to her. Imagine that!

"You're right, of course," she told him, emerging from her fog somewhat. "I had a lot to do with his success to start with, and when we broke up, I guess he was flat-out doomed."

"And that's why he's outta here," Mr. Place said, making an exaggerated hitchhiking gesture with his thumb. He also had an expression on his face that suggested he was far from sorry to hear of Harlan's imminent departure.

Periwinkle felt a certain resolve overtaking her, and it was reflected in her more confident tone. "I'm sure he was too proud to ask me for money. At least other than trying to get me to marry him. But I saw through that and didn't make the same mistake twice."

"Yeah, you did. And you have to believe that it all worked out for the best," he added, looking more smug than ever. "Maybe he'll find himself back in Texas. Maybe that'll bring out his better nature. What part of Texas is it, by the way?"

"Oh, East Texas," she said, flashing back to a more pleasant time in her life. Pleasant, to be sure, but she had been entirely too naïve for her own good. More than once she had reminded herself that it was a wedding and a marriage that never should have taken place. "Jefferson, Texas, to be exact. He took me there once to show me where he and his mother had lived. It was this tiny little nothing of a shack, not much bigger than Elvis's dogtrot in Tupelo. But we never returned. Actually, the town has a lot more charm than Cherico does. Part Deep South and an extra big helpin' of that special Texas spirit. I kinda liked it." The suggestion of a smile crept into her face. "We drove up and down the streets, and he pointed out all the house numbers. He said when he was trying to learn how to count, he couldn't get enough of 'em. It was a side of him I never saw again."

"Just you resist any urges to go back for old time's sake once he leaves," Mr. Place said, sounding almost fatherly. "That part of your life is over, Peri. You gotta know that for your own good."

She said nothing but nodded slowly. There was a finality to it all that was gnawing at her, and she was surprised by the emotions that were rising inside. There were strange spurts and pangs in the pit of her stomach. In some order or another she knew that Parker and The Twinkle were her future—one she was more than happy to pursue and enjoy. If that happened to be the case, however, why didn't she feel better about it? Why did she feel such a tremendous sense of loss?

Harlan John Lattimore had driven his big white truck to the edge of Lake Cherico a mile or so south of Justin Brachle's developments, the construction site of the new library and his own Marina Bar and Grill. That morning, he had put a closed sign on the front door of the restaurant and given all of his employees the day off without a hint of explanation.

"Don't worry now, and don't look so damned shocked. I'll pay y'all, too," he had told them when they showed up, and they had happily scooted off with their smiles in place—no questions asked.

Later in the afternoon he had made his phone call to Peri, and he could tell she was shocked by his news because she hadn't once smarted off to him. In fact, she had hardly said a word. That was truly a first—leaving Periwinkle Lattimore speechless. He couldn't help but chuckle at that, however briefly. It was the last sensation of humor he had allowed himself the rest of the day.

Now it was nearly ten o'clock in the evening, and he was parked beneath a couple of pines that stood over him and his vehicle in towering, protective fashion. He rolled down the window to listen to the sounds the lake and the creatures around it were making. The crickets, frogs, and cicadas had still not retired for the season, hanging on to their summer symphony as long as they could. He remained behind the steering wheel, staring at the distant lights north of him where people were doing such things as cooking and eating food, watching television, reading, arguing with each other over things both trivial and substantial, or even having sex in their bedrooms. It came to him that most all of them were reasonably content and not even close to questioning the routine nature of their lives.

Routine. That was what had gone wrong for him. Or rather, the wrong routine was the issue. This obsession with Peri had taken on a life of its own. He considered himself fortunate that it had not ended in even greater disaster already. There had been plenty of opportunities for the worst to happen. Not that Peri's refusal to marry him the second time had been easy for him to swallow. In fact, it was devastating. He was sure she was going to say "yes," and then there had been that business with the prenup she had sprung on him at the last second, and he thought his head might explode when it was all over and done with. It was the first time in a life of effortless and continuous conquests that he had failed to get his way with a woman.

Then there was the evening a first-time customer had sauntered in for a couple of beers and gone on and on about Peri and that Parker Place, damn him!

"I'm in town all week on business," the balding salesman with yellow teeth began. He was one of those types who thought bartenders just hung on their every dull, rambling comment. "Thought I'd give you a try. Had a great meal last night at that Twinkle place, and that dessert I had . . . wow! They're pretty friendly, too. The owner and the pastry chef stuck around and chatted with me. Do you know 'em, this being a small town and all?" The man could have no way of knowing how much his banter almost felt like a branding iron being applied to Harlan's backside.

Beyond that, Harlan was having serious trouble with the race angle—there was no way around it. He didn't like it one bit that his ex might be getting too friendly with this black man everybody was raving about. And that confrontation he had staged with Peri in the parking lot had only confirmed his fears. There was no longer room of any kind for him in her life, and it was driving him crazy.

After that, his obsession with Peri, Mr. Place, and The Twinkle itself had escalated exponentially. There were times when it seemed that someone else—maybe some crazed demon whispering schemes in his ear—was orchestrating everything, and he was helpless to do anything about it. He didn't seem to care that these premeditated actions of his might lead to some very serious and unintended consequences. If he got the sudden urge to go downtown and stand across the street staring at The Twinkle, then he went right ahead and did it.

Then there was that sneaky business of paying Barry Bevins's high-school friends, Crispy and Scott, to call in that fake takeout order and then tailgate the young man in The Twinkle's van out on Littlejohn Lane. It had taken some leg-work for Harlan to track them down, but he had managed to do it. He was his own private detective, working feverishly yet stealthily around town. And he had paid them well to go all out and throw caution to the wind.

"This'll make it worth your while, boys," he had said, handing them three crisp hundred-dollar bills each. "Your mission is to scare the hell outta him, ya hear? Stay on his tail 'til you make him pee his pants. And no matter what happens, you never met or heard of me. This is money under the table, so nobody can ever prove a damned thing. Just keep your mouths shut and don't go spendin' it all in one place at one time. Folks'll get suspicious as to where kids your age got it."

Later, Crispy had called him up and said that they wanted more money to cover the cost of the ticket the sheriff's deputy had issued them for reckless driving, and he had complied, although grudgingly.

"Just remember, this is the end of the money train. So don't either one of you fellas get in touch with me again!" he had told the boy, practically shouting at him.

Then there were all the forays into following Mr. Place's mother out to her house on Big Hill Lane. He had no idea what he was going to do, how far he would go at such times. Would he break in at some point and terrorize her for the hell of it? He had actually considered doing it and had even imagined the poor old woman clutching her chest and having a heart attack as a result. That would put the fear of God into the high and mighty Mr. Parker Place with all of his fancy recipes! How sick and unhinged was even thinking something like that, and what had Ardenia Bedloe ever done to him, except give birth to that annoying, pastry-making son of hers?

There were other times when he would park his truck on Myrtle Street, just behind The Twinkle, and watch Mr. Place pull out of the parking lot after work and head home by himself. That was the only way he could be sure that his rival wasn't sleeping with his Peri on that particular night. The idea of such a coupling made him want to stand atop his restaurant deck railing and scream out over the lake. Who knew? If there was some long-missing corpse mired in the mud at the bottom, maybe he could make enough noise to cause it to float to the surface with its skeletal smile. His mind was filled to overflowing with such creepy, unspeakable horrors, and it was just way past time to put an end to it all. Otherwise, his rapid descent into Hell was imminent.

There was only a half moon reflected in the waters of Lake

Cherico on this crisp, early autumn evening. But there was still enough light to remind him of that magical night when Peri had said she would marry him twenty-something years ago. He had her wound around his finger then, their wedding had been "storybook," as people were fond of saying, and he saw no end in sight to the cheating game he had started playing with her. But that point in time seemed to belong in an alternate universe now, and he was bogged down in this driven, compulsive routine that would allow him no peace, awake or dreaming.

Enough of this torture. It was time to move on, whatever that entailed, however it was accomplished. Was this peaceful spot by the lake going to be the site of his last hurrah? Somewhat tentatively, he opened the glove compartment and retrieved his handgun. The metal was cold to the touch as he handled it gingerly, but somehow it felt pleasant to him. Maybe it would be the last cold thing he would experience before the hellish conditions that probably awaited him for doing what he was about to do. He always kept it loaded in case anyone, anywhere tried to mess with him. It was practically a mantra in the Deep South among a certain class of men—*don't even think about messin' with me and my gun.* But he had never imagined that he would end up using it on himself.

He took off the safety, positioned the barrel underneath his chin, and put his finger on the trigger. Then he shut his eyes and began to count backward silently toward a destination unknown—the ultimate departure.

Ten . . .

Nine . . .

Eight . . .

Seven . . .

Six . . .

Five . . .

Four . . .

But he stopped just before he got to three and opened his eyes.

No, he suddenly decided. This was just not the right spot for leaving. He had a better idea. Cleaner. Simpler. No pain. No spatter. None of that grisly television forensic stuff that most of America swore by now.

He put the gun away, turned the key in the ignition, and mentally said good-bye to the lake as he backed up the car, heading toward the comfortable home he had built for himself during the plushest of his Marina Bar and Grill days. Those days when he had had Peri by his side, crunching the numbers ever so efficiently for him. It would only take him ten or fifteen minutes to get there, and then, without a great deal of fanfare, it would all be over.

Once he arrived, it flashed into his head with a clarity he had never before experienced just why he had insisted on adding that expensive closed garage to his house plans. Originally, he had only wanted an open carport—nothing fancy— just the extra space to organize and hang up all his yard work and other manly tools. He had seen the "turn on the car in a closed garage and go quietly to sleep" trick depicted hundreds of times in movie after movie over the years. There was really nothing much to it. It seemed to be universally touted as a quick and painless way to end it all. So that was the way it was going to be.

Yes, this is the way it's gonna be, he was thinking to himself once everything was in place and humming along a few minutes later. Particularly the engine humming along inside the closed garage. What was that other sound he was hearing? Was it coming out of his mouth? Was he actually humming a tune for this grand finale of his? Well, how about that? It was "The Eyes of Texas." They were upon him once again. He imagined they were the eyes of Jefferson, Texas—his boyhood home—as a matter of fact. On this, his last, live-long day.

"Are you—are you an angel?" Harlan Lattimore managed to ask the image now slowly coming into focus. It began to become clear to him that he was staring at a pretty young female face of some sort. Her dark hair was pulled back from her face, and she was all in blue scrubs, smiling down at him.

"No, Mr. Lattimore. I'm just your nurse—Myra," the soft female voice said. "Welcome back. Looks like you're gonna make it."

He made an effort to stir, but the IV drip in his arm and other telemetry drastically restricted his movement.

"There, now, Mr. Lattimore. You just relax and don't try to move. You've been through a lot."

"Where—where am I?"

"In triage in the emergency room at Cherico Memorial."

Harlan looked around to the extent he could and frowned. "You mean I'm not dead?"

The nurse laughed gently. "Not according to our definition of the word. But you did come close. You were saved in the nick of time."

"How? You mean carbon monoxide doesn't work anymore?"

The nurse pointed to the white curtain providing the triage room with what little privacy it had. "Well, there's someone out in the hallway who's been waiting to see you for a while now. If you feel up to it, we could let him come in and visit with you just briefly. But not too long now. You need to get lots more rest after what you've just been through."

Harlan frowned deeply. "Okay . . . I guess."

Nurse Myra pulled back the curtain, and Mr. Parker Place slowly entered, smiling gently.

"What? You?!" Harlan managed, his tone sounding both puzzled and slightly annoyed.

"Hope you're feeling better, Mr. Lattimore," Mr. Place said. "They tell me you are, anyway."

"You're the last person on Earth . . . how the hell . . ." But Harlan tailed off, his surprise overwhelming him.

"Just one a' those quirks of fate, I guess," Mr. Place told him. "Peri told me all about your closing down the restaurant and leaving town, and when I got off work at The Twinkle tonight, I decided to drive out to your place and wish you the best in Texas, tell you no hard feelings and all that kinda stuff, you know. At least I hoped we could tidy things up that way. I didn't know how it would turn out—in fact, I'm pretty sure if I'd told Peri I was gonna do it, she would've told me to stay the hell away. But I decided to give it a try anyway."

"How lucky for you, Mr. Lattimore!" Nurse Myra said in a patronizing tone peculiar to certain caregivers.

But Harlan was shaking his head, his eyes barely open. "I . . . still don't understand what happened."

"I just put two and two together, Mr. Lattimore," Mr. Place continued. "You didn't answer the doorbell when I got to your house, but then I heard your engine running in the carport. Don't ask me how, but it just came into my head what was going on. I dialed 911 on my cell, and the paramedics got to you in time."

"Just barely, though," Nurse Myra added. "A minute or two more, and you wouldn't have made it."

"Yeah, I couldn't even begin to pry your garage door open or tear a hole in it," Mr. Place added.

Harlan snickered. "Well, I had the deluxe model installed. You know, the kind made of metal with the fancy electronic opener and all that good stuff."

"Practically a safe room, huh?" Mr. Place continued.

But Harlan made no effort to disguise his conflicted feelings. "More like a death room as it almost turned out. And maybe it would've been for the best if y'all had just let me go."

Mr. Place remained remarkably composed. "I did what I had to do, Mr. Lattimore. If anyone else had happened by, they would've done the same thing. Life is important, you know."

"Does Peri know about this?"

"Not yet," Mr. Place told him. "Do you want her to know?"

Harlan thought for a while, gazing over at his telemetry to distract himself momentarily. "Since I wasn't successful at offing myself, I'd say no. Could you—will you keep this between us?"

Mr. Place nodded with a gracious smile on his face. "Of course. As far as I'm concerned, it never happened."

"Well, then . . . thanks."

"Don't mention it."

Harlan was groping for the right words but couldn't seem to find them. All of the poisonous feelings he had carried around for so long for Mr. Place seemed to have been sucked out of him by the effectiveness of his emergency room treatment. Suddenly, both his head and veins were clear. He was freed of his demons. Finally, he said, "I'm still leaving town, you know."

"I figured you were."

"But I . . . I feel I should thank you for making that even possible."

"You're very welcome, Mr. Lattimore. I'm glad I could be there for you, even though I had no idea things would happen the way they did."

Then Nurse Myra stepped between them. "Well, I think that's about enough for now, Mr. Lattimore. I don't believe you're quite ready for a full-blown press conference."

Mr. Place was about to make his exit when he turned at

the curtain. "Don't worry too much about your future, Mr. Lattimore. I got a feeling your hometown of Jefferson is gonna welcome you back with open arms."

"Yeah," Harlan said, managing a hint of a smile. "The open arms and eyes of Texas."

13

A Farewell to Palms

"We desperately need a new place to live," Maura Beth said to Jeremy as she surveyed the cornucopia of wedding gifts that were taking up all the space on her little dining room table. These days, the two of them were eating their meals on bamboo TV trays while they sat on the living room sofa. It was fun and cozy as a temporary measure, but hardly suited to the long haul.

Maybe the wedding would be a small one in relative terms, but those who could not attend had sent their presents as etiquette required. Miss Manners would have been proud. The "loot," as Jeremy kept calling it jokingly, was impressive so far: a crystal punch bowl, complete with cups and ladle; a crock pot; various pieces of silverware and china; a blender; a set of steak knives; bath towels; and any number of gift certificates to restaurants and department stores. Of course, there just had to be a clunker or two. The most obvious was the oversized, framed black-and-white photograph of herself that Cudd'n M'Dear had offered up.

"Can you believe this?!" Maura Beth had exclaimed, after unwrapping it and thrusting it in Jeremy's face. "She must be the most self-absorbed person in the entire known universe!"

Jeremy had looked it over and drawn back dramatically. "Geez. It was one thing to hear all those stories about her. But it's quite another to actually see what she looks like. She's not very attractive, is she?"

"Well, that part she can't help," Maura Beth had continued. "The homely part's in her genes. Her eyes are too far apart, her nose is too big, and when she smiles with those long bicuspids of hers, she looks like she's getting ready to bite your neck. You have to play the hand you're dealt, of course. It's just that she's chosen to make everyone pay attention to her every second she's around. I suppose it's her revenge. She's just a wearying person, that's all. You'll find out when she shows up."

"Then you must never leave my side," Jeremy had added. "My natural charm can only go so far."

The fact remained, however, that Maura Beth's Clover Street efficiency seemed more cramped than ever with the wedding presents taking up residence, and they still had made no progress in finding a larger place for themselves to live after they returned from their honeymoon. Although newly married couples were forced to do it all the time, Maura Beth did not want to continue fighting Jeremy for closet space and bathroom time. In short, they both needed some breathing room.

"I have a feeling something will turn up," Jeremy said, standing beside the table full of gifts with his arm around Maura Beth's waist.

She turned and gave him a skeptical frown. "And that's based on what? We've scoured Cherico from top to bottom, and there's just nothing out there. Every apartment we've looked at is as small or smaller than this one, and all the houses are out of our price range and way more space than we need right now. Maybe we'd be able to afford them in another lifetime."

"Buck up, Maurie. If you could be patient enough to put up with Councilman Sparks all these years, you can tough it out a little longer until we find just the right place to start our new life together."

Maura Beth managed a smile, but it lacked conviction. She didn't want to have to tell him all the things that had been building up inside. Such as she was annoyed he never cleaned up his pepper-like whisker remains in the sink after shaving; and, worse, kept rearranging her clothes in the closet, including sometimes throwing the coat hangers on the floor after he was done with them. Somehow, she had envisioned that someone so romantic and chivalrous would be tidy and organized in his personal habits. But that was simply not the case. Not to mention that she probably did little things that annoyed him, but he was too much of a gentlemen to call them to her attention.

However, it would all disappear the minute they abandoned her little efficiency that was barely practical for one. What a relief more closets and a second bathroom would surely provide!

Miss Voncille was in tears as she and Locke were driving out to Teddy Bower's Green Thumbery late in the afternoon. She had been inconsolable since she had made the decision, and all Locke could do was say soothing things to her every now and then, hoping she would pull out of it. But they had dutifully taken pictures of each and every one of the potted palms that graced her house on Painter Street, and now they were finally on their way to convince Teddy Bower to buy them all.

"Well, I don't have too much demand for potted palms normally," he had told Miss Voncille over the phone when she had first sounded him out on his interest. "People think they're too much trouble, what with all the watering and such. In fact, you're the only one who ever had me order 'em over the years. I really don't know what I'd do with fourteen of 'em."

However, Miss Voncille had been so choked up she could barely speak. "But you . . . you must find good homes for all of them. I'd do it myself, but there just isn't time."

Teddy's empathy was sadly lacking. "Geez, Miss Voncille, it's not like they're puppies."

That had caused her to pull out all the stops, unleashing her wrath upon him. "Now, you listen to me and you listen good, Teddy Ray Bower. These palms mean a great deal to me— more than you'll ever know or understand. They're not just plants I bought from you. But I have to be practical about this. I'm moving into Locke's house on Perry Street soon, and there's simply not enough room there for all my palms. Something's got to give, and I'm giving you the chance to make a little money on these creatures that have been so dear to my heart all these years!"

"Yes, ma'am, I understand," Teddy had said, his tone properly meek after being thoroughly chastised. After all, he had been one of Miss Voncille's history pupils way back when, and he was still conditioned to straighten up and obey when she barked orders at him. It was either that or be sent to the principal's office. "Why don't you take some pictures so I can see what kinda shape they're in? Then, we'll see what we can do out here at the greenhouse. I'll look forward to your visit."

But the closer they got to the Green Thumbery, the more apprehensive and conflicted Miss Voncille became. Of course she knew by now that Frank Gibbons was never coming home from Vietnam. Over forty-five years had passed, and his MIA status remained unchanged. It was all long over and done with, and this clinging to the potted palms as a way of honoring Frank's disappearance in the jungles of Southeast Asia had served its purpose. She was now Mrs. Locke Linwood, and it would be a dishonor to her new husband to fill his home—

now their home—with these tropical remembrances of things past.

But if Teddy Bower agreed to take them—well, all but one, since she and Locke had agreed to make room for the largest on his back screened porch—would she truly be able to say good-bye to them for good? Oh, maybe one or two of them might turn up in the homes of friends as a pleasant surprise, but she couldn't count on that. She had to be prepared to accept them as out of sight, if not out of mind.

"You know, Locke," she told him, sniffling as they turned on to the gravel road leading to the Green Thumbery, "I've really doted on those palms as if they were my own children. Isn't that silly?"

"I don't think so. You were just trying to keep Frank's memory alive. You said his letters to you about the beauty of the jungles over there inspired you."

"Oh, it was more than that," she added, calming herself with a deep breath. "He told me he wanted to come home to a house full of palms. Now, will you listen to me? I've bored you to death with these stories about Frank over and over again. It's for the best that I make a clean break."

Locke reached over and patted her shoulder gently. "Don't beat yourself up so, Voncille. You're doing the right thing."

"But I do so want Teddy to find good homes for all the palms. It would break my heart if he let them dry up in their pots and die."

Locke chuckled under his breath. "Oh, I expect he's a better businessman than that, and I expect he'll do his best to accommodate you. Pamela and I always found him to be quite reputable in our dealings with him. Why, he found us all those crepe myrtles in the front yard for a bargain, and we never had any trouble with any of the houseplants he sold us. Not a one of them ever shriveled up and died. I think he named his business real well."

Of course, Miss Voncille knew that Teddy Bower wasn't the issue. Her emotional stability was, and she had hit the nail on the head with this "clean break" business. "That he did, and I just need to get over myself. That's all there is to it. So, I guess the next thing we need to decide is when to tell everyone that we're married. I can't believe we've kept it hidden this long."

"Well, I think we pretty much have to now," Locke said, raising his voice slightly over the crackling noises the tires were making on the gravel below. "Tomorrow the 'For Sale by Owner' sign goes up in your yard. That'll get all those tongues wagging for sure."

"Won't it, though?"

Locke thought a minute longer, and then said, "Okay. Tonight, we start letting everyone know we eloped. I'll call Carla and Locke, Jr., and you can call Maura Beth and all the rest of your Cherry Cola Book Club gang, and you know it should spread like wildfire from there."

Miss Voncille momentarily turned to watch the forest of pine trees flashing by, as all sort of thoughts filled her head. Wow! She was really uprooting herself pretty late in life—palms, house, and all! But forget finding homes for the palms for a moment. What about her beloved house on Painter Street? True, it would remain close-by, and she and Locke could drive over and see it from the street any time they wished. But what about the character of the people who might buy it? Would they take the same loving care of it that she had? Or would they paint it some awful, gaudy color and even redesign it from stem to stern so that it was no longer even recognizable? All in one stroke, she would be saying farewell to a huge chunk of her life, and she knew she would never be able to get it back again once she let it go.

She came out of her reverie just as Locke pulled up in

front of the long row of opaque greenhouses that constituted the Green Thumbery; there was also an amusing, homemade painted sign featuring—what else?—a gigantic green thumb. Teddy Bower stood in the middle of the gravel parking lot, waving at them with an inviting grin plastered on his fleshy face. Miss Voncille found herself marveling at how much some people could change over the course of a lifetime. As her pupil many decades ago, Teddy had been the ultimate string bean, forever swallowed up by his clothes. Now, far too many extravagant meals later, he was always seen in overalls that looked one size too small. Or maybe they didn't make overalls any larger than the ones that seemed to be bursting at the seams trying to contain his bulk. In any case, he was a massive, lumbering presence wherever he went.

"Good to see you, folks!" Teddy called out, as they both got out of the car and shook his hand. "Thanks for coming all the way out here. I hope you didn't mind my askin' you to take those pictures, Miss Voncille. I just need to get an idea of the size and shape they're in."

Miss Voncille handed them over quickly, while Teddy took his time, perusing them one by one. "Gotta admit they do look real healthy to me. You sure have taken good care of 'em. Maybe I could find a market in some of the local stores for decorations and such. Maybe in the lobbies or in the seating areas."

"Then you'll buy them back from me?"

Teddy hung his head for a moment, looking somewhat embarrassed. "Well, no, not quite, Miss Voncille. I can't afford to put that much money into iffy inventory like that right now. But I will take 'em on consignment, and we can work out a split between us, that is, if you'll agree to it."

"You should definitely take the deal," Locke whispered, giving his wife a gentle nudge.

But Miss Voncille was in no mood to be told what to do and balked. "What if you can't sell them? What will you do then? I can't bear the thought of them being cast aside all brown and brittle for cattle fodder or something."

Teddy's brow furrowed as he tried to work things out in his head. "Well, how's this? If I can't move 'em after a decent length of time, I'll give you a call, and you can pick up any that's left to do with as you please. A' course, you'd almost be right back where you are now."

Locke gently elbowed her again. "C'mon, Voncille. It's the best way to handle this. We just don't have the room in my house, what with moving some of your furniture in, and you can't leave it up to the new owners to do the right thing by you. For all you know, they may hate potted palms, and you don't want to have to be negotiating the fate of house-plants with prospective buyers. They absolutely won't under-stand, believe me. They'll start to wonder what you're hiding in the attic and in the basement."

Miss Voncille's sigh was clearly one of concession. "All right, I'm thinking it over. I already know most people think I'm obsessed on the subject. And when you come right down to it, they're right." Then she leaned toward Teddy with plead-ing in her voice. "But I want you to promise me you'll try your best to place my beauties properly."

Teddy was clearly amused, struggling to repress outright laughter. "I'll ask for pedigrees from my customers if you want."

Miss Voncille thought about bringing him up short as if he were still her pupil but couldn't resist smiling herself. "You al-ways were a skinny little smart aleck, Teddy Ray Bower. I'd say you and Durden Sparks were birds of a feather in that regard—the smart-aleck part, I mean. But you were nearly as good a student as he was, and I know for a fact you run a top-notch nursery. So it's a deal. Just draw up some papers or whatever you need, and my sweet babies are yours."

Teddy and Locke both took deep breaths as Miss Voncille held her head up high, feeling braver and more adventurous than she ever had before. Not even her affair with Frank Gibbons had been this much of a leap. That had come under the category of youthful mistakes. This—this letting go of what might have been—now that was the mark of a mature woman who had truly taken control of her life.

Jeremy was finishing off a second square of Maura Beth's chocolate, cherry cola sheet cake at the kitchenette counter when the phone rang. He thought it might be his mother calling about the rehearsal buffet out at the lodge the following evening, but was surprised to hear Miss Voncille's voice at the other end instead.

"Is Maura Beth there, dear?" she continued after the usual pleasantries.

"Yes, but she's in the shower right now," Jeremy told her, swallowing the last of his dessert.

"Ah. Of course, I can pass the information along to you just as well," Miss Voncille added. Then she proceeded to tell him about her elopement with Locke and her house being put on the market.

Jeremy didn't miss a beat. Over the years he had become accustomed to surprises from his students, and Miss Voncille's revelations didn't appear to be any more difficult to handle. "Let me congratulate you and Locke then. I know I speak for Maurie, too. From what I've seen of the two of you since moving down to Cherico, I know you'll be very happy together. I also have to tell you that there have been a few moments when Maurie and I have felt like eloping ourselves. These weddings aren't exactly a walk in the park, much less a walk down the aisle. But I'm especially interested in your house news. Would you mind telling me how much you're asking for your place?"

Miss Voncille gave him the starting figure and her idea of an acceptable down payment.

"Is that, uh, written in stone?"

"My wish figures, I suppose. I've never sold a house before, but I imagine these things are negotiable. Do you think you and Maura Beth might be interested? I don't know why I didn't think of you before. Sometimes I think my mind has wandered off the plantation."

"That amount of money doesn't seem completely out of the question at this point, but let me think about it," Jeremy told her. "We might need some help."

There was brief silence at the other end; then Miss Voncille spoke up hesitantly. "Well . . . umm . . . I was just wondering. How do you and Maura Beth feel about potted palms? Fourteen of them, to be exact."

Jeremy frowned, taken by surprise this time. "I, uh, don't know. I've never thought about them before. Not even one, much less fourteen."

"They could come with the house if you wanted," she explained.

"Intriguing," Jeremy said. But what he wanted to say was, "What the hell are you talking about?" He had never been inside her home on Painter Street, but he had seen it from the outside driving by from time to time and had admired its simplicity; not to mention the tidy front yard that wouldn't need much mowing. It might just fit the bill as a starter house for Mr. and Mrs. Jeremy McShay.

"I assume you'll want to see the house first," Miss Voncille continued. "It's got two bedrooms and two baths—all pretty small, though."

Jeremy was thinking on his feet now. "Seems like Maura

Beth has mentioned your house a time or two. I don't remember anything about palms, though."

"It may have slipped her mind, I guess. Anyway, she's been over several times for various to-dos I've had. Just us girls, you know, and we've had some wonderful times. I know Maura Beth said she felt completely at home in my big yellow kitchen, and she loved the birdbath in the front yard."

Suddenly, everything fell into place. "Listen, Miss Voncille, if you'll bear me with me, I have a few phone calls I need to make. Just promise me you won't do anything about the house until you hear from me, okay?"

"I promise."

"Am I—are we the first ones you've called about this?"

She told him they were.

"Good choice, Miss Voncille. Good choice."

After they'd hung up a minute or so later, Jeremy felt strangely liberated, then empowered by Miss Voncille's news. He could still hear the water running in the bathroom, so he decided to go ahead and make that first phone call and try to get things under way. He had told his Maurie that he thought something would turn up for them sooner or later as a genuine prospect for their new home, and now he felt so confident about it all that he was about to burst.

Life was good for this idealistic teacher of the classics.

14

Relatively Speaking

On a day when the air had the crisp sensation of biting into a fresh apple, the improbable parade of wedding guests to Cherico began. Looming just ahead of the main event tomorrow were the early evening rehearsal and dinner afterward; or in this case, the buffet that The Twinkle would be catering at the lodge on behalf of Paul and Susan McShay.

Hands down, however, the most eclectic grouping among so many consisted of Father Will Hickock—who had seen his way clear to performing the ceremony—Cudd'n M'Dear, Lewinda Sojourner, and Mabel Anne Simmons. The latter trio were among the Mayhew cousins, however remote or removed. It was late afternoon by the time they all finally showed up in Father Hickock's car, and everyone had begun to worry that they might even have lost their way between Corinth and Cherico. But the throng of Mayhews, McShays, and other Chericoans awaiting them breathed a sigh of relief when Father Hickock tooted his horn a couple of times, rolled down the window, and waved energetically as he drove up with an hour or so to spare.

"I hope everything was fine with your rooms at the hotel

over in Corinth," Connie McShay was saying, after the new-comers had joined the gathering already inside the great room and introduced themselves.

It was Father Hickock who spoke up for his contingent as wine and cocktails were served all around. "Yes, the accommodations are quite nice. But I have to confess, I did take a wrong turn that delayed us. I'm usually pretty good out there on the open trail. As it turned out, it was all very scenic, and we were fascinated by that leafy green vine that seemed to cover everything on both sides of the road."

"That would be the kudzu," Maura Beth told him. Then she enjoyed a little chuckle. "I'm just glad you didn't break down. That stuff'll overtake you if you stay in one place too long."

"She exaggerates, of course," Connie said, joining the laughter that erupted. "But not by much."

Father Hickock continued his praise. "It was an exciting adventure regardless. Sometimes we forget to admire the diversity of God's creation."

"Well, we're awfully glad you could come up, Father," Cara Lynn Mayhew added, sidling up to him. "It means so much to us to have a little bit more of our New Orleans culture here for this special weekend."

Maura Beth decided to give her mother the benefit of the doubt on that one—the remark seemed pleasant enough—and made no comment. Instead, she focused on Father Hickock himself. She remembered him as having a lot more hair and being taller, although she realized she hadn't seen him since high school when she herself was always "looking up" to adults, both literally and figuratively. In the time that had passed, he seemed to have gone mostly bald by leaps and bounds, and also to have shrunk by a few inches. How the latter was possible, she could not possibly imagine—but nonetheless, there it was! The constants, however, were his ruddy, cherubic face and charismatic demeanor—traits well-suited to a man of the cloth.

"Well, we certainly believe our hospitality and scenery will make your visit worthwhile. We've been looking forward to it," Connie continued, her customary cheerful personality firmly in place.

"You know, it never ceases to delight me where some people choose to get married," Father Hickock told everyone. "I've performed ceremonies in pirogues, on beaches, atop mountains—even in a bowling alley once. Not while games were being played, of course. We certainly couldn't have had all the clatter of those pins while vows were being exchanged. But the entire place was rented out for peace and quiet. It's all the same to me, of course, since it's my belief that the spirit of the church exists everywhere."

What followed next was a stream of polite small talk, measured sipping of drinks, and munching of The Twinkle's hors d'oeuvres, but Maura Beth largely tuned it out for observations of relatives she had not seen in some time. Obviously, there was Cudd'n M'Dear, as homely as ever; but what in the world could she have been thinking with that outfit she was wearing? The beige color of the dress was acceptable enough, but it appeared to have tears and holes in it, from top to bottom, as if a weary seamstress had taken a knife to it in a fit of rage. Was it supposed to be like that, were people supposed to catch glimpses of her silk slip underneath, or had something traumatic happened to it on the trip up? What kind of wild ride had the good Father Hickock saddled up for and offered? Perhaps there was more than met the eye in that innocent smile of his. But then she thought better of such preposterous speculation and moved on.

As it happened, Maura Beth had never understood how she was related to Lewinda and Mabel Anne. Whenever she

had asked her mother about the connection, the explanation
had been so labored and incomprehensible that she had just
given up trying to figure it out—and eventually even caring.
They just appeared without fail at most family gatherings, possibly for the food and drink; for the truth was they never had
anything noteworthy in the way of conversation to add. Like
Cudd'n M'Dear, they had missed out on the attractive gene in
the family and remained unmarried, but at least Cudd'n
M'Dear had opinions and caused a stir wherever she showed
up. In short, she was nothing if not memorable, while they
were the very definition of forgettable.

Eventually, and much to Maura Beth's chagrin, Cudd'n
M'Dear forced a showdown about her outfit. "How do you
two like this?" she asked, after finishing off her second glass of
Merlot and cornering both Maura Beth and Jeremy as they
were about to go out on the deck. "I've been dying to wear
it someplace special, and I thought your wedding would be
just the ticket."

"Don't leave me," Jeremy whispered out of the corner of
his mouth, holding on to Maura Beth's arm.

"Well, I—uh—what . . . exactly is it, Cudd'n M'Dear?"
Maura Beth stammered, trying her best to steady herself.

"Oh, it's the latest. I found it in this little avant-garde shop
in the Quarter," Cudd'n M'Dear began. "I forget the name.
But anyway, this is what's called *distressed chic*. At least that's
what the saleswoman said. Now, why would she make that
up? Isn't it daring?" She whirled around completely to show
it off better—not once, but twice—her arms high above her
head. No belly dancer could have done better. "And it's really
very cool and comfortable."

Maura Beth wondered if the smile she was forcing on her
face looked as silly as she felt continuing the exchange. "With
all those holes I'll bet it is. So you're saying it's supposed to
look like that?"

"Oh, yes, of course, dear. The second I saw it in the window, I knew I had to have it."

"Well, I have to agree. It's certainly not fashion as usual," Maura Beth managed, fearful of where the conversation might go next.

True to form, Cudd'n M'Dear hitched a ride on an entirely different tangent, looking supremely smug. "Did your mother tell you I was in another fender bender last month? All the best people have fender benders, you know. It was my fourth this year, but who's counting? It was so exciting. I was trying to parallel park in the Quarter—which is practically impossible—and I just overcorrected and dented the car behind me. Actually, I don't remember it being there. I think it appeared as if by magic. But don't worry, I left a note on the windshield, giving them my name."

Maura Beth knew better but asked anyway. Why not indulge the woman? "And your phone number I hope?"

"Oh, heavens, no! I would never give that out. I've always been unlisted. An unmarried woman living alone gets all sorts of creepy, goose-bumpy calls. At least I have. But you'll be happy to know I was very friendly and courteous in my note. I wrote in very legible penmanship, *So sorry about the dent I put in your bumper. All the best, Theodoria.*"

"I thought you never used your real name anymore."

"I don't. But I wanted whoever it was to think I was a real person. You have to admit that Cudd'n M'Dear sounds completely made up."

Maura Beth nodded reluctantly, slightly concerned for her own sanity that she was able to discern a strange sort of logic in her cousin's ramblings. At the same time, she couldn't help but notice that the look on Jeremy's face was a combination of bewilderment and dread, and he continued to hold on to her tightly.

"But can you believe it?" Cudd'n M'Dear resumed,

clearly in her element. "My insurance rates haven't gone up a bit. That's because Phil Leblanc—he's my agent, you know—anyway, he always keeps in mind that I'm a Mayhew. He fudges things for me quite nicely. In return, I always send him one of my homemade fruitcakes doused with rum for Christmas." Then she suddenly focused on Jeremy. "Dear boy, would you mind getting me another glass of wine, please? I was drinking the red. If they're out, I'll settle for a nice blush. I believe I saw one somewhere over there."

Maura Beth noted that Jeremy didn't have to be asked twice. He nodded with a smile, quickly let go of her arm, and headed off to the crowded bar across the room. She sensed that he would not mind standing in line for a while to rustle up drinks. As a result, it was just Maura Beth versus her unpredictable, flighty cousin—the one-on-one she knew would happen at some point over the weekend. There was no telling what might be discussed now.

"So," Cudd'n M'Dear started up, leaning in with her wide-spaced, chameleon-esque eyes, "your mother tells me you're quite the independent woman these days. Wouldn't even consider a New Orleans wedding with all the trimmings. No Three-Hundred Club under the moss-draped oaks for you, my girl. I can tell you she's quite upset about all this. I don't know how many phone calls I've received from her these last few months. As if I could do anything about it."

"I'm well aware of all that, Cudd'n M'Dear. You should tell me something I don't know."

"Such as?"

"Surprise me."

"Well, how's this for starters? I think she's dead wrong to get so worked up the way she has," Cudd'n M'Dear continued, suddenly lowering her voice. "She should be proud of you. I know I am. I think it's thrilling the way you're striking out on your own while you're still so young and fresh."

Maura Beth was hard-pressed to keep her wits about her. This was the last thing she had expected to hear. Still, she managed a cogent, grateful reply. "Why, thank you. I'm flattered, Cudd'n M'Dear. I really am!"

Then the dishing began in earnest, and Maura Beth felt as if she were suddenly listening to an entirely different person. "Listen, sweetie, I'm nothing if not a realist. Most people think I'm off my rocker, but I know how the world works for a woman who looks the way I do. The truth is, no man ever took me seriously; and, yes, that hurt me deeply. They never even tried to discover the woman inside. But I got over it a long time ago. So, then the question became: What was I going to do with my life? I decided that if I couldn't be attractive, I could at least be interesting—even a puzzle for people to solve. Okay, so maybe I didn't make that sort of decision consciously, but it amounts to the same thing if you have a lot of time on your hands and follow your instincts. Don't you think I've succeeded?"

"I do. I really do," Maura Beth told her, genuinely delighted with the talk they were having. "If you don't mind me saying so, I never could even come close to figuring out what you were all about. But I was always fascinated and usually amused whenever I heard about your adventures from Mama. So why are you telling me all of this now? It's such a wonderful revelation."

Cudd'n M'Dear shrugged her shoulders. "What better wedding gift could I give you than my admiration? Along with my framed picture, of course. You'll also find I did put a little something extra in the card I'm giving you tomorrow. But the point is, you've stood up for yourself, and what's not to like about that? Plus, here you are getting married to that adorable young man with the pale, frightened face. It was all I could do to keep from giving him a big family hug to let him know everything was going to be all right. Was he afraid I was going to bite him with these teeth of mine?"

Maura Beth could not restrain her forceful burst of laughter and was happy to see Cudd'n M'Dear joining in. "He may very well have been. Meeting relatives under these circumstances can be stressful enough without certain people telling their exaggerated tales. I think I'm probably the guilty party here."

"I'm basically harmless, you know."

"I see that now."

"I just enjoy the drama of it all."

"You and Mama both. I think it runs in the family."

Maura Beth mulled things over further, keeping an eye on Jeremy all the while. She needed to do some plotting before he returned from the bar with the refills. "There's something I'd like you to do for me, if you wouldn't mind, Cudd'n M'Dear."

"Anything, sweetie. You just name it."

"Well, tomorrow, I'm going to introduce you to the man who runs Cherico—Councilman Durden Sparks. I'm assuming he'll show up like he said he would. Anyway, that devious so-and-so has done everything he could possibly do to drive me away and make life miserable for me—not to mention actually hitting on me—and I'm not sure I'm through exacting my revenge."

Cudd'n M'Dear seemed to be shivering with delight as she rubbed her hands together in imitation of a fly. "Ooh, I absolutely adore getting even. It's practically become my mantra."

"Just what I wanted to hear." Maura Beth drew herself up, still full of the endorphins her recent belly laugh had produced. "It's really quite simple. I just want you to be the Cudd'n M'Dear we all never understood. Do your befuddling thing as only you can do. I promised Councilman Sparks he'd get to meet all my relatives at their very best, if you catch my drift."

Cudd'n M'Dear looked as if she were about to swoon. "Oh, I can hardly wait. You really haven't seen me when I'm on a mission. But first, I want you to give me all the dirty little details about what he's done to you. I must prepare myself properly for this role." Then out of the corner of her eye, she spotted Jeremy approaching with her wine. "We'll get together later and huddle. But you just leave it up to me," she said quickly with a wink. "That councilman of yours won't know what hit him."

An hour or so later the rehearsal was finally under way, and everyone was lined up to march in a stately manner down the makeshift aisle between all the rented folding chairs. After much discussion, Jeremy had persuaded Maura Beth to choose *Symphony No. 9* by Beethoven as a classical change of pace for the processional. He was particularly a fan of the opening "Allegro ma non troppo-un poco maestoso" and even intended to use it for the recessional.

"I'd like for us to use the stretch starting about two minutes in," he had explained further, quite adamant on the subject. "After all, I think Mendelssohn's been done to death."

He had also insisted that they use his old LP of the *Complete Works of Beethoven* that he had discovered and bought for a song at an old flea market up in Nashville, and accompanying it was the turntable that reflected his attachment to outdated but revered technology.

"At least you're consistent about wanting to be born in another century," Maura Beth had told him, once the matter had been settled.

Thus, Renette, Nora Duddney, and Miss Voncille began their studied journey toward Father Hickock, who awaited them through the open doors out on the deck, his black and white vestments billowing in the breeze off the lake. Behind him, the blood-orange sun was squatting on the horizon but sinking fast; while beside him stood Jeremy, tall and sturdy—with Paul McShay looking on proudly as his son's best man. But the two eager bridesmaids were no more than halfway up the aisle when the LP began to show its age—namely, a pesky scratch that would not be denied. Caught in a loop, the allegro repeated the same brief strain over and over; both Renette and Nora stopped in their tracks, looking alternately amused and bewildered, while giggles broke out among the onlookers.

Jeremy couldn't resist, pointing emphatically. "I think my Beethoven's stuck in a rut."

Father Hickock quickly came to the rescue with that jolly smile of his and solemnly lifted his right arm, as if about to impart a blessing upon his congregation. "We know that God is patient with us in all our endeavors, but he has his limits when it comes to worn-out technology. Therefore, would someone kindly pick up that stubborn stylus, please?"

Douglas McShay sprang from his seat and rushed over, did the deed, and then crossed his fingers as the music resumed a few notes ahead. "No more stops and starts, I hope."

"As my mother the seamstress was fond of saying all the time—'the world could use a little more excellent needlework!' " Father Hickock called out, again indulging his sense of humor.

Fortunately, the LP was on its best behavior from that point forward. Becca, Periwinkle, and Connie soon followed as matrons of honor, peeling off to either side to join the bridesmaids on the deck. Finally came William Mayhew escorting his daughter as only loving fathers can do; then the recitation of the couple's original vows followed—all in one smooth take.

After Father Hickock had listened to what they had each composed, his eyes seemed to widen and twinkle at the same time. "Well, I do believe God enjoys the expressive use of English on these and many other occasions. That was some very creative writing. Not to mention quite moving."

Jeremy lifted his head proudly, as if the praise had been solely directed at him. "Thank you, Father. I like to think it's my mission in life to preserve and enhance the language."

"It's the English teacher in him, you know," Maura Beth said out of the side of her mouth. "He just loves the classics. Well, anything classic—old cars, music, you name it."

"You make a charming couple," Father Hickock told them. "And I'm so glad I was able to come up and preside over your ceremony, Maura Beth. To see how you've grown from the little girl who took her First Communion in my church into such a beautiful and accomplished woman warms my heart. Weddings and christenings are the greatest joys of my ministry. I look forward to performing your marriage ceremony tomorrow evening, and may that sunset be as lovely as this one was."

Everyone began to dig into the tried-and-true Twinkle buffet with gusto after the rehearsal was over: chicken spaghetti, stuffed mushrooms, tomato aspic, arugula and mandarin orange salad, and lemon icebox pie for those with a sweet tooth. In the aftermath of it all, Maura Beth could tell that Jeremy was overwhelmed by the many names and faces that were being thrown at him from her side of the family.

"Now, which one was Lewinda and which one was Mabel Anne?" he was asking her at one point while they balanced their plates on their knees near the fireplace. And, "But tell me again—who is Mrs. Salter? Is she another cousin or just the one who's your mother's best friend? Or am I thinking about Mimi Halloran? Or was it Harriman?" Maura Beth could have eaten Jeremy with a spoon, he was so earnest and eager to please her.

On the other hand, she had no such dilemma. Jeremy's parents and his grandparents on his father's side were the only ones attending from his family, since his sister, Elise, stubbornly continued to boycott the ceremony. Johnnie-Dell Crews and three other teachers from the Cherico High faculty rounded out those who had accepted invitations on Jeremy's behalf, being the newcomer that he was.

Somewhere in the middle of the rehearsal festivities it dawned on Maura Beth that as hard as they had tried to keep the wedding on the small and simple side, it had still managed to become more elaborate than they anticipated. There were still more people milling around, eating, drinking, and laughing than they really wanted; and yesterday evening's news from Jeremy that Miss Voncille and Locke Linwood had eloped was just about the simplest, sanest thing she'd heard in ages. But it was too late to turn back now.

It was, in fact, Miss Voncille—now Mrs. Locke Linwood—who helped Maura Beth put things in perspective after the crowd had thinned out significantly and people were heading back to their homes and hotel rooms.

"There's something very important we need to discuss," Miss Voncille began, as the two of them stepped out on the deck for a bit of the cool autumn air. "I guess you realize that I absolutely should not be one of your bridesmaids tomorrow, even though I went through the entire rehearsal without saying a word. Why, I didn't even bring it up once with Father Hickock, but I probably should have. It's just a fact we can't ignore any longer."

For some reason—perhaps it was the refreshing breeze off the lake that heightened her senses—Maura Beth got it right away and gave a little gasp of recognition. "Oh . . . of course. You should be one of my matrons of honor now."

"Right you are. I'm officially no longer a bridesmaid, I'm thrilled to say. That monkey is off my back."

They both giggled as Maura Beth leaned back against the railing, and said, "It won't change things much, though. You'll just walk in behind Becca and Connie and Periwinkle instead of with Renette and Nora. Oh, these wedding technicalities are such a drag, aren't they? I was just thinking how sensible you and Locke were to do it the way you did."

Miss Voncille looked skeptical, even slightly disapproving. "Yes, but don't lose sight of the fact that we're almost seventy. We couldn't fool around like we had all the time in the world. You and Jeremy are twenty-somethings. You should savor all the festivities this first time around. You'll both remember it for the rest of your lives. Forget the glitches and the hassles that have made you worry and maybe even want to pull your hair out. Just relax and enjoy it. As someone who had to wait most of her life for the big moment, I know what I'm talking about."

Maura Beth gave her an impulsive hug and exhaled. "Thanks for that, Miss Voncille. I know you're right." Then she remembered. "But what's all this I hear about you selling your house? Becca mentioned it to me just before the rehearsal and said Stout Fella wants you to list with him, but you wanted to go the 'for sale by owner' route. It all came as news to me. Did you tell Jeremy about it when you called us last night?" Maura Beth could tell that Miss Voncille was becoming decidedly uncomfortable, quickly averting her eyes.

"Well, as a matter of fact, I did," Miss Voncille said, trying for nonchalance. "I believe he said you were in the shower at the time."

"I was. But why didn't he tell me everything? He's the most organized, detail-oriented person I've ever known. That's just not the sort of thing he would keep to himself."

Suddenly, Miss Voncille glanced at her watch. "Ummm,

well, I wish I could go into it more, but I believe it's almost time."

"Time for what?"

Just then, Jeremy and Locke came out onto the deck with big grins plastered on their faces, and Maura Beth began to wonder if they'd had too much to drink. It often came with the territory where wedding hoopla was concerned. "They're ready for you inside," Jeremy said, tilting his head toward the door.

"Go on in," Miss Voncille added, the excitement rising in her voice. "We've been frantically planning all this for you around the clock. It's a little surprise. Actually, it's a big surprise."

Jeremy took Maura Beth by the hand, and what was about to unfold came to her at the precise moment he touched her, flowing through her in some unknown, intuitive manner. That was how connected they had become, and she knew she would remember that particular heady rush for the rest of her life.

15

A Pair of Scissors

There they all sat or stood as one—the members of the wedding party and the core of The Cherry Cola Book Club as well—waiting for Maura Beth in the great room and smiling to beat the band. Her parents soon became her main focus, however; her eyes particularly went to her mother, who looked happier than Maura Beth had seen her in a very long time. Had it actually been in her album of wedding pictures taken some thirty years ago? Way too long, of course, but was this current smile a genuine one or just more of her mother's machinations? Momentarily, William Mayhew spoke up for the group.

"Sweetheart, we have some wonderful news for you, thanks to the quick thinking of Jeremy and Miss Voncille. Your mother and I are going to give you the down payment to buy Miss Voncille's house on Painter Street, and we'll see to it that you get a good deal down at the bank. They'll have the papers all ready for you when you get back from Key West. Our wedding present was going to be money to use as you wished, but we just thought it might work out better for you this way. We hope you like the decision we made. Jeremy seemed to think you'd be pleased."

Although Maura Beth had already guessed what he was going to say, she played along magnificently, sounding genuinely surprised without going overboard. "Oh, I just love that little house so much, Daddy. I'm not just pleased, I'm overwhelmed—thank you so much!" She lost no time in hugging and kissing both of her parents and then followed suit with Jeremy. "So this is what you've been up to! You and Miss Voncille and . . . I guess the rest of you knew about this, too?"

Connie and Douglas raised their hands, and she said, " 'Heard it through the grapevine,' to quote one of my favorite rock lyrics from my era. You know how we book clubbers are about staying in touch."

"It was all I could do to keep from pickin' up the phone and spillin' the beans, girl," Periwinkle added. "You know how I like to spread the news around."

Then Becca spoke up. "We're so excited for you. You'll be surprised what owning your own home will do for your entire outlook. Gosh, I sound just like one of my husband's brochures, don't I?"

Stout Fella offered up his big laugh. "Well, that's my philosophy of life. You need to own a piece of the good earth to really feel connected to it, and I'm just the guy to sell it to you. Except you'll have to wait 'til you're in the market for another house, since I had nothing to do with this deal. Sure would have liked that commission, Miss Voncille."

"You have plenty of projects to occupy you right out here at the lake," Becca reminded him.

"It all happened so fast, it made my head spin," Miss Voncille explained. "I probably would have listed with you if things hadn't fallen into place the way they did." Then she focused on Maura Beth. "But just so you know, I'll have everything moved out and into Locke's house by the time you and Jeremy return from your honeymoon. Including the potted palms."

Maura Beth recalled her first impressions of Miss Von-

cille's intriguing "jungle." "I think I'd like to keep a couple if
you don't mind."

Miss Voncille dramatically clasped her hands together.
"That would be wonderful. At least two more of my babies
will have a good home!"

"I like the way they looked in that big, bright kitchen of
yours. Everything was all yellow and green and full of life,"
Maura Beth added.

"I think kitchens should be cheerful. It's not debatable. We
spend enough time in them. And whenever I'd let something
boil over on the stove, I never worried. I knew all that steam
would be very beneficial to my palms." Then Miss Voncille
turned to Becca. "Although I have to admit I don't spend as
much time in my kitchen as I used to when *The Becca Broccoli
Show* was on the radio. I was there with my cup of morning
coffee at my counter listening to every show. I miss the recipes
and the cooking tips—and all the humor you put into everything."

Becca pointed to her growing baby bump and laughed.
"I do appreciate that, Miss Voncille. In fact, WHYY tells me
they're still getting calls and letters all the time begging me to
come back. But as you can see, I've got a different kind of bun
in the oven now. But don't forget about my cookbook that'll
be coming out in a few months. That way, you can have me
with you year-round."

"Will it be coming out in time for Christmas?"

"I'm going to try my best. It would have been out earlier,
but I have to admit my pregnancy has been my main priority.
That, and making sure my Stout Fella here sticks to his nutri-
tion regimen."

"I can vouch for us both," Stout Fella said. "She eats the
stuff she's supposed to for the baby, I eat my stuff for my burn-
ing feet, and I'd say we're doing just fine. She keeps gaining
weight, and I keep losing."

"I see that. Looks good on you, Justin. Well, just keep on gaining and losing, and don't get them mixed up," Maura Beth said. "And, Becca, we're definitely going to have that book signing at the library for you when the time comes."

"I'll hold you to that."

Maura Beth continued to circulate among her treasured circle of friends and soon found herself bonding as she had so often in the past with Periwinkle, who was overflowing with advice as she worked her gum.

"Girl, movin' is the pits. But here's a really good tip. You go out and buy yourself lotsa trash bags and keep an eye out when your movers come. If you don't, they'll wrap up everything in sight, including the leftovers in the fridge, and charge you for all of it to boot. Take my word."

Maura Beth was laughing now. "It's been so long since I moved up from Louisiana, I'd practically forgotten about all that. But I know you're right. They boxed up everything in my wastebaskets last time. Imagine—old, crumpled-up pieces of paper wrapped in new crumpled-up pieces of paper!"

"But can you believe it? You have your own home!" Periwinkle continued, nudging her friend playfully.

"Not to mention a wonderful husband and a new library going up a few hundred feet away."

The two of them enjoyed an impulsive hug, but Periwinkle soon pulled away, frowning. "Which reminds me—did you invite His Majesty to your big to-do tomorrow?"

"Who?"

"Our beloved Councilman Sparks."

"Oh, yes, I did, as a matter of fact, and he says he's coming."

"Do you think he'll behave himself, considering his track record regarding the library and the book club?"

Maura Beth looked wickedly smug. "Trust me. I have a little treat planned for him at the reception."

"Well, it looks like everything is finally goin' your way."

Maura Beth thought about Periwinkle's words, indulging a warm inner glow as she moved about the great room in and out of conversations and soaking up this milestone moment in her life. It all confirmed once again the rightness of her decision to stick it out in Cherico personally and professionally over the past six years.

There were a couple of loose ends that Maura Beth needed to tie up, however, and the first concerned Mr. and Mrs. Locke Linwood.

"I'm just curious," Maura Beth said, sidling up to them with a smile. "Where did you two end up on your elopement honeymoon? You haven't said a word, and I'm just dying to hear all about it."

"Ah, that!" Locke answered, after a sip of his wine. "Well, we just got in the car and drove up to Memphis and then headed west to Little Rock. But we didn't stop there, did we, Voncille?"

"No, indeed. We were eagles flying high and free. We just kept on going until we got off the interstate at this little town called Altus. They billed themselves as the Wine Capital of Arkansas, or something like that. So we toured a couple of wineries, did a lot of free tasting of the grape, and then spent the night in this quaint little country inn. Although I have to admit, we didn't get much . . . sleep, so to speak. It was all just too glorious. We were like teenagers on a lark!"

"Sounds like a lot of fun. I hope Jeremy and I can have your outlook when we get to be your age."

Locke put a finger to his temple and winked. "It's all up here, and don't let anyone tell you otherwise."

The second loose end was certainly the more important, however. There was still that unfinished business to address with her mother. Yes, Cara Lynn Mayhew had smiled right along with the others when her father had unveiled their spectacular wedding gift. There had been a hug and kiss exchanged between mother and daughter that had felt genuine enough. But Maura Beth knew she simply could not leave it at that, not with the wedding and honeymoon fast approaching, not with any number of things left unsaid and truly unexplored.

It was upstairs in the guest room that Maura Beth and her mother faced each other, sitting on the edge of the quilted bed with its rough-hewn, cedar posts that faced the lake below. Oddly enough, it was Cara Lynn who had come up to her daughter at one point and initiated everything.

"Maura Beth," she had said, gently taking her arm, "I'd like to tell you a few things in private. Let's head upstairs."

Once they had settled in, Cara Lynn retrieved a pair of scissors from her purse and laid them out on the patchwork quilt. The gesture was at once puzzling and—for a brief moment—seemed just a tad bit ominous.

"What are those for?" Maura Beth wanted to know, cocking her head but still managing a smile.

"They're kitchen shears that Connie was good enough to lend me. No, I don't ordinarily go around carrying them. Don't worry—I'll get to them soon enough," Cara Lynn said. Then she took a deep breath, straightened her posture, and rested her hands in her lap, looking thoroughly relaxed. "But first I want to start acting like a mother instead of a prima donna."

Maura Beth made a half gesture of protest, but Cara Lynn quickly waved her off. "No, sweetheart. This is long overdue. Let me have my say. Or at least the right kind of say, for once."

"Please, Mama. Go ahead."

Then the words started coming, and it occurred to Maura Beth that everything about them was natural and welcome—with not a single syllable forced. "When I was first married, I wanted to have a big family. I didn't particularly like growing up an only child myself. Maybe things would have been different for me if you hadn't been our only child as well. Your father and I wanted a brother or sister for you—well, we probably intended to have as many as possible—but I wasn't able to have any more children. Just one of those things that sometimes happens in life. It breaks your heart a little, but you move on."

"I know, Mama. You told me a long time ago that year I asked you if I could have a little brother or sister for Christmas."

Cara Lynn reached over and took her daughter's hand, and again, everything felt right to Maura Beth, as it rarely had before between the two of them. "Once you arrived, I think I expected you to be just like me. I was going to dress you up in style, and you were going to be the social leader of your generation. But I knew from the beginning that you weren't like that at all. A mother knows such things and doesn't have to be told. And it wasn't just your red hair and obstinate temperament." Cara Lynn briefly looked away and chuckled. "I remember clearly that your father and I spent a lot of time researching both of our family trees for a while there. Oh, we shook them and shook them to see what would fall out. We thought maybe that way we'd discover just where you came from. Isn't that silly?"

Maura Beth saw the humor in the remark at once and shook her head. "No, I don't think so. I understand. I know I've always been a handful."

"I think your father truly appreciated your uniqueness long before I did. Whenever I'd say to him, 'What are we going to do about her?' he'd just shrug and say, 'We'll let her be whoever she's going to be.' And when you turned out to be a small-town Mississippi librarian—wonder of wonders—I just didn't know how to handle it. I didn't see how you could possibly be happy up here in Cherico so far away from the world you'd grown up in down around New Orleans."

Maura Beth realized that she had heard some of her mother's words before; but this time—and maybe for the first time—she was hearing them from the heart—both hers and her mother's.

"But despite all my stubborn protestations," Cara Lynn continued, "I want you to know that I truly see how happy you are up here, what Jeremy means to you, how you fit in so well with these friends of yours you've made on your own. When I heard the words you and Jeremy had written for each other this evening, they took my breath away. I remember what it was like to have something or someone take my breath away. His name was William Morrell Mayhew, and I still feel the same way about him as the day I married him."

Maura Beth gently squeezed her mother's hand. "It's all there in your wedding pictures."

"Your father reminded me of that before we came up again. We went through the album together—we hadn't done that in a long time, you know. And then he turned to me, and said, 'That's all our little redhead wants. The same thing we had—and still have. Forget about the trappings and what the wedding looks like. Let's just take tons of pictures of her looking as happy as we looked."

"This is just about the best conversation we've ever had," Maura Beth said, the affection flowing from the light in her eyes. But she soon returned to the scissors with an impish grin. "And I can't wait to see how those fit in to all of this!"

"Oh, those!" Cara Lynn picked them up and stared at them as if they were expensive jewelry. "They're just symbolism, so to speak. I hadn't thought about the idea in many years. First, your father told me he thought I should go see Father Hickock about all of my wedding resentment and see if I could get some help. 'You need to do something, Cara Lynn,' he said to me. 'This could affect your relationship with Maura Beth the rest of your lives.' Or something like that."

"So I took your father's advice, and it was Father Hickock who brought up the scissors. You know, there's really a great deal of wisdom behind that jolly disposition of his. What he said was that all I needed to do was cut the cord, and then I'd be fine with everything."

"The cord?"

"The umbilical cord. The tie that binds a child to its mother. Sometimes it's the child that has trouble cutting the cord. Sometimes, it's the mother. You were out there snipping away on your own early, sweetheart—my only baby. Maybe just too early for my tastes, and that's what I had so much trouble with all these years. But . . . it's high time I let you go . . . and let you be you."

Cara Lynn pointed the scissors gently in her daughter's general direction and made a gentle snipping motion. "There, now," she said, her voice not unlike the way a mother speaks to a newborn cooing up at her. Then she put the scissors down on the quilt, exhaled deeply, and smiled. "All done."

Maura Beth felt the release in the form of a surge in her blood, and it overwhelmed her for a few moments. But soon enough, she and Cara Lynn were embracing, as the long years of tension between them dissolved into tears of joy.

"I've finally gotten you back," Maura Beth said, pulling away slightly and sniffling. "The Mama that used to read *Adventures of Uncle Wiggily* to me every night at bedtime. You planted the seed, you know. That's when I started falling in love with books. And when you took me to the library and enrolled me in summer reading, I was done for—a librarian in the making. It wasn't all on me."

"I know that now," Cara Lynn said, wiping the tears away with the tips of her fingers. "And I want you to know that I

am proud of what you've done with your life. I had no business coming up here thinking I could change that and force
you to do things my way—the New Orleans way. Please forgive me for all the dramatics—especially the way I stormed
out of the library that night. Sometimes I think I should have
majored in Theater Arts at Tulane."

They both enjoyed a much-needed laugh. "Of course I
forgive you, Mama. And it's not like we haven't included our
New Orleans upbringing at all. We have your wedding dress
and Father Hickock to remind us of all that. And I was just
thinking—maybe we could ask Miss Voncille to show you her
house before you leave—well, I guess it's my house now. But
we could draw up some diagrams to see where the furniture
goes and that sort of thing."

"I'd love that. Only promise me one thing."

"What's that?'

"If your father and I decide to contribute a piece of furniture now and then, let us do it. Let us help you and Jeremy
enjoy your house and your life together. Don't be defensive
when we give you things."

"It's a deal."

Another hug followed, and suddenly, Maura Beth felt like
she could conquer the world. This was the one ingredient that
had been missing in her life—a resolution to this awkward,
drawn-out standoff between herself and her mother. Now,
with the snip of a pair of scissors, the dilemma had been cut
out of her life for good. She must remember to thank Father
Hickock for the excellent counsel he had given her mother;
then she found herself laughing out loud.

Cara Lynn drew back, somewhat astonished. "What's so
funny?"

"I was just thinking about our Sheriff of St. Andrew's for
a moment there. I guess you had to be inside my head to appreciate it."

"Apparently. So let's go join the others, why don't we?"

But mother and daughter had only gotten halfway down the stairs when Cudd'n M'Dear appeared at the bottom, dramatically gesturing their way. She almost looked and sounded like she was in the midst of some classic Shakespearean balcony scene. "Pray tell, where on earth have you two been?"

"Let me take this one," Maura Beth murmured to Cara Lynn out of the side of her mouth.

"Gladly."

"We just had one of those last-minute wedding talks," Maura Beth said, once the three of them were face-to-face on the great room floor. "You know, lots of motherly advice and all that sort of thing. I wouldn't have dreamed of getting married without it, you know."

Cudd'n M'Dear was not appeased in the least. "Well, I trust you haven't forgotten, Maura Beth."

"About what?"

"Please don't tell me it's slipped your mind. We were going to huddle about that councilman of yours."

In fact, the cathartic session with her mother had the effect of wiping out practically all her other modest concerns. Councilman Sparks suddenly seemed like a footnote at the bottom of the pages of her life. But she still intended to unleash Cudd'n M'Dear on him. It was only fitting.

"Yes, so we were. Mama, if you'll excuse us, we have a bit of dishing and plotting to do. Just an old score to settle."

Maura Beth's spirits were soaring now. At last—the first documented, constructive use of Cudd'n M'Dear's machinations at her disposal!

16

Into the Sunset

Jeremy thought it was the funniest thing he'd heard in a while and said as much with a note of laughter in his voice. "I guess you think some conventions should be upheld after all, Maurie."

It was the morning of their wedding day, and after they had finished a paltry breakfast of cinnamon toast and coffee at the kitchenette counter, Maura Beth had surprised him by laying down the law with a smile. "This is the way it's going to be, Jeremy. I'm spending the rest of the day at your Aunt Connie's. She and Mama and your mother are all going to help me get dressed when the time comes. Everyone knows it's bad luck for the groom to see the bride until the ceremony. I don't know what you're going to do to occupy your time, but I'm sure you'll figure out something. Maybe you and your father could do something together."

"It's perfectly fine with me," he continued. "I mean, I didn't have a bachelor party, you didn't have a bachelorette party, and we're not doing anything else by the book. And since I know I can dress myself, I guess I'll be seeing you out on the deck at sunset. But I'll still miss you."

"I'll miss you, too," she said, giving him a lingering kiss.

"But I think I need to do it this way. It'll mean a lot to Mama, especially since I'm wearing her dress. I know you understand, sweetheart."

An hour later, Maura Beth had kept her word and headed off to the lodge in a virtual whirlwind with everything she needed to become the beautiful bride of the day. Jeremy was about to call up his father to come over for some last-minute male bonding and manly encouragement when the doorbell rang, and the smile on his face was nothing short of smug. Was it possible for a woman to go anywhere without forgetting something and having to backtrack? But in another instant he found himself frowning as he realized that his Maurie never went anywhere without her key and had made quite a to-do of dropping it into her purse before leaving.

"In case I need to come and go, and you're not here," she had told him just before making her hurried exit.

So who was that ringing the bell on his wedding day? Had Paul McShay read his son's mind? If so, more fatherly advice would be just the ticket.

When Jeremy opened the door, he felt like pinching himself. There she was after a five-year absence in his life, looking the same as ever: her blond hair parted down the middle and hanging nearly to her waist, no makeup of any kind as usual, and her garment of choice—a floral granny dress—covering her tall, thin frame. But there were a couple of new and uncharacteristic things to observe. His sister, Elise McShay, had a smile on her face for once, lighting up her delicate features. In fact, when she wasn't frowning, she was a very attractive young woman. In addition, she was carrying an envelope in her hand.

"Hello, Jer. I bet you I'm the last person in the world you expected to see here today," she said

"Leesie!" he managed. "We . . . I thought you weren't

coming! I mean, you told Mom and you told me that . . . well, what the hell are you doing here like this at the last minute?!"

She arched her brows and gestured toward the living room. "May I come in, or are we going to conduct this conversation here in the doorway like I'm trying to sell you a vacuum cleaner?"

He gathered himself and stepped aside. "Oh . . . sure . . . come right in." Then he went ahead and did it almost as a reflex action—he offered up an embrace that she accepted without a moment's hesitation. Considering their past history, that was indeed a refreshing change.

Once inside, she looked around and nodded approvingly. "Well, you certainly don't go in for pretentious trappings, Jer. I like it. It's the new, simpler you. My place in Evansville isn't much bigger than this."

"This is actually Maura Beth's place. We're moving into a real house after the honeymoon, thanks to my in-laws. More like a starter house, actually. One of those little ole schoolteachers lived in it before. But can I . . . offer you anything? Orange juice, something for breakfast?"

"No, thanks, I stopped for something on the road," she told him. "But I will take a seat on this charming, rust-colored sofa. This has to belong to your Maura Beth. You would never buy something this shade. Simply not conservative enough for you, am I right?"

Jeremy took a seat beside her and couldn't help but snicker. "You're right, I wouldn't." Then he took a deep breath and dove right in. "Leesie, I'm bowled over by this. You've got to fill me in. I can't believe you drove all the way down here from Indiana. What in the world changed your mind about coming? And do Mom and Dad know you're here?"

She shook her head but still kept her smile. "The answer

to that last question is, 'Nope, they don't.' You're the first to know. But I was hoping your Maura Beth would be here so I could thank her."

"For what?"

"Well, she's the reason I decided to come after all. You have no way of knowing this, but she got my address from Mom and wrote me a letter, which I got just the other day. I don't think she'd mind you reading it, so I brought it with me." She handed it over and waited as he opened the envelope. "It's not often that anyone changes my mind about anything, as you know. That's why I can't wait to meet your Maura Beth. I think you've found yourself quite a strong woman and not just some echo of yourself. Good for you."

"Thanks for saying that, Leesie, and you're right—she is very strong." Then Jeremy eagerly dug into the letter:

> *Dear Elise,*
>
> *I know we've never met, but Jeremy has told me enough about you that I feel I know who you are. You and I have a lot in common—we set out on our independent paths in life and haven't looked back. My mission has been to be the best librarian I can possibly be, and that has not been easy for me. Here in Cherico where Jeremy and I work, the local politicians do not view my library as the necessary community resource that it is. Far from it—they think it is expendable, as is my job. So I have had to fight for what I believe in. I have not let other people's opinions determine my outlook. I believe you feel the same way about your life and career.*
>
> *Jeremy tells me you teach courses in Sociology and Women's Issues at the University of Evansville, and that you have your own strong opinions of the roles that men and women should play in our culture. I*

have to respect that because I have never defined my-
self in conventional terms. I've had this long-running
feud with my mother about what kind of daughter I
should be to her, and I hope someday to make peace
on the subject. At any rate, it's on my bucket list.

Meanwhile, I want to re-extend the invitation to
attend our wedding to you. I know that you and
Jeremy haven't seen eye-to-eye for a long time now,
but I believe it would mean a lot to him to have you
there as a witness. You certainly don't have to march
down the aisle holding flowers, if that's not your style,
but I know that both of us would appreciate you be-
ing there watching everything unfold. We've written
some very original vows, and I think you will enjoy
the way we've reinvented the marriage ceremony.
Neither of us intends to let other people define our
marriage.

Elise, I hope you will take this letter in the spirit
in which it was written and that I will have the privi-
lege of meeting you soon as part of the McShay family.
Sincerely,
Maura Beth Mayhew (soon to be Maura Beth
McShay)

Jeremy put the letter in his lap, and the expression on his
face was one of exaltation. His Maurie was practically a mira-
cle worker. What other term could describe someone who
had brought together a polar-opposite brother and sister with
a few paragraphs of prose?

"I wonder if you know what you're getting into, Jer,"
Elise said, after a brief period of silence had passed.

"What do you mean?"

"I mean that your Maura Beth is her own woman, and
you're never going to be able to take her for granted the way

some men do once they get married. Or even the way you used to do in high school and college with your girlfriends listening to you spout poetry. You always had to be the center of attention—like the main character in one of the classic novels you worship so much. Most men have to have everything revolve around them, you know."

Jeremy had to restrain himself. Now there was the Leesie he knew and had argued with over the years until they were both blue in the face—the militant sociologist who never let up on her talking points. A woman determined to change the world one debate at a time while not letting it get in one word edgewise. But he was equally determined not to let her drag him into yet another confrontation that might keep them from communicating with each other for another five years as a result.

"I'm not 'some men,' Leesie. At least not anymore." Then he told her all about the serious wreck he'd had out on the Natchez Trace that had totaled his car and made him straighten out his priorities for good.

"Yes, I knew about your wreck," she confessed. "Mom told me everything that had happened, but she said you were going to be okay and that it was more a scare than anything else. So I decided not to get in touch with you. I thought maybe with all the bad blood between us, you wouldn't want to hear from me out of the blue. Maybe that was a bad call on my part."

Jeremy lifted his chin and eyed her warily. "When you've had a near-death experience, you need to hear from the living, believe me. They keep you connected to your sanity because you keep asking yourself the same question over and over: Why am I still here? It could so easily have gone the other way."

"I'm sorry if I stayed too much in the background at that

point," she said, hanging her head. "But . . . I'm very happy you're still with us, if that means anything to you at this point."

"It does. And . . . well, I really am glad to see you— especially under these circumstances. Thanks for coming." He gave her a furtive glance. "But I think maybe you'd agree that we shouldn't discuss politics of any kind while you're here. Could we just . . . sit back and enjoy the sunset? That's when the ceremony is taking place, you know."

"I think I can manage to do that," she said, flashing a smile. "But I wonder if Mom and Dad will faint dead away when I show up like this unannounced?"

"You mean like I almost did?"

"I guess I had that coming. Maybe you should phone ahead and lay the groundwork for them."

Jeremy pursed his lips thoughtfully. "I think that's a very good idea. Maura Beth's already gone over to Aunt Connie and Uncle Doug's lodge, where they're staying. It'll give you a chance to meet and visit with Maurie. Oh, that's my very special nickname for her."

"So I gathered. I guess I've underestimated you, Jer. Maybe you've gotten your act together after all."

Jeremy raised an eyebrow playfully. "Well, Leesie, I think the fact that you've shown up for my wedding means maybe you have, too."

She cut her eyes at him and smirked. "Touché!"

Maura Beth stood at the bottom of the lodge stairs in her mother's classic wedding dress and veil, holding the bouquet of white crepe myrtle flowers that Miss Voncille had fashioned for her from her husband's front yard.

"I made one just like it for my little ceremony at Henry Marsden's office," Miss Voncille had explained just before handing it over in the guest room upstairs. "Now, you don't have to take it if you don't want to. No pressure. It's just a little gesture I thought you might appreciate."

"And it's a wonderful gesture, too," Maura Beth replied, discarding the pedestrian nosegay she had planned to carry down the aisle with her. "This is uniquely Cherico, and that's good enough for me."

There was also unexpected humor once the actual ceremony got under way. The sight of a jittery Douglas McShay hovering over the turntable to make sure the needle didn't get stuck again was worth a chuckle or two; and in truth, his services were needed when the ancient LP of Beethoven's *Symphony No. 9* briefly went another round with that same ornery scratch. But this time everyone in the processional was prepared and did not miss a beat.

Maura Beth was also working through the sensory overload of the rainbow-hued fashion show that marched up the aisle before she did. That was the price paid for disdaining cutesy coordination, but it was much more interesting and entertaining this way. Renette looked every inch the sweet prom queen in pink chiffon, all blushing and giggly; Nora Duddney had completed her rapid transition from dowdy to glamorous in a royal blue cocktail dress; Connie had chosen a conservative silver suit with a peplum that helped disguise her plump figure; Becca had selected an emerald green Empire design to accommodate her baby bump; Periwinkle had gone all floor length and lavender, which somehow managed to take years off her appearance; and finally, Miss Voncille had topped them all in a mocha evening gown, complemented by a Billie Holiday-esque gardenia pinned just behind her ear.

But for Maura Beth, there was nothing like the moment when she took her father's arm and headed toward Father Hickock, Paul McShay, her groom-to-be, and the setting sun, all awaiting her outside. Although the journey could not have been more than twenty-five feet from staircase to deck door, everything seemed to slow to a crawl. Here and there someone waved at her subtly with the tips of their fingers, and the gesture went into a freeze frame in her head. Somehow, she was able to scan the room and catch every little nuance that came her way.

Among the many familiar faces turning in their chairs to take it all in were the Crumpton sisters, preening and elegant as ever; stylist Terra Munrow and her biker boyfriend, Ricky; James Hannigan of The Cherico Market; Councilman Sparks and wife, Evie—keeping his word that he would indeed show up for the festivities; Mr. Parker Place and his mother, Ardenia Bedloe; the leaner-than-ever Stout Fella; Locke Linwood, who had never looked so distinguished; the mothers of the bride and groom—Cara Lynn and Susan; the surprise guest, Elise McShay, who had not changed out of her granny dress for the ceremony, however; and finally, Cudd'n M'Dear, who blew Maura Beth a kiss that she caught somewhere beneath her sternum in the form of a warm spurt of emotion. The undivided attention was all so intoxicating. Wasn't there some way time could be suspended indefinitely so that this spectacular procession of admiration and approval never had to end?

But end it did. And suddenly, Maura Beth was facing her beloved, tuxedoed Jeremy, after William Mayhew had offered up his tender, fatherly kiss on the cheek, and softly whispered, "I love you, sweetheart."

"I love you, too, Daddy," she told him, letting go of his arm with a lump in her throat and cutting the cord herself in an entirely different fashion.

Father Hickock's traditional opening words tumbled by quickly—Maura Beth hardly heard them at all. She was still rehearsing in her head the vows she had written, but soon enough her big moment arrived, and she was more than ready as Jeremy lifted her veil to reveal her peaches-and-cream glow.

"Jeremy, the journal I have kept in my heart throughout my life always seemed earnest enough to me. In it, I described to myself what sort of person my lifelong companion would be. First and foremost, he would be kind. He would not know what it was like to be mean-spirited toward others. He would also be visionary—expecting the best of himself and those he dealt with—never growing cynical when disappointments appeared, as they must. But most of all, he would see himself reflected in my eyes—the eyes of abiding love and commitment—just as I would see myself in his. We would need no other mirrors for the rest of our lives. So having found you, I will no longer search for completion. It is done. We are one."

There was a whispered excitement throughout the room when Maura Beth finished her vows. She turned briefly to get a glimpse of her mother's reaction and focused on the affectionate smile that Cara Lynn was beaming her way. The words "We are one" might also have applied to the Mayhew family at long last.

Then Father Hickock nodded graciously, inviting Jeremy to begin, and the room fell silent once again.

"So, here we go, you and I, sailing off into the sunset, launching our lifetime of expectations together. I have no doubt that we will fulfill those expectations because I know we were meant to do so. Our paths have crossed, and, to be truthful, there have been times when it has felt like we have not merely crossed, but collided. But in dusting ourselves off, we've found that our hearts and souls have been revealed to each other, and we've both liked what we've seen. No marriage is without hard work, but we are nothing if not hard workers at life. The sunset behind us is our witness, along with all of these good people in front of us. There could be no greater joy than for the two of us to join forces and let the world know we're here for a purpose. And so, my sweet Maurie, let the journey begin."

Again the room responded, but this time there was a decidedly more female reaction in the form of a chorus of "Aww's!" Maura Beth continued to drink it all in, at one point closing her eyes briefly to capture and remember the moment forever. She doubted that Douglas's camcorder would come close to doing it justice from any angle. Only with her eyes could she sear it on her brain.

Father Hickock called for the rings, which Paul McShay quickly provided. Then came the exchange, followed by the more traditional vows and "I do's!" And, at last, Father Hickock's seal of approval: "I now pronounce you husband and wife. You may now kiss your bride."

Jeremy leaned in gently, lightly brushing Maura Beth's lips at first; but he returned to linger and apply a bit more pressure. The timing of it all was just perfect and properly romantic.

"Ladies and gentlemen," Father Hickock declared after they had separated, "may I present to you Mr. and Mrs. Jeremy McShay."

The applause rang out enthusiastically, as Douglas again positioned the phonograph needle. Then the recessional began. As if on cue, the sun sank below the horizon, surely unwilling to play the poor sport and steal the spotlight from the newlyweds.

Strangely, Maura Beth found herself thinking about page 25 of her college journal in spite of the dizzying input of the last fifteen minutes or so. Perhaps it was time to put it aside for good, retiring it to the attic of their new home on Painter Street after they moved in. Time to put aside girlish things now that she was a married woman. She had a wonderful husband on her arm and a state-of-the-art library to run going up next door. She must learn how to balance both aspects of her life, but it was what she had been wanting for so long. As for the redheaded bambino she had hoped for since before puberty, well, he or she just might have to wait a little longer. But it was nothing to worry about—Jeremy had put it succinctly in his vows: They were sailing into the sunset together, and what a memorable journey it was going to be!

17

Parting Glances

Maura Beth and Jeremy had just finished feeding each other messy mouthfuls of Mr. Parker Place's "grasshopper pie" wedding cake in the lodge dining room—not once or even twice, but several times over while Douglas insisted on recording them from every conceivable angle.

"After all, this is for your children and grandchildren," he told them, jockeying for position among the guests surrounding them.

"Enough, Douglas!" Connie finally said. "They'll have crème de menthe hangovers!"

But William Mayhew and Paul McShay were also nearby, snapping pictures for posterity with their smartphones, and it did not take very long for Maura Beth to feel the buzz.

"Let's just pose with the cake from now on," she told Jeremy. "I don't think I should swallow another bite."

Jeremy nodded. "Gotcha! I can certainly vouch for the fact that's some powerful stuff right there."

Indeed, it was the talk of the buffet as people lined up for a piece, and Maura Beth caught snatches of Ardenia Bedloe's praise as they sampled it. "My baby boy made that cake. Yes, he did. My Joe Sam down at The Twinkle. Y'all should drop on by anytime, y'hear!"

At some point Maura Beth and Jeremy began circulating on their own, and Councilman Sparks was at the top of her list of unfinished business—even a glancing blow to land. She caught up with him as he was making short work of his piece of wedding cake.

"Isn't that scrumptious, Councilman?" she said after greeting him—and his Evie as well.

"Pretty wild and wicked, Miz Mayhew," he told her, running his tongue over his lips. "Although I have to admit I figured you more for the traditional white almond cake type."

"I'm only traditional in spots, Councilman."

"Well, it was a lovely ceremony with the sunset and all," Evie added. "You were framed just like a portrait out there."

"Yes, we were, weren't we? I could have stood like that forever and had someone do us in oils."

Maura Beth craned her neck and spotted Cudd'n M'Dear tied up with Lewinda and Mabel Anne at the other end of the buffet table. "Meanwhile, I have someone who's just been dying to meet you, Councilman. Why, she told me she just couldn't leave Cherico without talking to you!"

"Really?"

Maura Beth caught her cousin's eye and motioned to her. "Oh, yes. And here she comes now." Then Maura Beth made the introductions, and Councilman Sparks looked thoroughly confused.

"I didn't quite catch all those names," he told Cudd'n M'Dear, who began laughing uncontrollably.

"I'm sure," she said, catching her breath. "No one ever remembers all that. But you will, won't you, Councilman? At any rate, that was Theodoria Agnes Montaigne Mayhew, but you may call me Cudd'n M'Dear. Everyone who's anyone does, you know."

Councilman Sparks continued in his confusion. "I'm to call you . . . Cudd'n My Dear?"

"No, not My. It's Muh, as in *M* with an apostrophe." She boldly reached out with her thumb and forefinger, squeezing his lips between them. "Now, say, 'Muh, Muh, Muh.' That's it . . . make a mouth like a little goldfishy swimming around in its bowl."

He tried to repeat the word, but her severe pinching and squeezing were making mincemeat of his efforts.

Finally, Evie stepped in protectively. "I think you should stop manipulating my husband's lips like that."

Cudd'n M'Dear continued making a putty face of his features. "Oh, he looks so cute this way. I just can't resist." She pouted her own lips in an exaggerated fashion. "Muh, Muh, Muh. Just like a great big batch of Play-Doh."

Evie's eyes narrowed drastically. "Well, perhaps you should seriously think about trying."

"Why, of course. I will admit I do get carried away sometimes. It's just that my name has always been a mouthful, and I want to give everyone the opportunity to get it absolutely right."

Maura Beth was barely able to suppress outright laughter as Councilman Sparks's face returned somewhat to normal. "Oh, Cudd'n M'Dear has cut a wide swathe between here and New Orleans, haven't you?"

"Indeed, I have. I've been on a mission of sorts, you see. Would you like to hear all about it, Councilman?"

He made a weak attempt at smiling after flexing his jaw a few times. "Yes . . . of course."

"Well, on the way up for the wedding, I had Father Hickock get off the interstate and stop at several of these small-town libraries. Oh, I strictly played it by ear. And do you know what I did, Councilman?"

He shook his head warily.

"I went right on in, announced myself to those librarians, and made donations to them all. Wrote checks to them right then and there. You see, I'm rather a wealthy woman, but I'm very particular about how I spend my money. Because I fully realize that I actually didn't make a cent of it myself—I inherited just oodles of it. Luck of the draw, I suppose. But then it always makes you feel a bit guilty when you go around living high on the hog on someone else's money, pretending that it's yours and acting like you're a big deal, don't you think? Or do you not happen to know anyone like that?"

Maura Beth could see that Councilman Sparks suddenly had his guard up. She knew that calculating expression of his only too well. Nonetheless, she fully intended for the fun to continue, or—as they were fond of saying in Cherico—the dogs would keep howling at the raccoon they had just treed.

"Ummm-hmmm," he said, cutting his eyes at his wife.

"And so," Cudd'n M'Dear continued, "what better use of my money could I make than to support libraries. They are, in fact, the repositories of our culture. They tell us where we've been, where we are now, and where we're headed, don't you agree, Councilman? Or are you a 'fill the potholes only' kind of public official? We have a lot of that down in Louisiana, you know. It's the ghost of Huey Long on the prowl, I always say."

He hesitated briefly, obviously steeling himself. "I can confidently state that I serve the public in various ways. That's always been my objective, and I believe I've lived up to it."

"Oh, I'd say he definitely has. After all, our new library will be named for Durden," Maura Beth said. "And a few others who've also inherited lots of money. Amazing what a little guilt will do, right, Councilman?"

He again exchanged glances with his wife and cleared his throat. "I think generosity would be a better word to use at this point, and I'm sure those libraries greatly appreciated your contributions. But for now, I think I've commented suffi-ciently on the situation at hand."

"And I was thinking," Cudd'n M'Dear added, almost as if she hadn't heard the councilman's response. "Perhaps I should consider making a substantial donation to the public coffers of Cherico."

Councilman Sparks snapped to attention as he always did under such circumstances. "Oh?"

"Yes, but only under certain conditions, you understand. I'm a stickler when it comes to my money."

"And what would those conditions be?"

Cudd'n M'Dear filled her chest with air and lifted her profile dramatically. "That there must be a quarterly account-ing of the money's investment and return, and that it only be available as a slush fund for the new library. Under no circum-stances should it be used for the general fund or for any other purpose. In addition, it is to be drawn upon annually for cost-of-living salary increases for library employees only. If there are any violations of these policies, I will come after the Cherico powers-that-be with a vengeance. I just love my lawyers to pieces, and you wouldn't believe how fond they are of me, what with the retainers I lavish upon them. So, are these terms acceptable to you, Councilman? I'm talking a mil-lion dollars here. A supervised, fully accounted for million."

"I can certainly accept those terms, My Dear," he stated as evenly as possible, though his ever-widening eyes gave the game away.

"Now, don't make me have to play with your lips again, Councilman. Remember, it's Muh, Muh, Muh," she said, making a crab claw of her fingers and bringing them per-ilously close to his face. "Repeat after me—Muh, Muh, Muh."

Councilman Sparks managed a passable imitation of the sound, but then shot daggers at Maura Beth.

"There. That wasn't so hard, was it?" Cudd'n M'Dear said with a playful lilt. "I do believe I'll stay over a little longer so you and I can talk a little business. These dotted lines can be so bothersome, can't they?"

Maura Beth continued to play the game. "Isn't that thrilling, Councilman Sparks? Why, I don't believe City Hall will ever have to worry about the library's finances again!"

"Yes," he answered, his jaw set firmly. "No worries for the Cherico Library ever again."

Then Cudd'n M'Dear sallied forth with another of her grand non sequiturs. "And speaking of Huey Long, I feel it is my duty to point out the tendency of men in a position of power to abuse their office. Particularly when it comes to the subject of women working under them." She winked smartly at Evie as if they were best girlfriends. "The wife is always the last to know."

Evie bristled. "Excuse me?"

"Oh, nothing, sweetie. I've been bombarded with all these rumors ever since I arrived this weekend. But I wouldn't worry about it if I were you. There's probably nothing to them. You know how people will talk when they've gotten a few under their belts."

Maura Beth sensed that both Councilman Sparks and Evie had reached their limit, and she decided to call off the dogs at last. "Let's have no more idle gossiping on my wedding day, Cudd'n M'Dear."

"Yes," Evie snapped, "let's don't!"

Momentarily, Councilman Sparks recovered his composure, and his customary vote-getting smile returned. "Well, this has been most pleasant meeting you, *Muh* Dear," he said, "and you must call me Monday so we can talk about your generous contribution. But right now, the wife and I must make the rounds and chat with all the constituents, you know."

"I completely understand," said Cudd'n M'Dear. "A politician is always dabbling in something or other."

Councilman Sparks managed a quick nod in her general direction. "I'll look forward to your call. Talk to you then."

Once he and Evie had blended into the crowd and were out of earshot, Maura Beth flung her arms around Cudd'n M'Dear's neck. "You definitely missed your calling. You should have been either an actress or an international spy. I thought I was going to explode trying not to laugh when you did that rubbery thing with his face. That was a complete surprise."

"Oh, just a spur-of-the-moment inspiration. But you kept describing him as always having a smug expression, so I decided to do something about it. I must admit I enjoyed it tremendously. It was like kneading modeling clay or even finger painting—the sort of thing children like to do in nursery school."

Maura Beth pulled back and gazed at her cousin admiringly. "Seriously, though, I can't thank you enough for what you're going to do for the library. I could easily picture myself fighting Councilman Sparks every year for employee raises. He would find some excuse not to give them. But that will no longer be an issue—you've taken it out of his grubby hands completely."

Cudd'n M'Dear looked nothing short of triumphant. "You've toughed it out up here. You deserve for good things to happen to you. And a little birdie told me that you and Cara Lynn are on the same page at last on your career and life here in Cherico. I'm so glad I came and could do something to help in any way, Maura Beth. Meanwhile, I believe I'll go for another piece of that boozy wedding cake of yours. Could I bring you another one, too?"

Maura Beth clutched a hand to her décolletage dramatically. "Oh, dear God on a party cracker, no. If you do, I'll have to be carried up the stairs to change my clothes!"

Just as Cudd'n M'Dear wandered away laughing, however, Nora Duddney came up with a somewhat stout, shy-looking older man in tow. "Maura Beth, I'd like for you to meet my very own Wally Denver," she said. "Now, forgive him if he doesn't bubble over like I do these days. I think your very original wedding has overwhelmed him a little."

Maura Beth extended her hand, and her best public servant, librarian skills kicked in. "I'm so glad you could come, Mr. Denver. Or may I simply forget the formalities and call you Wally?"

"Please," he answered, averting his eyes. "I'd, uh, I think I'd like that."

Maura Beth could easily see why Nora had fallen for him. He had the persona of a sweet, huggable teddy bear, an overgrown children's bedtime toy, and she had to fight every impulse to keep from hugging him herself.

"Then Wally it is. And you must call me Maura Beth. Just remember that I'm a McShay now. You'll have to remember that, too, Nora."

"Yes—Miz Maura Beth McShay. It just occurred to me that you won't even have to change the monograms on your towels."

They both chuckled, and Maura Beth said, "And don't you dare believe those rumors that that's the real reason I decided to marry Jeremy. So, Wally, what brought you to our little town of Greater Cherico?"

"Well, um, I just retired, but some friends of mine—the Milners out at the lake, you may know them—anyway, I've visited them a time or two during the summer, and I thought to myself—Wally, whenever you stop running yourself ragged being a stockbroker, this might be a nice, quiet place to spend the rest of your life. And so here I am."

"Wally was living in Memphis, then in Collierville after his recent divorce," Nora added, hanging on to his arm tightly. "He's staying in the Milners' guesthouse until he can find a place." She wagged her brows. "He's playing it by ear for now. Oh, and guess what—he's a long-time library user! Another patron for you, Maura Beth. And a new member of The Cherry Cola Book Club, too. Isn't that all just too exciting for words?!"

Maura Beth was just about to answer when Jeremy came up and hooked his arm through hers. "Excuse me, folks, but it's family picture time. All the McShays and all the Mayhews in the same frame, if it can be managed. It's all about the wedding album, you know. Or the video or whatever's in vogue these days."

"Don't forget to say cheese!" Nora called out as the bride and groom hurried away.

So the day's festivities had now boiled down to this: Maura Beth at the top of the stairs getting ready to throw the bouquet to the bevy of clamoring females below. Among the candidates were Terra Munrow, Renette Posey, and Nora Duddney, and Maura Beth would have been thrilled to have had any one of them catch it. Not surprisingly, Elise McShay was standing on the far edge of the action with her arms folded and a look of supreme disinterest.

"I'll just sit this one out, if you don't mind," she had even told Maura Beth as the group gathered.

But deep down, Maura Beth hoped Nora would be the one to out-jump and out-hustle the others. Both Terra and

Renette were young—so very young—and would likely have many chances to get lucky in love. Now that Nora had introduced her Wally Denver around, however, Maura Beth's intuition told her that the two of them might just be a match. And though catching a wedding bouquet actually had nothing to do with the rightness or wrongness of that perception, Nora winning out just seemed like it would put an exclamation point on the day's activities.

"Get ready, ladies. Up on your toes, now!" Maura Beth called out, turning her back to them.

There was an outburst of high-pitched, squealing noises from down below, and then Maura Beth shut her eyes and tossed the bouquet over the balcony. By the time she had turned around, she saw that the impossible had happened: She was so off the mark with her fast and furious throw that the bouquet had landed in Elise's hands.

"How did that happen?" she asked Jeremy, who was standing beside her, rolling his eyes.

"Actually, you almost hit Leesie in the face with it. Did you by any chance play fast-pitch softball? She practically caught it in self-defense."

"You have to have a do-over!" Elise cried out, brandishing the flowers as if she were handling a skunk. "I don't want this!"

"Nah, Leesie. No do-overs," Jeremy told her, leaning over the balcony. "Just go ahead and toss it over your shoulder. That'll work just as well!"

Elise quickly did just that, and this time in all the confusion and jockeying for position, Nora did manage to catch it, much to Maura Beth's great pleasure. The others applauded amidst scattered cries of "Brava!" "Way to go!" and "We'll be sure and save the date!"

"I guess I don't know my own strength," Maura Beth said, turning to Jeremy while the commotion continued below.

"Well, Leesie was right, you know. You *are* a very strong woman. And I want to thank you again for writing that letter to her. She'd never let on, of course, but I bet she's having a good time down there in spite of herself. After all, she got to make another of her political statements by refusing the bouquet."

Maura Beth couldn't help but ask. "Do you think she'll ever fall in love the way we did?"

Jeremy gave her a conspiratorial wink and leaned in. "When she least expects it. That's the way it happened to us, you know."

"Yep, we kinda became an instant item."

It was then that Cara Lynn and Susan emerged from the guest room, both pointing to their watches. "All right, you two—enough of this cozy chitchat. Time to change and catch that flight. I'm pretty certain they're not going to hold that plane for you," Cara Lynn said, pointing to different ends of the hallway. "Off to your separate corners right now!"

Maura Beth and Jeremy quickly blew each other kisses, knowing that the next time they saw each other, their subtropical honeymoon would officially have begun.

"Do you really think you'll get that much writing done when we get to Key West?" Maura Beth was asking her new husband once the plane had reached cruising altitude and the lights had been dimmed. The cabin had a surreal, cocoon-like quality to it at the moment. "I'm thinking maybe I'll be a little disappointed if you don't get creative mostly with me."

He laughed good-naturedly and sipped his tiny, way-too-expensive cocktail. "And I'm thinking maybe I could end up building an entire novel around our honeymoon. It could be that fantastic, you know. They say the best writing always comes from life experience."

She leaned over and kissed him lightly. "That's what I wanted to hear from you, of course."

"The way I see it, I can fully pay my respects to Hemingway and my wife without any problem or conflict. I envision them as two entirely different forms of special adoration."

"Oh, you do know just what to say to a girl."

They sat back for a while, listening to the steady roar of the engines. Finally, Maura Beth said, "I hope our first year together is all we think it'll be. I do have this undeniable thing for Cherico, as you know. But it amazes me how often that crazy town finds ways to disappoint me just when I think everything is going my way. Do you think all those years of dealing with Councilman Sparks have made me paranoid? Say something soothing and reassuring to me. I've been put through the wringer when you come right down to it."

Jeremy gave her an amused yet skeptical frown. "I think the worst just has to be over, Maurie. What could possibly go wrong now?"

"I have no earthly idea," she told him, gently resting her head on his shoulder. "But when we get back from the honeymoon, let's don't let our guard down for an instant. I mean not for anyone or anything."

He put his drink down on his tray table and took her hand gently into his. "No way we do that. I've got some young high-school minds to educate, and you'll soon have a wonderful new library to move into. You'll have the thrill of watching it take shape week by week and month by month. I'll be building my way, and you'll be building yours."

Maura Beth smiled as she mentally pictured the finished facility on the shores of Lake Cherico. She imagined herself walking hand in hand on the deck with Jeremy as they took it all in. The rippling water. The willows bending in the breeze.

The towering pines and hardwoods nearby. Whoever was out fishing or swimming or skiing that day. Of course, that unforgettable setting sun that had adorned their wedding vows with such vibrant colors. All of those things would be a part of the new rhythm of their lives.

More Treats from The Twinkle

Our third recipe installment from Cherico, Mississippi, features a few more goodies from the menu of The Twinkle Twinkle Café, affectionately known as The Twinkle to all Greater Chericoans. This time, you'll find everything from a dip perfect for cocktail parties to a scrumptious, elaborate cake, ready-made for an outside-the-box wedding. In between, there's a treasured family recipe for chicken salad and two versions of Caprese salad. Little did my relatives know they would one day be working for an imaginary café in an imaginary town and having their recipes find their way into the homes of readers all over the country. Such is the universe created by fiction!

Periwinkle's
Chicken Salad

Ingredients you will need:

1 half-pound fryer
2 tablespoons seasoned salt
2–3 ribs of celery
¼ onion
¼ bell pepper
5 lemons
4 eggs
Dash of salt and pepper
1 cup of mayo (preferably Hellmann's)
Dash of paprika (optional)
Lettuce (optional)

Cover fryer with water and simmer until tender; add seasoned salt, celery ribs, onion, and bell pepper. Continue simmering until vegetables have softened. Remove fryer and cut 4 cups of chicken using kitchen scissors. Remove vegetables. Cut celery ribs into 2 cups of chopped celery. Finely chop onion into 2 tablespoons—more if desired. Finely chop bell pepper into 1 tablespoon. Juice 5 lemons and set aside. Boil 4 eggs. Finely chop the eggs. Mix chicken, all veggies, all seasonings, lemon juice, egg, and 1 cup of mayonnaise together. Best served chilled. May add dash of paprika on top and a leaf of lettuce on bottom.

—Courtesy Helen Byrnes Jenkins, Natchez, Mississippi

Periwinkle's
Artichoke Party Dip

Ingredients you will need:

1 can artichoke hearts (buy variety with hearts only, no
   leaves)
1 cup mayonnaise (preferably Hellmann's)
1 cup grated Parmesan cheese
1 pie pan or Pyrex dish
Paprika
Corn chips

Drain and mash artichoke hearts. Mix in mayonnaise and
cheese. Spoon into pan or dish and bake at 350 degrees until
bubbly. Remove from heat, dust with paprika, and serve with
corn chips.

—Courtesy Lucianne Wood, Natchez, Mississippi

Mr. Parker Place's
Crème de Menthe Cake

Ingredients you will need:

1 18-ounce package white cake mix (may substitute yellow,
   if desired)
2½ tablespoons crème de menthe liqueur or flavoring
1 16-ounce can chocolate syrup
8 ounces fat-free whipped topping
1½ tablespoons crème de menthe liqueur or flavoring
5 or 6 hard peppermint candies (optional)

Prepare cake mix per package instructions, but stir in crème
de menthe instead of water. Bake in 13 x 9-inch pan according
to instructions. When cake is done, remove and immediately
poke holes throughout cake top with toothpick; pour chocolate syrup across top so that it will seep into the holes. When
cake is cool, mix whipped topping in bowl with 1½ tablespoons crème de menthe liqueur or flavoring and spread over
cake. Refrigerate until ready to serve; also may freeze, if desired.

Optional: Pulse 5 or 6 hard peppermint candies in food pro-
cessor until in shard or powder state; dust shards or powder
over top of cake.

—Courtesy Lauren Good, Mobile, Alabama

Periwinkle's
Crazy Caprese Salad

Ingredients you will need:

1 12-ounce can roasted red peppers
12 slices fresh mozzarella cheese
12 slices ripe tomatoes
25 leaves fresh basil
Olive oil
Salt and pepper

Julienne can of red peppers and arrange in any pattern on platter as a base for the salad. Layer slices of cheese next; atop that layer, place tomato slices; final layer should be basil leaves. Splash olive oil, salt, and pepper to taste. Serve by scooping up portions of all layers per person.

—Courtesy Marion Good, Oxford, Mississippi

Periwinkle's
Super Crazy Caprese

Ingredients you will need:

All of the Crazy Caprese ingredients in previous recipe, plus:
1 ripe avocado
Worcestershire sauce
1 container (regular size) roasted red pepper hummus
   (preferably Sabra)

Prepare Crazy Caprese salad according to previous recipe; then julienne avocado and add slices of ripe avocado atop basil leaves. After olive oil and salt and pepper have been added, splash Worcestershire sauce over all ingredients. Atop each serving of salad, place a generous dollop or two of red pepper hummus.

—Courtesy Marion Good, Oxford, Mississippi

Mr. Parker Place's Frozen Key Lime Pie

Ingredients you will need:

1 8-ounce tub whipped topping
1 can condensed milk
½ cup key lime juice (fresh squeezed is best)
Prepared graham cracker crumb pie shell

Mix together whipped topping and condensed milk in bowl.
Add in lime juice slowly until all is thoroughly mixed. Pour
into pie shell; freeze. Pie is best if allowed to thaw for about 5
minutes and then served still frosty. Do not overthaw, as pie
will become runny. Garnish with mint leaves or fruit of any
kind, if desired.

—Courtesy Sissy Eidt, Natchez, Mississippi

THE WEDDING CIRCLE

Ashton Lee

ABOUT THIS GUIDE

The suggested questions are included to enhance
your group's reading of Ashton Lee's
The Wedding Circle!

DISCUSSION QUESTIONS

1. How did your wedding preparations and issues stack up against Maura Beth Mayhew's? Easier, or more difficult?

2. Have you changed your mind pro or con about a character in this, the third *Cherry Cola Book Club* series installment?

3. There were several new characters introduced in this novel, among them, Cara Lynn Mayhew, William Mayhew, Cudd'n M'Dear, and Elise McShay. Which one most caught your imagination?

4. What is your favorite sequence in this novel?

5. What was the biggest surprise for you in this novel?

6. What would you like to see happen in the next novel?

7. If you had to change one thing about Cherico, what would it be?

8. Do you agree that all the wedding hoopla doesn't really prepare people for life after the honeymoon? Why or why not?

9. Do you think Maura Beth and Jeremy would make good parents? Why or why not?

10. What character would you like to know more about in this series?

Please turn the page for a very special
Q&A with Ashton Lee!

What inspired you to write a series with a librarian as your heroine?

Many writers have day jobs to support themselves until and even after they get published. I made what I think was a very smart choice of careers in becoming a vendor to public libraries in six Southeastern states. Libraries have budgets to buy all of the materials that patrons often take for granted. They must pay for reference materials, periodicals, best-sellers, research titles, audiovisual materials, furniture, computers—indeed, everything that makes a library complete. And they rely upon library vendors to sell them these materials within the confines of their budgets, which are generated through taxes. Over the years I have sold everything from DVDs to large-print books to research titles to libraries, and that has helped me pay the bills while pursuing a writing career full-time.

As a result of this work, I learned quite a bit about the inner workings of libraries—but particularly their budget issues. Many libraries are woefully underfunded, and their budgets are the first to be cut when there is a municipal or county shortfall. My agent suggested to me that an entertaining series about what librarians have to endure in this arena might sell successfully and educate the public about how libraries work as well. I believe that libraries are the repositories of our culture. They tell us where we've been, where we are now, and prepare us for the future. New technologies will be incorporated into their mission, but cannot ever replace it.

How have libraries responded to your series?

Since I have hundreds of librarian friends because of my vendor work over the years, the response from libraries has been phenomenal. I have been invited to give book talks and do signings at many libraries, but I was most honored to be invited by the Louisiana Library Association to be their Luncheon Speaker at their Public Library/Trustees Section at their 2014 Convention/Conference in Lafayette, Louisiana. At that function I explained in great detail how my career as a published writer has been intricately interwoven with my library vendor work. One has complemented the other, and I have every reason to believe that that will continue indefinitely.

When did you first realize you wanted to be a writer?

In elementary school, believe it or not. I would spend my allowance on buying ruled tablets and Ticonderoga pencils at the five-and-dime store. Then I would write these little stories with illustrations. There wasn't much to them, but it definitely indicated someone who wanted to tell stories rather than do anything else. When I learned that my father had been an editor and writer in New York briefly after World War II, writing what is now known as pulp fiction, I began to realize that perhaps this urge to write was in my genes. My best grades were in English, and I majored in English at Sewanee—the University of the South. I suppose a lot of aspiring writers major in English, but I didn't have to think about it twice. It was always my best subject.

Other than your father, did you have any other influences regarding your writing at an early age?

Yes, my mother. She enrolled me in summer reading at the library in my hometown of Natchez, Mississippi. I got caught up in reading to earn ribbons for prizes, and I loved the books I read. Then, she would also read to me every night. My favorite of all time was *Adventures of Uncle Wiggily.* I loved the way each chapter ended with a cautionary statement such as, "And if all the trees in the forest don't fall and the river doesn't flood, Uncle Wiggily will be back to live another day." Or something on that order. I also loved the fact that each Uncle Wiggily chapter was titled. To this day, I title each of my chapters. It helps me focus on what I want to accomplish with my characters and the plot in that segment of the novel. And I also think it intrigues the reader if the chapter title is particularly unique. For example, in the second novel in this series, *The Reading Circle,* there is an early chapter titled "Hieroglyphics and Empty Pajamas." Several readers have told me that they couldn't wait to find out what that chapter could possibly be about.

Your hometown is Natchez. Many other writers have hailed from there—such as Richard Wright, Alice Walworth Graham, and Greg Iles. Is there something in the water down there?

If you're implying that we drink the Mississippi River water and that makes us a little crazy, that's not true. Natchez gets its water from deep wells. But I do think Natchez is a laboratory for writers. It's the oldest city on the Mississippi, founded in 1716, two years before New Orleans. As a result, there's a lot of history that has taken place there, and the people who live there reflect that. Old Southern cities, particularly river ports, have seen it all and generally have a more laid-back attitude when it comes to human behavior. If you're a writer and have the knack for listening and observing generations of people, you have a leg up on those who want to get published. In fact, you may have to water down some of the characters and episodes drawn from growing up in a town like Natchez so that they will be believable. As in—the truth really is stranger than fiction.

Finally, how would you like to be remembered as a writer?

I'd like for my readers to find themselves in some manner or other in my writing. Perhaps it would be a character who reminded them of themselves or a family member. Or an episode that rang true because it happened to them or someone they knew. I'd like for them to be entertained and, if possible, educated now and then on some subject or issue. Most of all, I'd like for them to disappear in my writing, come up for air, and think, "Thanks for that little vacation in my head, Ashton. And it only cost me the price of your novel!"